# Out of My Skin

▸ a novel ▸

# Tessa McWatt

The Riverbank Press

Cover and text design: John Terauds

Canadian Cataloguing in Publication Data

McWatt, Tessa–
Out of my skin

ISBN 1-896332-08-0

I.      Title.

PS8575.W37O97  1998        C813'.54        C98-930944-4
PR9199.3.M33O97  1998

The author gratefully acknowledges the
Canada Council for its support.

This is a work of fiction, and the characters in it are solely the creation of the author. Any resemblance to actual persons is purely coincidental. Certain events in the novel are based on historical events, but some liberties have been taken with details for the purposes of the fiction.

The Riverbank Press
308 Berkeley Street, Toronto, Ontario, Canada  M5A 2X5

Printed and bound in Canada by Métrolitho

For my parents, Cicely and Errol McWatt

I would like to thank the many people who contributed to the development of this novel in various ways during its gestation: Susan Shipton, Irene Cox, Lynne Cohen, Andrew Lugg, Clayton Bailey, Barbara Muirhead, Catherine Marjoribanks, Faye, Gregory, and Errol McWatt. Special thanks to Cicely McWatt and Tony Brown for their support and inspiration. I am deeply grateful for the generosity, enthusiasm, and unwavering support of Jackie Kaiser. To Attila Berki, my profound gratitude for his faith in the manuscript, his careful and sensitive editing, and his gentle persistence. Finally, thanks to Michael Flomen, Max, Annike, and Lucas, for sweet friendship."

Acknowledgements:

I would like to acknowledge *People of the Pines*, by Geoffrey York and Loreen Pindera (Toronto: Little, Brown & Company (Canada) Ltd., 1992) which provided important elucidation of the events of summer 1990.

The excerpt on page 113 is from *A History of Native Claims Processes in Canada: 1867-1979*, prepared by Richard C. Daniel, for Research Branch, Department of Indian and Northern Affairs. (February 1980). Reproduced with the Permission of Public Works and Government Services Canada, 1998.

The excerpt on page 165 is from "A Gulf showdown," by Holger Jensen, published in *Maclean's* (August 6, 1990). Reproduced with the permission of *Maclean's*.

Bird descriptions quoted from *Eastern Birds: An Audubon Handbook* by John Farrand Jr. (New York: McGraw-Hill Book Company, 1988)

Quotations from *Jane Eyre* are taken from the Penguin Classics Edition of *Jane Eyre* by Charlotte Brontë (London: Penguin Classics, 1985).

Quotations from *The Song of Hiawatha* by Henry Wadsworth Longfellow are taken from *The King's Treasuries of Literature Series*, General Editor, Sir A. T. Quiller-Couch. (New York: E.P. Duton & Co., and London: J.M. Dent & Sons, Ltd.,1923).

The poem on page 134, "I Wake and Feel the Fell of Dark Not Day" is by Gerard Manley Hopkins (1885).

The excerpt from "Tool-Using Bird: The Egyptian Vulture," by Baroness Jane van Lawick-Goodall, is from *The National Geographic Magazine*, (May 1968, Vol. 133, No. 5).

We end in earth, from earth began.
In our own entrails, genesis.
    – Derek Walcott, "The Castaway"

# Crescent

Up close it was all disappointing. Two chintz-covered chairs kept to their own corners of an awkward Oriental carpet that refused to lie flat against the floor. The carpet undulated like a flat, wide snake inching its way toward the kitchen. A plastic standing lamp lit the arm of one chair and its gleam strayed toward the edge of the rug where it warmed an oversized, green-and-orange wooden frog holding a mushroom umbrella. Patterns of Mexico adorned the frog's insipid stare. It didn't resemble the frightened frogs in the swamps around Thirty-one Mile Lake in the hills of the Gatineau. It was a southern frog, smiling and placid. Desire-paraphernalia for tourists. She wanted a lake. Closing her eyes, she conjured up a montage of lakes from everything she'd seen in magazines, camping stores, or on television, but with those images came the tackle-shop pickerel and bass stuffed and mounted on wood, staring back accusingly, puffed up and indignant. Daphne sighed.

The sigh fizzled into a light moan. The room had nothing appetizing, no corner of rubble that gossiped or told her how its occupants measured time on tedious evenings as they stared into faces that had become family, faces that couldn't be avoided. Nothing warbled from the walls. It was the third house that week with a photo of a couple dressed in 1940s clothes kissing in front of the Hôtel de Ville in Paris. One house in Notre-Dame-de-Grâce, one in Outremont, and now this one. So many houses where kissing was foreign and ancient.

She looked back at the insolent frog and tried to wipe its grin from her sight, but was surprised when her hand hit the glass. She lifted her head from the windowpane and rubbed the condensation from the glass. Feeling the prickle of a shrub on her thigh, she remembered that she was on the outside. Inhale. Exhale. Funny how moisture could sprout from dry breath, how heavy breathing could make the transparent opaque. Just then, spontaneously, the inside of her thighs quivered, but the sensation passed as quickly as her hand over the glass.

She backed away from the window and retreated over the shrubs, across the dark lawn, onto the sidewalk, and strode unevenly through the spongy, saturated air. At the corner, with the triplexes ignoring her, she paused to stare at the stars splattered around the hanging crescent moon. The feeling came back, the one of falling between cracks, of stepping and missing. The same feeling that had persisted throughout most of her life: that sensation of images preceding words in an out-of-sync movie, when objects fall but the sound is heard too late. A gaping hole in reality. Recently the feeling had surfaced more regularly and the crack had grown wider. Tonight the sensation stayed with her, lurking around her pelvis as she made her way through the neighbourhood under the grimacing moon.

Her foray last week in Outremont had been slightly better. She'd witnessed an unvarnished moment and felt as if she could almost reach across the crack to touch the other side. With her nose against the window, she'd watched a couple in an oak-panelled room arguing, their arms slashing the air about them. The red-haired woman, eyes blazing, kicked the television set when the man turned and left the room. She'd smashed the screen but continued yelling at the top of her lungs. The sounds penetrated the glass, and Daphne watched the woman cry on the couch, her long, red hair heaving up and down on her shoulders, the curve of her back like untouched terrain. Somewhat nourished, Daphne had then retreated, crept back across the lawn, and tripped over the sprinkler hose.

Tonight she hadn't run into any sprinklers spitting and spraying the lawn like the guardians of property. *Guard snake. Garter snake. Guard-er-snake.* At the lights she considered the possible etymologies, but when the walk signal flashed she lost the connection and turned down avenue du Parc.

❦

Her detour into the park beside the mountain was brave at this time of night. Closer to the woods the air was sharper. She slipped out of her sandals, could feel the cool green of the grass between her toes, and felt comfortably abandoned by the night. *Hhmm, hhmm hhmm*, the vibration tickled her nostrils as she hummed. But then a single doleful note, *ooooooo*, and a frightened fluttering by her right ear interrupted her song. Just before it dissolved into the darkness of the woods she glimpsed a reddish round-faced bird with eyes almost bigger than its head.

The image fixed itself in her mind as she ran back to the sidewalk, her sandals still in hand. Crossing the wide avenue, she dodged the noisy cars that disturbed her silence like annoying insects in the night. Running through the underpass and across avenue des Pins to her building near St. Laurent, she concentrated on the glimpsed face. Long strides up the stairs, a push, lift, and turn to make the key work in the lock, then she was at her desk in the living room of her small apartment, where *An Audubon Handbook: Eastern Birds* lay open. She sought out the right page and read:

> *Eastern Screech Owl*
> *8 1/2″. Smallest owl with ear tufts in the East. Has two color phases — red and gray. Widespread and common in wooded areas, including backyards. Strictly nocturnal. Often responds readily to imitation of its call. All plumages have small ear tufts, yellow eyes; bill usually light. Adult plumage varies from rusty to gray brown; paler face edged in black; white spots on wings, tail like back but indistinctly banded; underparts rusty to pale gray with dark streaks and fine barring. Very young birds resemble adults, but barred (not streaked), with smaller ear tufts. Long, monotonous, rolled whistle; also a quavering, dropping whinny.*

Standing beside her desk near the open balcony door, she attempted its call. Trying to settle on the right timbre, her voice was unwittingly loud and carried down the street. The whinny was the part she had difficulty with; she moved outside toward the railing bellowing a quavering *oooo* that dropped in pitch near the end. She associated a whinny with a horse and couldn't reconcile the soft nighttime sadness of the rolled *oooo* with a wide and open neigh. The night's only reply was a sputtering motorcycle engine. She returned inside, closed the book, and placed it on a pile that included several volumes about Greek mythology and a picture encyclopedia of Eastern seabirds.

"Eyes the size of dollars," she said aloud.

She knew that the Greeks believed that souls travelled in the form of birds. Eyes as window to the soul. Dollars. What could this have meant about owls?

Morning cracked open like an egg – too soon – and Daphne opened her eyes a sliver to get used to the light. She shuffled down the narrow hallway, bumping her knee as she turned the corner. Mornings were difficult, as though deep sleep had deleted all consciousness from a file in her memory. For that reason she kept few mirrors in the house – a casual, early morning encounter with a likeness of herself was startling. Shiny appliances were to be avoided whenever possible; she had painted her kettle red, her toaster matte white. Everything in her apartment had been dulled and muted, safe from reflection.

She filled the coffee machine, clicked it on, and plodded back along the hallway to the bathroom, bracing herself momentarily at the door before confronting the mirror. The first thing that always came into view was the nose: large, wide, and fleshy, nostrils asymmetrical, one an imperfect oval, the other circular. Her grape-coloured lips were full and perfectly pleated – almost beautiful. She moved them apart and together again, puckering for herself. Small slanted-acorn eyes peaked out from under her curly brunette bangs. In the summer her hair frizzed and kinked with the humidity, and on breezy days flew wildly around her head. Her skin was brown, not a permanent, wealthy tan, but rather copper-coloured in the summer and sickly olive by February. She was small-boned but had a bouncing, high-rumped gait. A trace of Africa. Although not unattractive, she lacked what she yearned for: looks that would drive someone to carve her name on his arm. Instead she inspired a pat on the head.

Jeremy had done that, and daily, for three years, she had punished him for his seeming indifference. She had tested and challenged his attraction to her as though some hidden disloyalty would soon be exposed and her suspicions confirmed that love would always betray her. It had been like that with every boy, every man, every lover she'd ever had, dipping into them, then pulling away – fear, attraction, repulsion, rejection. All suitors were caught in the ticklish filaments of her disynchrony, in the gulf between picture and sound, inside the stepping and missing. Like the others, Jeremy had been confounded by the pushing and pulling, the to and fro that in the face of his commitment had seemed like a taunt. His head-patting had been only a gesture of his own fear, which her abrupt move from Toronto to Montreal eight months ago had legitimized. She suffered a moment of guilt, but expertly slipped sideways, tossing it off, and stood back from the mirror to examine her body.

Even at thirty Daphne had a girlish appearance, with her midriff contributing an anachronistic pre-adolescent bulge – a hurricane-lamp shape starting at her chest and continuing to her hips. *Cado-belly* she'd begun to call it, in an accented pronunciation of avocado. She'd stolen the phrase and accent a couple of weeks ago from a voice that had nested in her brain. An invented voice, with the playful rhythm and scorn of the islands, it had taken on a life of its own, coming and going unannounced and uncontrolled. Daphne had recently been considering her connection to the Caribbean but was more accustomed to seeing herself in classical terms. She longed for the ancient beauty she'd seen in statues, not for the virtue of fruit or vegetables. Certainly not an okra.

*You could boil it, fry it, mek a coocoo wid it…*

The woman with the dreadlocks had offered a pitiless grin while delivering those words. A few weeks earlier, Daphne had been drawn into a greengrocer by the ripe mangoes piled up in the window; inside she'd been accosted by loud ska music and greeted by arrangements of unfamiliar fruit and vegetables. The woman behind the counter was teasing a man leaned over the melamine countertop. Daphne eavesdropped on the couple as she picked up a thin, felty green vegetable under the sign: OKRA. The woman giggled and the man's voice was chastened with hurt pride.

"How come yu cyan mek me mout say such stupidity? Yu know I dun talk like dat wid every girl, just so." His wool hat of green, black and gold stripes, rising a foot above his head to contain all his hair, bobbed along with his words.

"Stupidity does as stupidity says, dun' matter who he talkin' to," the woman said and gave the man's cheek a mock love-tweak.

Daphne carried the okra to the counter, holding it up for the woman to see. "Excuse me, could you tell me the best way to cook one of these?"

The man and woman glanced at each other then grinned almost as one.

"Well, you could boil it, fry it, mek a coocoo wid it..."

Their giggles were barely contained.

"Never mind, thanks," Daphne muttered sheepishly, then replaced the strange vegetable and quickly left the store. But the cadence of the woman's voice had stayed with her.

Rubbing her belly as though it were smooth stone, she recited from her book of Greek myths, "The breath of the west wind bore her," as Homer had said of the beautiful, golden goddess Aphrodite, whom the wind had carried over the sounding sea. With Aphrodite, beauty came, and all bad winds fled. "The breath of the west wind bore her," she repeated, stroking her hips and navel, "the breath of the west wind." Her belly, soft and comforting to touch, had become a companion through many years. She had been born from herself – it was a conviction that had sustained Daphne through childhood and adolescence, and up until recently, before she'd contacted the adoption agency. But lately when she'd stroked and stroked her belly the genie of comfort had not answered. She'd been losing weight these last few weeks. Losing weight and her own gravity. Her body had started to feel transparent, leaving her fleshy nose exposed to attention, so at the beginning of the summer she'd begun to wear conspicuous clothing, tops that would reveal her belly to distract attention from her face. Even so, there it was, her nose appearing first in all glimpses of herself in public mirrors. She had never accepted its intrusion on her face.

Lathering her hands with soap, Daphne scrubbed her wide forehead, round cheeks, and delicate chin, then opened the faucet to rinse her face. She had lingered too long in the bathroom and was going to be late for her appointment and then for work. She would have preferred to stay home and just read, but she forced herself to get ready and was soon out the door, locking it behind her. A few steps down the stairs she detected a whisper in the air, as if someone was speaking to her. She turned around to find the stairway empty and still.

By the time she arrived at the agency, sweat had glued the T-shirt to her ribs. She breathed in deeply as she stepped inside the elevator and pushed 9. In the rush upward, she wiped her neck and forehead and pushed back her hair. The cool office air that flowed through the gradually parting doors was a relief. Forcing one timid foot in front of the other she approached the receptionist.

"I spoke to a Mr. McIntyre on the telephone. We have an appointment."

The receptionist checked her list and told Daphne to sit down. Daphne searched the coffee table for a distraction. She picked up a magazine, then replaced it. The familiar lifestyle glossies of doctors' and dentists' offices seemed out of place here where medicine couldn't touch her. Here nature and nurture were being reconciled; she was about to confront nature. She crossed her legs, uncrossed them, looked at her watch, compared it to the clock on the wall. There were a few others in the waiting room, all, she guessed, squirming on the inside too. She tried to imagine their births. It was a habit she'd acquired when confronted with adopted children, envisioning them taking their first breaths, screaming their first screams, getting severed from their first blood, and then being passed into the hands of a stranger. The scar would be the same each time: an invisible strain, a quiet line that passed from the forehead, through the eyes, and over the lips like a shiver, detectable only to those who'd studied it as she had, each morning in the mirror. Who had carried these people? The wind. "The breath of the west wind bore her," she repeated to herself to affirm her noble lineage, even in the face of what she was about to find out.

And what would that be? *Breathe, breathe.* She suppressed the urge to bolt and saw the same urge in the squirming bodies of the others in the waiting room, all of them wanting to know, yet surging with guilt. She'd effectively delayed the knowledge for so long, why did she need it now? But the other breath, the voice, had already begun its challenge. *Cado-belly* was only one of its phrases.

For the last few weeks the voice had accused and admonished in motherly tones. It wasn't unwelcome, but it startled her when it made comments about passing strangers. *Look at dat silly dress de woman is wearing; she don't care how she look?* Then Daphne would smile to herself, to the air that brushed her cheek.

"Daphne Baird?"

Daphne stood up quickly and followed the receptionist into the office. The case worker was a middle-aged man who was wearing a thick wool cardigan even during this, the longest heatwave of the summer. He stayed seated at his desk as Daphne entered and motioned her to sit in the leather chair across from him. He fussed with files, seemingly having misplaced something. Finding a folder, he began speaking, without looking up, in a thick Scottish brogue.

"Some things we can know about birth, the rest will always be a mystery; same for those who know their parents and those who don't – even though nowadays all these children have the whole thing on videotape. Poor bastards, all of that mystery stolen from them."

*The breath of the west wind bore her.* A short breath escaped as Daphne made an effort to speak, but the man didn't look up, and she couldn't see his eyes. He continued.

"So, let's see here . . . yes, Daphne Baird, born May 24, 1960." He paused, staring at the form.

"To whom?" She tried to sound casual, but her words came out like the salutation in a formal letter. The man took a few too many seconds to answer, so she preempted him.

"I mean, what about *them*, my parents?"

In her voice the word *parents* sounded foreign. She gripped the leather cushion with both hands. The man took out another sheet of paper from the file. Daphne suddenly giggled. A bad habit, the need to laugh at fear. She wanted the man to make her laugh and deflect the tension the way her father would, the way Bill Baird would guffaw at uncomfortable moments just to defuse them. Her giggle had no effect in this instance.

McIntyre looked up over the rim of his glasses then down again. "The registry certificate lists a mother – Muriel Eyre – but not a father."

"Muriel," Daphne said to herself. Something in her shifted with the utterance of the word. Suddenly she wondered how she'd arrived here, to hear the name of the woman who'd conceived her. The possibility of knowing that name had nagged like a sore tooth over many years, but she'd ignored it, thinking it might go away. She'd always known the place of her adoption but hadn't considered learning more until one night in front of a house in Outremont a few months ago, when she'd peeked over a window ledge to watch a teenage boy playing Scrabble with an elderly woman who must have been his grandmother. Something about the rightness of the scene, the boy's polite sympathy toward the old woman, had sent her home with the nagging ache becoming a throb. A few days later she'd called the adoption registry and received this appointment with such ease that she was still unprepared for it.

Mr. McIntyre continued, "Muriel Eyre. Daughter of Mary Eyre." He pronounced the names as if reciting a roll call. She noticed how the *r* on Eyre ran on and on – a wild horse under his tongue. She dared another question.

"You mean, if they don't know who the father is they put that on the form?"

"Well, in some cases they stipulate UNKNOWN, but that's only in a few cases. Those who don't want to state it just leave it blank. Your mother left that section blank. Good name she had . . . Eyre . . . very good name."

More *r*s trotted through his mouth. She wanted to bolt from the office and warn all those faces in the waiting room about opening the lid of that tight jar of entitlement. Warn them of the release of pressure that, like breath held for so long, suddenly exploded into the shape of strange names. Cocking her ear to her right shoulder, she hunted for the voice – her mother's? – but couldn't find it. She touched her belly; it was lean, hungry.

The man had still not looked up at her. Having found something more in the file, he continued, "British Guiana, now Guyana." He listed the country of her mother's origin as though it was a land he'd discovered himself. For Daphne it was only a name bearing more air. McIntyre added that it was a country of many cultures, Chinese, African, Indian, Portuguese, British, as though explaining Daphne to herself, but she didn't notice at first.

"And brothers, or sisters?" she dared.

"That's possible, but you'll have to find out yourself. There's a listed party to contact . . . someone who's willing . . . An aunt. Sheila Eyre. Your mother's sister. Lives here in Montreal, or at least used to. Can't be sure she's even still around after all this time."

He wrote the details on a piece of paper and gave her the name and a number. Then he was silent again and closed the file. For the first time, he looked into her eyes, and Daphne could feel her heart move up in her chest.

"Well, that's about it," McIntyre said.

"That's it?"

"Yes, unless of course you want us to arrange a meeting, but that's an extra fee, and normally something we do only if the parties haven't indicated agreement to contact."

*Next*, she could almost hear him saying in a passport-office voice, calling up the person behind her in line. McIntyre cleared his throat to signal that the interview was over. He stared at her, waiting for her to get up and leave, presuming she'd be happy to have made this one contact to her blood. Daphne stood up and backed out of the room, bumping into the door frame, then turning around to exit, saying nothing more to the man.

In the hall outside the reception area, Daphne stood with the slip of paper in her hand. She looked down at the name — Sheila Eyre — written above the seven expectant digits and moved slowly toward the payphone. A fleshy, heavy woman was talking on the phone, words flying out of her like spit.

". . . too many different tribes . . . they didn't keep the same records . . ."

Daphne strained to hear, pretending to search for something in her pocket as she moved closer to listen.

". . . to hook up with other provinces, but it's not . . ."

She tried to piece together what the woman was talking about but couldn't catch much. After a few seconds of silence the subject of the conversation seemed to have changed.

"You're kidding . . . anyone hurt?"

Silence, waiting.

". . . teargas . . ."

Silence.

". . . after the raid what'd they expect? There's gonna be hell to pay."

More waiting. Daphne couldn't put it all together. She relished the sound of the woman's voice, so kept one ear on the conversation and looked again at the name of her aunt on the piece of paper.

"He always said he'd stay on the bridge, to hold the highest point."

The woman's accent was strange — rural, with sloped vowels. The sounds bounced everywhere, and Daphne gave up trying to listen.

The woman finally hung up and Daphne faced the receiver.

She dialled the number. A Caribbean voice asked her to leave a message at the sound of the tone. She hung up quickly. As she was about to leave, she noticed a manilla file folder left on the ledge of the phone booth. Looking around before picking it up, she slipped the file under her shirt. In the washroom down the hall, she slid into one of the three cubicles, locked the door, and removed the folder. She didn't have to pee, but sat down anyway and opened the file.

Skin. Photographs of skin upon skin. Glossy, pocked-grey closeups of an arm, a leg, a torso, all of which had been scarred from burning or tearing, each scar puffy yet shrivelled, a keloid minefield. It hurt. She felt the wounds as if they were her own. Remembering that the woman at the phone had worn long sleeves, she wondered if these were her arms and to whom she'd come to show these pictures. Had McIntyre looked up long enough to take them in? Had he said a name to her that then exploded? Daphne touched the surface of one photo, running her finger along the scarred arm. A sensation under her fingers made her close the file quickly and leave the cubicle. Habit washed her hands while she stared blankly at the flowing water, wondering if the receptionist could be trusted with such evidence of the past.

"Shit!"

The whispered expletive made Daphne jump. She turned around and followed the fleshy woman's stare to the counter above the sink where the manilla file lay exposed. Daphne felt blood rush to her cheeks. The previous fifteen minutes coalesced for the woman, and Daphne began to perspire.

"I was going to give it to the receptionist. I didn't know whose –"

"You enjoy this kind of thing?"

"Honestly, I just had to go to the bathroom. Then I was –"

"Did you get a good look at them, all of them, I mean? I can show you more if you like, this time live, right here, a little private peep show for the little peeper."

The woman began to unbutton her shirt, but Daphne offered up the file to stop her. Her mind sought for the right thing to say as the woman flipped through her photos to verify their safe return.

"I didn't show anyone," Daphne said feebly.

"And that's supposed to make it all better?"

"No, I didn't mean . . ." She tripped on words.

It was McIntyre who shouldn't have seen, who wouldn't have had the right sounds under his tongue to say skin in a way that wouldn't be cold. She wanted to tell the woman that the photos were safe with her, but the woman continued, "What the hell. Don't care who sees them now. The more the better, I guess."

Daphne saw the woman's face soften. Her skin was dark brown, darker than Daphne's, and her eyes tapered off dramatically at the side of her face. Flesh hung in extravagance from the cheeks. The excess was disconcerting, even repulsive, yet Daphne was drawn to it.

The woman shook her head and smiled to herself. "It's Sister Isabella who should be ashamed. She made that fucking mess; candles . . . churches got a lot of candles . . . nuns love that shit . . . burnin' light, burnin' bushes, burnin' flesh . . . makes 'em feel like Jesus. They're kinda like jealous wives."

"Does McIntyre know?"

"What?" said the woman irritably.

Feeling the woman's anger rise again, Daphne scrambled to repair the moment. "You had an appointment too?"

"Yeah. Not much help. You?" The face jiggled into a question mark. Daphne nodded, relieved at having righted the error of her first question.

"It's creepy stuff . . . did they find anything?"

"Yes."

"Lucky you . . ."

She stared at Daphne a deep, long second then went into a cubicle. Daphne heard the sound of a zipper. The moment was ripe for her to escape her embarrassment, but the woman started to talk over the sound of pee and Daphne found herself staying, her curiosity winning.

"Born beside water?" the woman asked as the stream of urine became a trickle.

*Mmm?* Daphne looked up at the cubicle door via the mirror over the sink.

The woman didn't wait for an answer. "That would be a hoot to find out. My Mohawk friend says that if you live near water you have a better chance of having children whose hands and feet are the right size – with all the parts in proper proportions; brain and heart balanced, organs that behave. And you get a spirit that doesn't cackle, just giggles. She says landlocked people are off kilter, have babies that cry too much and grow up to hate their parents. I'm hoping for an ocean, not just a lake or a river."

The sound of the toilet-paper roll spinning made Daphne uncomfortable. She looked back down at the tap and washed her hands again. The voice resonated in the stall, rising above the water.

"You, you look like it could've been the Mississippi, or somewhere in the deep south. A Delta gal, you look like to me. There're some Indians there look like you, but you also got some Chinese or some slanty shit happenin' in those eyes."

Daphne turned off the water. "The Caribbean . . . well, actually, Guyana . . . South America."

"Hey, salty water everywhere. Congratulations. Salt adds another benefit. Preserves you. You'll live to a ripe old age."

Clothes rustled. A reluctant fly gave in and *zzzzzip* it was up. The toilet flushed. The woman opened the cubicle and walked to the sink, breathing heavily with the effort of carrying all her weight. Daphne wanted to touch her, to feel the skin and the heat. She imagined burying herself in folds of flesh and for a second closed her eyes while the woman washed and dried her hands. Then Daphne threw her hand out for a shake, a touch.

"I'm Daphne Baird. Well, I guess, Eyre, Daphne Eyre."

"Like Jane . . ."

"No . . ." The detonation of another name rattled her. "Surefoot."

The response was puzzling, but Daphne held firm to the woman's warm hand, which wriggled to be released.

"That's my name. My Indian name. Had to give it to myself; they called me Isabella, but this one suits me. Look at these feet

– have to hold all this skin."

The keloid skin jumped back into Daphne's mind: "I was going to turn them in, really."

Surefoot pulled her hand away and studied Daphne's face again. "Look, Daphne Eyre, no hard feelings. One thing you learn about at a convent is forgiveness."

She pointed to her palms. The graceful sweep of her fingers after touching each palm mimed the flow of something. While repeating the gesture at her side, depicting blood flowing from her body – stigmata – she turned her gaze heavenward, almost rolling her eyes up into her head, mocking the beautiful smile of an icon. A giggle escaped from Daphne.

"In a convent forgiveness seeps out."

With these words Surefoot turned and left the washroom, leaving Daphne with her smell, the tangy, minty odour of her clothes. Daphne opened the stall Surefoot had used. Here the smell was stronger: sweet and sour. She turned to examine her face in the mirror. Her hair was being obedient today. She fingered the bangs then touched her ribs, feeling them piercing the cotton. The pounds were leaving. Checking her buttocks, she rubbed them as she had her belly, reluctantly beginning to relinquish her descendance from a Greek goddess. Her real mother had probably been part Chinese, part White, and part Black. She touched her cheek and drifted in and out of the ingredient colours of her mother's skin: yellow, white, black. *Yellow, white, black* – it reminded her of the game with the variable winner: *scissors, stone, paper . . . scissors, stone, paper . . . paper.* She left the washroom and headed down the stairs of the building, descending each of the nine flights very slowly, absently, her mind sticking on *black*, on *paper*, and wondering how it ever won.

It had been during reading period in the second grade when she'd first heard the word Negro. She had lost interest in the story being read by her teacher and was imagining riding her bicycle through a ravine. But the teacher had stopped reading to ask the class a question, and the long silence of ignorance snapped the perpetually dreaming Daphne back into the room; she sought out her teacher's voice, which repeated the question.

"Well, does anyone know what a Negro is?"

Again silence. A few seconds passed before Kenneth Darcy said, "Yeah, Daphne."

"Oh no, no, not Daphne," the teacher corrected. "No that's different. Quite different."

Daphne felt heat rise in her cheeks. The teacher paused before addressing her, "What are you, anyway, Daphne?"

Daphne sat mute, her cheek beginning to quiver, her eyes to water. She'd never before considered the question. Her teacher soon sensed her discomfort and tried to help. "I mean, are you, say, Brazilian? Mexican? Now dear, people are certain things, like Japanese, Chinese . . . things like that."

*They are? What things?* Daphne folded her arms on the desk and cradled her head in them. No one had ever told her how to answer such a question. The fact that the woman she'd known as mother was Scottish had never meant much more to her than if she'd been a housewife, like Bev Campbell's mother. Some mothers worked, they were Scottish; others didn't, they were housewives.

When she got home that afternoon, she approached her father with the question and the options the teacher had provided for the answer. Puzzled, he put down his magazine, pulled her up on his knee, and asked her what she meant. As Daphne described the scene in the classroom, Kenneth Darcy's assertion, and her own confusion, his pink face grew red. He told her she shouldn't pay attention to people who thought things were so simple, but when Daphne insisted on an answer he grew flustered, then irritated. Gently, he lifted her off his lap and rose from the armchair to leave the room, saying, "You're a Canadian, and don't you let anyone tell you otherwise."

She went to bed confused and woke feeling frightened to go back to school. Kenneth Darcy would pay for singling her out.

Her reluctant walk to school the following day, each tempered step an attempt to never arrive, brought her slowly to the end of her street where she looked for the familiar shape of the flattened squirrel she'd been observing for days. It was still there. Almost a week had gone by since a car had crushed it, and all that remained was dried bones matted into a stiff, hairy carcass. She picked at it with her fingers. The head peeled off the asphalt and broke away from its torso. Later that day when Kenneth Darcy screamed, only Daphne knew what he'd found in his desk and how it got there.

It had begun that day: the appearance of the crack, the question *what are you* nudging it wider each time she asked it of herself. Events accumulated like clouds. Every gesture of belonging that other children showed prompted a repetition of the question. The intensity burst and she found herself in puddles of her own confusion. Her parents had explained what it meant to be adopted. They explained and explained until she lost all the other words except *wanted*. She had been *wanted*; she was to remember that, and they ensured that she did. It was her special status. But *wanted* hadn't been a good enough answer all the times she'd been asked *what are you*, or asked why she looked so different from her parents. So she began to invent better answers, and events conspired to confirm them.

Heat had always made Daphne itch, and in the middle of one July night when she was eight years old, the irritating rash underneath the elastic waistband of her pyjama shorts became intolerable, forcing her out of bed to walk around the sleeping house. She could hear her father snoring in the bedroom down the hall. Quietly she headed down the stairs, scratching and scratching. She went outside, down the front steps into the night air.

The whole world was asleep, and in the stillness her steps sounded gigantic. Listening intently to her footfalls, she crossed the street, lost track of where she was, and was suddenly in the park – High Park – and she could feel the soothing emanation from the lake. Even so, the air was still, dense, almost congealed.

The darkness was a giant sneaking up on her fledgling soul. Fear struck. Whimpering gave way to full-out crying. She wasn't lost, exactly, but was paralysed, terrified to take another step on the grass. She imagined things lying in wait for her, waiting to grab her legs and curl around them, dragging her down into the curdled earth. Huge mounds of dog shit, she remembered, had fallen – moist and steamy – from the backsides of German shepherds and collies, and she was certain to go sliding into some, slipping through the warm paste that would gush between her toes, ruining her white pyjamas; then she'd really be in trouble. So she hollered. She hollered with the pink and electric urgency of midnight fear. A seagull hollered back.

In the gulp for air amid her panic she heard grunting and smelled urine. A man approached, his pungent, sour smell growing stronger with each step toward her. He was tall and dark with shiny, straight black hair, and when she could see his face, she saw that it was pot-shaped and gently stained with moles. He spoke softly to her, asking what she was doing out in the middle of the night, but she refused to answer, obediently following her parents' directive regarding strangers. The man talked anyway. Talked on and on, about things she didn't understand, about "stupid people." Her knee stopped trembling as she listened to his thick, musical accent which finally made her giggle uncontrollably. He asked her if she wanted to hear a story. Keeping her lips shut tight, still obedient, she giggled and nodded. He suggested they sit on the swings and led the way to the playground set. As they swung slowly back and forth he began his tale.

It's a story about a too-sassy spider named 'Nansi, who is always playin' crazy tricks. You see 'Nansi was out lookin' for food, and he ran into Candlefly, de one who shines a beam of light in front of she as she moves through de night. Candlefly always had fire, was always showin' de other animals de way home. One day, 'Nansi ran out of matches when he was cookin' something good for his little trickery self to eat. He begged Candlefly for some fire, sayin' it was fa' his mother to start a fire for her cooking. Candlefly gave him de fire, and also gave him some eggs that she'd fetched in de valley de night before. Now 'Nansi went home with de eggs and fire, but 'next day, came back to Candlefly askin' for more fire and wantin' to know where she had got those delicious eggs. Candlefly gave 'Nansi fire and four eggs, but didn't tell him how she got de eggs, or where.

So, you know that 'Nansi, he was back de following day, asking again for fire and "please just one egg Candlefly, just one." Well, she was kind, so she gave him one, but half way home he stopped, put out de fire, ate de egg, and went back again to Candlefly.

"De fire wasn't good; it went out," he said.

Candlefly gave him fire again. 'Nansi waited to be offered another egg, but he waited and waited, and waited — in vain. Finally, he begged cousin Candlefly to give him one egg to put on de burn he said he was gettin' from de fire. Candlefly gave him another egg and added that "since you like them so much, I'll take you to a place where you can get eggs easily, as many as you like. But we must go at night. I cannot take you there in de day."

De next day 'Nansi waited and waited for night to fall. He couldn't stand it, he was so eager. He sat with his giant bag underneath de ackee tree and shouted at de tree frog to start whistling and beckoned de cricket to tune up as he saw de sun sink slowly behind de mountain.

Finally, Candlefly took 'Nansi to Egg Valley, and every time she lit up an egg 'Nansi cried out: "It's mine, it's mine, I saw it first," and put de egg in his bag. Soon, 'Nansi had 50 eggs while Candlefly had none. Each time Candlefly found an egg, 'Nansi cried "It's mine, it's mine; I saw it first," and Candlefly, being weaker than 'Nansi, could not take de egg away from him.

When 'Nansi had about 100 eggs in his bag, Candlefly said "Mr Anansi, since you are so greedy, you will have to find your own way home without a light. Good Night." And Candlefly flew home.

There was no moon in de sky and rain clouds covered de stars. 'Nansi was not sure which way to go, or where to put his foot. He was lost and open to all de perils of de jungle. He was scared, scared, and he sat down on one of de larger eggs and cried.

And you know, even though that trickery spider found his way home when de light started to come up through de trees, he didn't learn a lesson, he wasn't sorry. He still tries to do things he thinks he should be able to do but that he's not born to do. And, you know, to this day Candlefly will not give him a light, and he is de only creature in de jungle she will not help.

After the story, he said "right, right, now where yu livin'?"

Daphne told him, and he delivered her to her horrified parents. Her mother's usually calm ivory face turned yellow, and she sobbed. Her father put Daphne to bed, saying only that she shouldn't do things like that to upset her mother, and then he left the room. A few minutes later her mother came in and, without a word of rebuke but with a shaky voice, sang a soothing lullaby. Just before drifting off, Daphne asked her mother what the man was.

"What do you mean?" asked the exhausted Jennifer.

"I mean, the way people are things, like Japanese. He has a funny accent."

"His accent . . . West Indian, I think."

"An Indian?"

Through a wide yawn, Jennifer nodded. "Now go to sleep."

The next day Daphne searched her encyclopedias and any source she could find, researching Indians, investigating their food, clothing, customs, but she had forgotten the qualifier: West. She fashioned saris out of bedsheets and wore them around the house, saying words like *curry* and *tandoori* over and over like a mantra. Or she would appear in the den as her father watched sports on TV and admonish him with *chutney, chutney*, pointing her finger and shaking it along with her head.

She continued with Indians until she'd exhausted her young powers of investigation and discovered the ancient Egyptians at school. Soon invention was separated from her quest for belonging, and it thrived on its own impetus. The chivalric knights of the crusades needed her; she could feel the Grail within her grasp. She named herself Galihadia and trotted through the park with an imaginary lance tucked under her arm. Later, she dropped the Arthurians and started to bind her feet at night, becoming a Chinese concubine suffering the absence of her wealthy master. At puberty, when hair first started to appear on the region above her labia, she was horrified. The impurity disgusted her, so she plucked each one – a weekly task as they started to grow back – and remained a clean, smooth China doll right through high school, after which she dropped the whole wardrobe of fantasy.

One step forward, two steps back. Soon after starting work at Copie Copie in Montreal, she fell upon the Greeks. She had been given simple copying jobs, nothing double-sided or specially collated. One of them was a long manuscript by a classicist at a university who was hoping to repopularize Homer and Virgil in a forgetful age and to provide a pocket-book guide to the myths of the ancients. When Daphne confessed to her co-worker Joanne that she was intrigued by the manuscript, she was surprised that Joanne suggested she make a copy for herself and take it home. Joanne, who was close to completing her M.A. thesis in communications, frequently used the store for her own work, and Daphne was happy for the encouragement. She made a copy of the manuscript, reading it over lunch hours and sliding it into her small knapsack to take home, where she highlighted passages that appealed to her.

*The Thracians were the most musical peoples of Greece.*
*But the only musicians to rival Orpheus were the gods*
*themselves. He was the embodiment of the sublime when*
*he sang, and a part of his instrument when he played.*
*No one and nothing could resist him.*

*In the deep still woods upon the Thracian mountains*
*Orpheus with his singing lyre led the trees,*
*Led the wild beasts of the wilderness*

*Everything animate and inanimate followed him.*
*He moved the rocks on the hillside and turned the rivers*
*in their course.*

That first Christmas, alone in Montreal, she had walked to the summit of Mount Royal and had seen skipping streams and dancing boulders that had been inspired by Orpheus. Branches tittered, snowflakes pirouetted. The gods became her family. She imagined she saw a nymph through the trees. Near the summit she beheld a naiad's face when she bent over the frozen pond. Later, at the Museum of Fine Arts, she absorbed the look and feel of ancient statues, lingering until the end of the day when other visitors had left and sneaking past the rope barriers to rub the arms and bellies of their cold, smooth bodies. She returned their fixed gazes. By the time the museum guard made his rounds to turn off the lights, she would be rigid with longing, her jaw tight, her knees stiff. The apparitions were each mercifully flawed, just shy of perfection. The Greeks had made gods in their own image – all sublime, yet all distinctly natural, satisfying desires with the things of the world: the earth, water, food, men and women. Could heaven be an unfamiliar place with such human gods? Even on earth, their grace proliferated – exquisite forms peopled the fields, the forest, the rivers, the sea. The entire immortal cast was entrancingly, humanly beautiful. And there was laughter. The wine of Dionysus lightened the hearts of the maenads who worshipped in the wilderness, and Daphne sought to follow them. That winter she had yet to let the sensation of the widening crack invade her. She had pushed it away and had read and re-read the idyllic descriptions of an ancient pantheon where everything had a human explanation, one born of irony. It all made sense. In all of it, Daphne had been able to place her own marginal beauty. Her name, after all, had Greek origins. Her own features could be explained in mythological terms: her bulbous nose made her as vulnerable as his heel made Achilles.

The heat of the day was overwhelming, the soupy air choking her as she stepped out of the building and back into the present.

As Daphne walked away from the adoption services building, up into the heart of the city toward Copie Copie, she gulped in the wet air and felt for the smoothness of her belly, touching protruding bone and pockets of flesh instead. The scarred flab of the fleshy Surefoot stung her fingers. She pulled her hand out from under her T-shirt, tied her scattered hair up into a bundle on her head, and crossed the busy avenue, heading north.

The morning's yolky film hovered over the entire region. In Châteauguay, a suburb on the south shore of the St. Lawrence, the engines of cars had turned over, one by one, in a spark-plug chain of activity ending in the earlier-than-usual combustion of the neighbourhood. The sickle moon still hung like an emblem of labour over the lampposts.

At one end of town, amidst rows of similar raised-ranch bungalows, one home stood out as unique, its garden of tall waving blue flowers distinguishing it from everything else in the neighbourhood. Standing on the lawn, Daniel checked his watch, diverting for a split second the spray of the hose from the soft indigo flower beds. The petals fluttered in the spray, their colour deepening above glistening stems. Daniel's face was shining. He wiped sweat from his thick eyebrows.

He had started the day by pulling out weeds and fertilizing the soil, an aura of violet generosity around him. The early sun had warmed his back, but now it was retreating behind the humid haze that had turned the city ethereal all week. He checked his watch again, then reluctantly wound the hose in a perfect tight spiral around its mounted hook. At the car he surveyed his splendid garden before getting in. With the air conditioning turned up high, he revved the engine before pulling out of the driveway.

On the road, his mood began to shift. Traffic was already heavy miles before the detour. Commuters to Montreal were getting an irritable early start to the long and tedious drive in. Mohawk warriors on the South Shore, in support of their brothers in a standoff with police at the town of Oka, had sealed off the highways that passed through their reserve and thereby access to the closest bridge. The Mercier now belonged to the Mohawks, and commuters were having to find alternate routes to bridges farther east to get into the city. Stuck on the service road to the highway, Daniel watched in the rearview mirror as cars settled into a row behind him. As he brushed his bangs back with his hand, he spotted a small white eruption in the crease of his nose and cheek. Angling the mirror for a better view, he took the white spot between his two fingers and squeezed. The puss shot at the mirror, then oozed out slowly until gone. He wiped the mirror with a tissue and turned it back to the lengthening line-up of cars. The traffic inched forward. The hills in the distance were yellowing with the coming light. Daniel released air, first through his mouth, then onto the car seat. By the time he arrived at Sherbrooke and Parc, his earlier contentment had given way to an odorous *mauvaise humeur*.

He was an hour late, even allowing for the seven-minute advantage he always gave himself. His watches and clocks were set precisely seven minutes fast, just to be sure. His father had been an overly punctual man, and Daniel had learned the value of beating people to appointments, arriving early for dinner parties, and being first at work. But since the blockade he had been knocked off schedule. He arrived in the newly renovated, champagne-coloured office of Copie Copie just after ten o'clock. Being the manager, no excuses were necessary, but he still felt the need to announce himself.

"*Bonjour*, sorry I'm late. *Maudits sauvages!*"

"Daniel!" Joanne's reaction was immediate.

Daniel looked around the store. No customers. "I won't asked to be excused."

"Why not?"

"I am a taxpayer."

He walked past the service counter, past Daphne, who stood at the large copier watching them, to his desk at the back of the store. Joanne followed.

Daphne saw Joanne's thin, meandering lip curl into a canine snarl. Joanne's hair, which she'd dyed upon arriving in

Montreal, was pitch black with a hint of plum that set off her translucent skin and balanced the naturally invisible eyebrows pencilled over in black. Her passion was discourse, both political and personal, the two always intertwined like a magic rope rising by the force of conviction alone. The current crisis and Daniel's comments appeared to rile her like teasing a pitbull.

"What do you mean by that?" she asked.

"I pay for bridges so that I can get to work. I don't see why I have to pay for this mess," Daniel defended.

He looked over at Daphne, his eyes searching for support, but she was no help, so his gaze skipped back to Joanne, then to his feet, as he became suddenly self-conscious. Red blotches appeared on his cheeks. Why was he always at odds with her? His words were reasonable, he was sure, but why did they always come out wrong? He was rubbing her the wrong way again.

"Oh, so it's a mess – and somebody else's, I suppose," Joanne continued.

"That's right. I'm in business, not politics."

"But you vote, don't you?" Joanne wouldn't let up. "It's the government that won't do anything. You *do* vote, don't you?"

She glared at him, waiting for his response, but he was silent for a long time, searching for facts . . . *Je me souviens.* He'd lost track of who belonged where.

"Listen, Joanne, no one would have to do anything except get to work on time if these Indians knew how things were done. You can't just seize a bridge to get what you want. It's got to do with law, not traffic."

"Law. Right. Your law?"

The others pretended to do their work but, despite the drone of the air conditioner working in overdrive and the swishing of the copiers, sound still carried throughout the open-concept layout. At his desk just behind the main counter, Marc jiggled his mouse and clicked on the cursor as he prepared a graphic for the printer. Across from him, Sylvie, after a voluble sigh of annoyance, determinedly focused on adding up receipts and entering the totals in the ledger on her desk. Daphne moved from the large copier to the paper shelf to replenish the supply.

Only the high-pitched statements of the argument could be deciphered as they busied themselves. All week long they had been collecting an anthology of the two perspectives on the blockade. There had been no certainty since the police raid that had begun the standoff, and the whole city relied on debates, along with *La Presse*, to keep them informed. By the end of each day, Joanne and Daniel were no longer speaking to each other or to anyone else, and opinions shifted like worn gears throughout the store. They all found themselves resorting to an unabashed anger at the government.

Daphne had started the fourth job of the day – two hundred copies of a four-colour technical manual for employees of a security alarm company – and the conversation faded out of her consciousness. She had paid little attention to the two Mohawk blockades – the first northwest of the city, in Oka, the other on the South Shore bridge. She felt the filmy tension in the streets during the day, but slid through it, absorbed by her own riddles. She had bypassed street demonstrations and had flipped past the front-page photos in the *Montreal Sun* that howled *Standoff*, hurriedly seeking out the secrets in the back pages of the paper. The Mohawk crisis was like a foreign event; she was seeking something closer.

The whiz and swish of the copier comforted her. It spread rhythmically around the room like a white net. She had been learning to use the Macintosh computer, and Marc was training her to do desktop publishing for the English customers, but she preferred the large copier. Here she could dream standing up, fantasizing without interruption.

Before Montreal, Toronto had been her whole life, from her childhood near High Park to her life with Jeremy in Parkdale – a narrow expressway of experience along the lake. Perhaps, she thought now, she had unconsciously stayed close to the lake. Landlocked people are off kilter, Surefoot had said in the washroom. Daphne looked around; nobody was watching. She bent at the waist, her body dividing perfectly in half as she reached for the floor, legs apart, her hands lining up beside her feet. Fine. Everything in proportion. Her hamstring muscles contracted as she straightened up. In Toronto she'd begun to detect slight darting pains in her legs, like the ones her mother had called growing pains when she was a child. In the middle of the night, with Jeremy in bed beside her, she'd wake to soft spasms in her calves. They'd stopped when she moved to the island of Montreal. To escape Jeremy, she'd been looking for something else into which she could dissolve, but after her first long, cold winter and a subsequent dreary spring, she'd collided with the thick, wet heat of July.

Near the beginning of the month, seeking to escape the heat, she had gone for a walk down avenue du Parc. It was towards dawn, but the sky was still black. The city felt deserted, and the stillness hung like fog. But some sounds penetrated. One in particular: the sound of a couple frantically having sex several metres from the sidewalk, on the grass just near the playground. She walked quickly so as not to startle them, not realizing that they were oblivious to her passing. Then farther along, closer to the park, she thought she heard it again, but this time a different couple, a different style: slower breathing, quieter moaning. *Black-winged night rising out of chaos.* It was right out of one of her books.

> *Night danced on the seething depths. The dance of Night*
> *stirred up a great serpent wind Ophion which Night*
> *embraced and warmed between her hands. The wind grew*
> *lustful, coiled around Night and joined in the dance. Then*
> *Night assumed the form of a dove brooding on the waves*
> *and laid a silver egg, and Ophion coiled seven times around*
> *the world egg until it hatched and split open, the bottom half*
> *becoming earth and the top half the sky, sun, moon, and stars.*

She had been embarrassed by the sounds, but excited at witnessing a creation of sorts, and the images began to mingle in her imagination. The lines in time began to waver. She rushed home to read, to search for Aphrodite and her birth from sea foam, but instead she ran across Ovid's story of Daphne.

Loved by Apollo, the nymph Daphne would not be possessed,

and she fled from the deity's embrace. In the final chase, as Apollo gained on her, she called to her father, the river god, for help, and within moments of her plea could feel her feet take root in the earth, her body grow bark, and her arms sprout leaves. By becoming a laurel tree – inviolable, glossy green with foliage – she had successfully escaped. Daphne thought of Jeremy wrapping himself around her before sleep, often touching her belly – trespassing. In spite of her efforts to breach the moat of the things they didn't share, she had remained, finally, like a tree, unable to bend, unable to cross over.

A loud crack, a sputter, then a low whine startled her out of her musings. Paper had jammed in the bowels of the machine. She opened the front of the copier, pulled out the blotched sheets and discarded them.

"You could die!" Joanne's voice came from the front of the store.

"Oh, stop exaggerating," Marc said.

Daphne restarted the copier and joined the others at the service counter.

Marc's broad fingers were struggling to unlock the write-protect tab on a computer diskette, which Joanne grabbed from his hands, gracefully clicked open, and handed back to him before continuing.

"You could smash your head on a big rock or slip down the side of one . . . break your neck. Then you'd just sink and drown."

Daphne had been eagerly awaiting Marc's promised invitation to his cottage in the Gatineau. He'd described for them the two-hundred-foot rock face, the clear, deep lake, the sound of loons at night, and now they'd make plans to visit. Daphne moved closer to Marc.

"Well, okay, so I promise we won't jump off any cliffs, do you want to come or not?" he asked Joanne.

"How long does it take to get there?"

"About two and a half hours, if the traffic around Ottawa isn't backed up."

"Sounds great to me!" Sylvie got up from her desk with a voracious look. "What weekend are you planning to go?" She twisted her torso wistfully in front of Marc as she leaned in against the counter. He glanced at her then turned back to Joanne and Daphne.

"Last year we went the first weekend in August, but it may have to be near the end of the month, 'cause I'm late in arranging it. I need to know who can make it . . . to warn my parents. Can you come, Daph?"

"Sure. I want to hear a loon."

The word itself was magic. *Loon, loon, what tune, tune . . .* but there was also the rest. The smell. She'd be in the woods on Mount Royal and smell the mixture of pine needles and earth – like a proffered meal – and she'd arrive ravenous at the summit. She'd imagined loon calls brewed into the smell of water and longed to experience all the elements together. The weekend at Marc's cottage would be her chance.

"We could sleep outside on pine needles," she added. The others were awkwardly silent, but she barely noticed. "Are there berries you can eat there?"

"Oh, Daph, you're such a romantic."

Daphne's neck muscles tightened, pricked by Joanne's comment. "What do you mean?"

"All I can think about in the woods are bugs and ants, and that there's nowhere to shit properly. I've never heard anyone talk like you before, always making things sound better than they are."

Joanne started to clean up as she spoke, saving Daphne from making any response. Never comfortable with idleness, Joanne was efficiently active, a quality that impressed Daphne. She found herself riveted by Joanne's hands as they briskly swept up the paper remnants and loose sheets discarded beside the paper cutter.

"Were you born beside water?" Daphne asked.

"Hell no, not unless you consider Alberta an island . . . although, God knows, anyone other than a cowboy might feel shipwrecked there. Why do you ask?"

"Just wondering."

Joanne's hands had begun to grow under her gaze, bloating like a waterlogged corpse. As they gathered a scattering of paperclips they lost their fine lines and angles, becoming smooth gloves of flesh. Daphne grabbed one of the paperclips, saving it from the slippery peril of the fingers, then shook her head quickly. The hands returned to normal. As the others continued the conversation, Daphne bent the paperclip back and forth between her fingers until it snapped.

"My weekends are getting booked up quickly, so we'd better firm up plans now," Joanne said. The sound of a chair scraping across the floor silenced the group for a moment. Joanne turned toward Marc and said in a quiet voice, "He's not coming, is he? Better not be."

"That would be unbearable," said Sylvie in a low, hoarse whisper.

Marc shook his head to reassure them. Daphne watched Daniel move from his filing cabinet back to his desk. She was reluctant to turn against the first person to whom she'd confessed her guilt over Jeremy. But she too was increasingly wary of the rising spike of his moods, which had turned as prickly as the heat, while his eyebrows had begun to weigh down his face.

"What do we need to bring?" she asked, changing the subject.

"Hats. I'll bring hats: essential to outdoor survival, the ones that cover your neck at the back. Ozone's bad up there, one of the worst spots. Let's see . . . four of us." As she spoke, Joanne jotted down a reminder to herself of her generous offer, then tucked the piece of scrap paper into her pocket.

"I was thinking more in the way of food," said Daphne.

"Oh." Joanne paused, then added, "Oysters. I know they're not cheap, but I'll get them. Don't worry."

"What about marshmallows for the fire," Sylvie suggested.

"Oh brother," said Joanne under her breath.

Sylvie hadn't heard, but Marc jumped into the conversation. "Don't worry too much about the food. My parents always leave the cabin well-stocked, but you could bring booze – beer, or rum for cocktails."

Sylvie moved closer to him, tossing her golden hair as she did. Daphne noticed Joanne's lip curl in distaste. Glancing around, Daphne sought a distraction from the sudden tension. Marc too felt the negative undercurrent that rendered the counter electric.

"I can borrow my parents' car . . ."

"I used to go to a lake with my parents every summer," Sylvie interrupted him. "They rented a cottage, the same one, every year. We all sat on the dock and watched the stars every night, and I used to wish. I used to say 'God, make me an angel, please make me an angel.' I wanted to be able to fly up there and visit all the stars."

Joanne's eyes almost disappeared into her head with each eye roll of irritation. After a few seconds of caustic silence she threw out, "Yeah, sure, stars can do that to people."

Daphne tuned into the sound of the air conditioning, visualizing the wires that ran through the system to create a tight static universe. The conversation hissed around her until the door opened and a customer entered, bringing in heat and the sound of traffic, which broke up the group and sent them back to their jobs. Daphne moved to the Macintosh to work on the resumes of a commerce graduate from Concordia, an actress, and a cosmetician. Each new customer brought in a surge of noise and conversation. The talk was all of Oka. Daphne remained in the hum of white noise, absent from the news and discussion.

In the afternoon she took a break to read the paper, turning past the headlines about the Native blockade – *Defiant Mohawks dig in. . . No Deal at Oka, Mercier stays blocked* – to the letters to the editor, where she reviewed the opinions of several citizens on issues not associated with the blockades: *Teachers are not to blame*, someone from Westmount wrote, deflecting criticism of the school board. She flipped past international news – *Gorbachev reduces role of politburo* – past the life section – *Beating the heat* – past business – *Stock markets post healthy gain – Dow Jones index closes at record hight of 2969.8* – past the list of new movies – *Total Recall, Robocop 2, The Cook, The Thief, His Wife, & Her Lover,* until she reached the obituaries. Part of her afternoon routine was to scan the pages for names she liked or deaths that might have been unusual. In the *R*s, followed by *tragically, in her twentieth*

*year*, she noted the full decade by which she had outlived poor K.D. Rochelieu. She read other notices, seeking out the names and occupations of loved ones, deciding how much the deceased was loved, or if he'd be missed at all, and trying to imagine the moment of dying, the moment when love became meaningless and the drudgery of blood through veins ceased. By the time she made her way to the passing of Andrea Woodlock and *according to her wishes, there will be no funeral service,* her throat was constricted and ink-blot tears stained the newsprint.

Daniel left the store early in the afternoon to avoid the worst of the traffic. Toward six o'clock, Sylvie and Joanne left, and Marc asked Daphne to close up, so she stayed alone to finish the last resume. The relief of space. She wandered around the store, turning over manuscripts and reading letters on Daniel's desk: *Dear Sir, Please find enclosed a copy of the invoice you requested from your May order . . . Dear Sir, I would like to take this opportunity . . . Dear Sir, Pursuant to our telephone conversation of June 22 . . .*

She enjoyed the solitude but not the silence. Marc had switched off the large photocopier and the room felt empty. With a push of its power switch the accelerating hum took over. She tried her hand first, reducing it to 75% of the original. Then she put her finger on the glass and enlarged it to 150%. Next, she bent over and stared into the light as the flash copied her nose onto the paper that shot out of the machine. It was larger than life, and it startled her to see it feathered out on the page, even the pores visible in the reproduction. She set the machine to 25% and again pressed her nose against the glass. It was this copy that she would pin up beside the bathroom mirror when she got back to her apartment.

On her way home she passed the neighbourhood library and found herself turning back. Inside it was cool, and she felt safe among the tons of paper laden with print. Files of pre-digital memory, tangible, redolent. She browsed the colourful rows until she found the beginning of the fiction section. Brontë:

Emily . . . Charlotte . . . There it was: *Jane Eyre.* A burst of print released by the loosened lid on the jar of names. She pulled the book from its spot on the shelf and examined the cover, a portrait of a woman with white skin, black hair, a Victorian frock, embroidery on her lap. Storm clouds were building in the background landscape. She opened to the first page:

*There was no possibility of taking a walk that day . . .*

Then to the last page, as was her habit.

*"My Master," he says, "has forewarned me. Daily He announces more distinctly, 'Surely I come quickly,' and hourly I more eagerly respond, 'Amen; even so, come Lord Jesus.' "*

Back to the beginning. The language surprised her; its odd syntax and resolute politeness made progress slow. She struggled with Jane's manner, with her curiosity for solitary churchyards, and the *newly risen crescent attesting the hour of eventide.* The world of childhood was terrifying, damp, and lonely, but within it Jane would always find fire and exclamation. So many exclamation points, thought Daphne. Soon she was engrossed in the red-room itself, the room in which Jane had been locked up by Mrs. Reed, and in which the carpet was red, the bed covered with crimson cloth, and the walls blushed with pink. Jane's orphan sobs provided accompaniment to the lyric prose in which every moment was measured, every action accounted for. The words were like keys that gradually unshackled Jane from her predicament in a century uneasy with freedom, and Daphne began to share Jane's fastidious contempt for insincerity and to be restless with the tedium of days lived waiting for an unnamed change, a leap to a higher plane.

*It's a very strange sensation to inexperienced youth to feel itself quite alone in the world: cut adrift from every connection, uncertain whether the port to which it is bound can be reached, and prevented by many impediments from returning to that it has quitted . . .*

*Well, looka who dat is here . . . yu tink she mind if we read about she?* The bouncy accent of her mother invaded again. Daphne looked around, expecting a presence over her shoulder, but there was only a girl shelving books at the far end of the stacks. She shivered, suddenly feeling the cold air that blasted through the library with vengeance, battling the humidity that threatened to curl pages. She put the book back on the shelf, having begun to like this Jane, this fiery girl. But her name was too ordinary; Daphne didn't want her name.

That night, with the erratic noise from St. Urbain grating on her idleness, Daphne left her apartment and walked up Esplanade toward the mountain. A couple was playing tennis under the lights of the large public court near the park, . On the street to her right a light shone from the second-floor apartment at number 4557. Steadied by the thick air and the muffled, punctuating *tock* of the felt ball against the rackets, she crept up the stairs. Stepping on the lower bar, she leaned over the wrought-iron railing to look inside. Someone was in the lighted kitchen at the back of the apartment. Late at night it's always the kitchen that's occupied. For Daphne kitchens were escorts into the night. The monotone drone of the refrigerator was a substitute for chatter, even – and sometimes especially – at parties. There conversation already existed, about food, about dishes, about the colour of paint. Kitchens offered work to do, tasks to complete, small-talk to avoid. Even in the dead of night a sense of company inhabited them. Daphne could see a bare arm, bent, resting on the table, a beer at hand and a cigarette burning in an ashtray. A female arm. Long thin brown hair fell over the shoulder as the arm reached for the cigarette. The fingers folded around it tensely, tightly pinching the filter.

There was barely any furniture in the front room. An old couch with invincible oversized arms sat against the wall, covered by a flowered sheet. All the furniture faced toward the television: two vinyl folding chairs were placed at eye-blinding closeness to the screen. A small tricycle, draped with cloth dolls, rested in a corner, and other toys were scattered over the floor: Lego; plastic rings of bright yellow, orange, and green; a tiny shovel and accompanying rake; and a bucket whose purple butterflies were gradually disappearing from the plastic surface. Unframed posters covered cracks in the wall: Jim Morrison, a skier descending a deserted white mountain, and a torn one of a cat hanging from a bar. *Hang in there baby*. Crayon scribbles in a line around the walls, about three feet above the floor, marked a certain territory. The room stammered with exhaustion. Daphne stood for several minutes with her hips pressing against the railing. She could imagine the woman waking early, rushing, feeding, playing, working, alone even in the company of giggles. She saw the progress of the day right up to this moment alone with the chatter of the kitchen – the interminable wait for a huge wet swig, a long heavy drag like a sigh.

She backed down from the railing and walked past the now empty tennis court toward home.

In bed she remained wide awake, tossing to stop her thoughts, the heat so bad even the cotton sheet was an annoyance. She tried counting things. After counting tricycles, cats, and cigarettes, she settled on fingers, the fingers of everyone she could think of. Starting with the woman at her kitchen table pinching her cigarette, to Joanne's bloated digits, to Surefoot's fat thumb – but skipping Jeremy – she counted into the eighties, but soon found her own fingers moving over her hot belly, down her pelvis, and between her legs, carefully examining for traces of hair.

Several were sprouting in a line above her labia. Months ago she had started to attend to them again but had forgotten in the last week, and now the spiral black hairs were breaking the surface. She bent her torso forward and propped her head up with some pillows, then reached for the tweezers on the bedside table. She carefully plucked the few burgeoning hairs until she was completely smooth, clean, devoid of any traces of a normal tuft. She rubbed herself. *The breath of the west wind bore her.* The skin was marble sleek, sculpted. In the sweep of her hands her fingers stumbled on her clitoris, tapping and alerting it. She began to fondle it, fingering it like a rosary. Slowly, she brought herself to a climax, disappearing into a cracked and peeling wall, releasing a silent supplication – the *ohh, ahh, ahh* that signals the sedative of touch.

# Quarter

6:42 – the same configuration every morning when she opened her eyes. Her internal alarm went off just three minutes ahead of the clock radio a few inches from her head. The next three minutes flipped over like destinations on a train station marquee. 6:43. 6:44. 6:45. The radio announcer's sentence was ending: "and the Expos downed the Cubs 9-3." Daphne listened for a few minutes, but the volume was low and the noise of traffic was growing. She dozed through the seven o'clock news.

"This morning, the sliced curve of the fading moon looks wide, refracted through the hazy, moist air here near the Lake of Two Mountains. While provincial officers and Mohawks stare at one another through binoculars from behind their respective barricades, the people of the village of Oka and the native settlement of Kanesatake try to go about their daily business . . ."

The blockade was now more than two weeks old. One native woman had become the mediator. A West Coast lawyer, she had come to Oka in a show of support, but she'd soon been asked to negotiate with the Sûreté du Québec officers who had set up a counter-blockade outside the town after the raid. Mohawk leaders remained in the woods – the gravesite and land of their ancestors known as the Pines – surrounded by warriors and women banded together to protect the bones of their dead from the bulldozers that threatened expansion of the Oka Golf Course. The lawyer rode her all-terrain vehicle back and forth between the Natives huddled among the trees and the police beyond the gate. The reporter described her swerving between the trees, grazing her elbow on one of the pines. She was delivering messages for both sides.

The secondary blockade on the Mercier Bridge, south of the city, was still standing. *Déjà vu.* Cowboys and Indians. The gunfire in Oka on the day of the police raid had lasted just twenty-three seconds, but one officer had been shot and killed. (*I think we got one.*) Within hours, warriors from the Kahnawake reserve had seized the Mercier and threatened to blow it up if violence resumed in the Pines. No one knew who had fired the first shot, but both sides were scared and had agreed to negotiate. Letters were sent back and forth, government ministers were called in. In an attempt to defuse the crisis, the federal government purchased the graveyard from the town of Oka for a dollar. "You know you can't talk to the Indians," said the mayor.

The police were stopping food from getting through to the reserve on the other side of the blockade. Starving them out. *Déjà vu.* One of the messages delivered by the lawyer was from a white resident. It said that the Klu Klux Klan was driving north toward the Canadian border; men from Texas, Louisiana, and Illinois were coming to Quebec. There was no turning back now. The warriors were afraid of what the police would do to them if they surrendered. Revenge was a matter of interpretation from here on in.

And every day the traffic was getting worse. With the Mercier Bridge blocked, it was taking hours to get into Montreal from the South Shore community of Châteauguay. Rancour had become another toxic fume on the highway. In Oka, the garbage piled up on the streets and supplies in the stores were running out. The days refused to rain. War had become the mad accident of geography.

"*Calice de tabernacle!*"

Daniel entered the store dishevelled and sweating. He rarely swore, especially in French. Swearing, he'd said, was for people who weren't smart enough to communicate in any other way. Daphne looked up and watched him slam his briefcase on the counter, take out a handkerchief, and wipe his brow. He looked shorter than usual, and his light brown bangs were plastered down by sweat above his green eyes. Always a clear indication of his mood, his eyebrows were aligned in a single bar, the space between them vanquished by his frown.

Daphne had seen Daniel alternately grow and shrink since she'd started to work for him. In the first few weeks he had seemed enormous, a giant of efficiency dignified by the duties of management. She had loved to watch him with customers, to hear him switch effortlessly between French and English. His charm would carry the store. In the spring term, he'd begun to take evening courses toward an MBA and would arrive in the morning at Copie Copie speaking of rationalization and AIDA – Attention, Interest, Desire, and Action; not the opera. But these buzz words diminished him like stolen clothes that didn't fit. He wore them as camouflage, and Daphne distrusted his belief in them. After all, it had been Daniel who had said during her job interview that words were products like anything else – they could be assembled like toys or widgets for whatever purpose. It was the packaging of the words that made the difference. She had been envious of his clarity and had watched him every day packaging his perfect bilingualism, his pronunciation flawless in either language. But recently he seemed to be stumbling, his tongue tripping over the enigmatic concepts of management.

His father had been English, and Daniel had gone to English schools even though French had been the language used at home and what he still spoke to his mother and sister in Sherbrooke. He had described them to Daphne as *habitants*: "They're old-fashioned," he told her. "You know, Christ, and Mary, and maple syrup – very simple." Daphne heard sleigh bells when he spoke of them, and smelled Christmas goose and *tourtière*. His mother and sister lived in the family home Daniel had persuaded them to keep after his father's death. Aside from speaking French with his family and with customers, the rest of Daniel's life was conducted in English. Daphne understood that for him family was the repository of all that he'd left behind – the museum to which he could return to be reassured that a part of him was being preserved. He seemed to save French for special moments, so she was surprised by his outburst.

"*Hostie!*" The word burst open like flimsy cellophane, and the bitterness poured out.

Joanne suppressed a yawn as she watched Daniel from the counter, where she'd been skimming the pages of a newspaper. She looked tired and hot, her face puffy, not seeming to care whether or not Daniel noticed her dawdling. Daphne sensed that today there'd be no sparring with "Danny Boy," as Joanne called him. Joanne detested the heat as much as the very cold. "I'm moving outta this damn country as soon as I get enough money. California, or Spain, even. Somewhere where they know how to live," she kept saying to Daphne. Would she let her hair grow back in blonde? Daphne wondered. Joanne moved away from the counter as Daniel passed and strolled over to Daphne who stood at the coffee machine pouring her second cup of the morning. Both of them watched Daniel settle down at his desk, fling open his briefcase, then reach for the phone. A customer at the front counter was speaking to Marc, and the patter of the shop reached its comfortable working pitch. Daphne caught Daniel's eye, but he quickly averted his gaze and stared into the receiver which he held expectantly. She felt guilty and dropped her eyes to her coffee cup.

"You know what's going on down there, don't you, Daph?" Joanne spoke conspiratorially, making Daphne feel she was being let in on something.

"Mm?"

"There, on the South Shore, you know, things are getting worse. But if you look at it, it's really quite simple. It's like the strain exerted on a bridge or structure that depends on balance. If it's built badly it just gives. But it takes a kind of mutual conversion."

Daphne looked up from the small curdles of milk she'd spotted in her coffee. "Mutual conversion?"

Joanne followed Daphne back to her desk. Daphne pushed the power button on the Macintosh and – *click* – was no longer paying attention. It had happened again: the click – something hyper-aural – that always pulled Daphne out of events into a protected dreamspace. She had been clicking out at all words surrounding the debate and the factions growing over the blockades. She would swirl above the day's events as if in a dream. A word inflected in a particular way and – *click* – all of a sudden she'd be sucked up above the room, unable to come down.

"Mutual conversion. People don't commit themselves too far before trying to find out how everyone else around them feels. Just like kids really . . ."

Daphne floated above Joanne's lecture, up and up, until she was looking down on the spot where she was supposed to be, watching Joanne standing by the computer far below. She could hear Joanne's voice, but her words meant nothing here.

"Say you have one kid who gets a failing mark on a test. Poor sod feels like a loser, until he finds out that others aren't doing too great either. He starts to dig around to see how the other kids are feeling. 'Do you like the teacher?' he asks. 'I dunno, do you like him?' asks the other. 'Not too much,' says the first. 'Na, I don't like him at all,' the second one finally admits. And it snowballs from there. Each kid commits himself a little further and all of a sudden the teacher is an ogre, totally unfair, giving good marks only to kids he likes. Judy becomes 'teacher's pet,' and they all start hating Judy until it's Judy who thinks she's the one having trouble in school. That's what's going on in Châteauguay, you can bet your life on it."

Joanne looked at Daphne's blank stare, shrugged her shoulders, then turned away. Daphne finally sat down at her desk and began to input data for a résumé. She played a game with the document, inserting experiences from her own life into the job descriptions.

*WAITER: Cousteau's Restaurant – I waited and waited and waited, and Cousteau refused to serve me. I walked out; he lost a big tip.*

She highlighted her changes, deleted, and then saved the document. Self-invention continued.

The day droned on with the whiz of photocopiers and the in-and-out of customers. Late in the afternoon, Daniel threw his calculator at the wall, picked up some papers and tossed them into his briefcase. Before the Mohawk blockade, Daphne had never heard Daniel speak badly of anyone, and he rarely raised his voice. He was charming to faithful customers and subtly solicitous to new ones. The previous week, when everyone else had gone for the day, Daphne had stayed late trying to finish formatting a newsletter using the template Marc had set up for her. Thinking he was alone in the store, Daniel spoke loudly and very quickly on the telephone as he ordered supplies. There would be a delay. His pause was heavy and his self-control gave way in an explosive, "I don't give a fuck what delays you have to deal with, I'm finished doing business with you," after which he'd slammed down the phone. Daphne was embarrassed for him. That tension had remained floating about the store all week like stale air, his temper a pending storm.

She started to connect other odd moments to Daniel's new mood – one event in particular, at the Bistro St. Denis on Marc's birthday. It had been February, after an icestorm, and the ice on the sidewalk in front of the bistro had to be chipped away before the door could be opened wide enough for them to squeeze through. Despite the weather, Daniel had been determined to celebrate, and when they were finally seated he jovially ordered a round of drinks for everyone. His treat. The meal arrived, and they were halfway through when Daniel stopped in mid-sentence. A morsel of cartilage from his hamburger appeared on his tongue, and he picked it off delicately with his fingertips. At first he remained calm, even amidst jokes from Joanne and Sylvie, but slowly his eyebrows slid closer together. He called the waiter over, handed back the burger quietly, without ceremony, and followed the waiter to the kitchen. The others sat smirking and anxious, checking their own meals, and in a few minutes Daniel returned. The waiter brought him onion soup and a salad. Daniel was sullen for the rest of the evening, becoming thick and singular like his eyebrows, and leaving Marc, with his usual graciousness, trying to fill the uncomfortable silence that had descended on the table.

Hearing the calculator hit the wall, Daphne turned around to scrutinize Daniel. Her eyes reached his ankles and stuck there.

Slowly, his shoes began to swell, transforming into enormous clown-like feet stamping the floor in a vaudeville dance. She blinked hard several times and the feet returned to their proper size as Daniel marched out. The store returned to normal for a few hours, with the hum of machines lulling away the afternoon. But when the courier arrived with rumours that Premier Bourassa was not going to back down and would ask the federal government to intervene, Joanne became animated and drew Marc into a heated discussion. Marc did his best to calm her down. Daphne ignored them and remained absorbed in typing Antonio Barbusi's résumé.

LANGUAGES: *Italian, English, French*
ACTIVITIES AND INTERESTS: *Dancing*

Dancing. His diploma was in Business Administration. She wondered if dancing could be the potential upper hand in the job application, the edge he was looking for over the other applicants. She envisioned him at his finest, most alive moment at Chez Swan, his arms rising and bending just to his ears on the beat, his fingers snapping, an intense look of concentration on his face. His suit has small, iridescent speckles that shimmer in the light of the room, and it is this same suit he is wearing – not having made it home in time to change – when he arrives at his job interview at 9:30 the next morning, a little tired but calm, all cells settled comfortably in their plasma. No one can notice the dried sweat on his forehead and neck. No one needs to get that close in an interview. Daphne couldn't help but admire him. She clicked the cursor on SAVE and exited the program with a smile.

Her dress stuck to her after only a few minutes in the open. Sweat. Odour. She trudged through the pasty air. When her stomach rumbled she knew it was time for coffee. Coffee for breakfast, coffee for lunch, for dinner, coffee to help pass the hot afternoons. It had become her routine, with the occasional plate of pasta or French fries late at night when a cloudy hunger called for starch and the air was cool enough for solid food. Her plan was to cut coffee out at the end of the summer when eating made sense again. For now it was all she could ingest and still feel comfortable. *Déjeuner 2,50$. Café. Take Out.* She pulled open the lettraseted glass door of the diner on the corner. The place smelled of grease and stale smoke, despite the air conditioning. A couple sat in a booth examining menus. At the counter, Daphne ordered a coffee to go from the blue-smocked waitress. She was about to pay when she heard a voice from the corner, near the grill.

"Hey . . . following me now?"

Daphne turned, surprised by the familiar voice and then by the sight of Surefoot. On her huge frame the white apron that stretched across her belly appeared as a mere patch. Daphne moved toward her, attracted by something, not sure what: the loudness of skin, the crude extravagance of such a huge body? Surefoot must have sensed something.

"Still peeping?"

"I wasn't . . ."

"No, just lucky."

"I don't know about lucky . . ."

"Like I said, saltwater in the blood. But luck forgets about people who forget it. Take it from me. What can I get you?"

"Just coffee. I'm on my way home. It's too hot."

Surefoot's forehead corrugated into a frown. "No one should take just coffee from a real kitchen. Kitchens are important, deserve respect. If not, they'll fight back, make or break a home. Some kitchens are wicked, the food doesn't cooperate, and all the family's stomachs can turn sour. Those that don't get respect . . ." Surefoot shook her head and wagged a warning index finger, then wiped her fat hands on her apron, adding a print over her navel. She waited for an answer.

Daphne blushed and looked into the glass display case hoping to find something made with potatoes that she could eat later, but all she saw were desserts and drinks. She timidly pointed to a homemade snack pack of tapioca pudding and watched Surefoot slide the refrigerator unit open, remove the container, then slide the glass panel tightly shut. Daphne noticed the blackness of Surefoot's short-cropped hair and the way her triceps jiggled with each movement of her arm.

"Met your folks yet?" asked Surefoot, handing over the pudding.

"No. You?"

"Complicated. But Natives live long, like long summers. I'll find 'em. By the end of this summer – I'll pray to the right ancestors."

"I have an aunt."

"Yeah, good."

Daphne wanted to say the name Sheila Eyre, to have it bounce off Surefoot's belly and back into her own ears, but she couldn't.

"Haven't phoned her yet."

Surefoot looked surprised. Daphne noticed how the folds in her neck piled up on each other.

Surefoot shook her head again. "Make sure you do. Don't put it off. Blood is blood. Spills easily, be careful. You call her."

The waitress called out "steak, medium," and Surefoot turned automatically to the grill. Daphne waited a few moments, hoping she would turn toward her again, but Surefoot had focused on her work, her arms moving at jiggling speed over the grill. Daphne paid the cashier for the pudding and coffee. She looked back one more time, hoping to get Surefoot's attention, but no luck. Surefoot flipped the steak over. Daphne slipped off the thin silver bracelet that had dangled around her wrist since her twenty-first birthday and left it on the empty counter near Surefoot. She snuck away without another word and pushed open the door to a rush of wind that blew dust into her eyes.

# Half

Heat seeped through the city like leaked fuel, dangerous, ready to ignite and send the metropolis blasting to the stars, the splinters doused in the St. Lawrence River as they fell, one after another, back to earth. By night the city smouldered. Daphne's sleep was fitful as she struggled with the sheet that had twisted into a wick at her feet. The singeing treble of car radios on St. Urbain sent her head under the pillows, making it almost impossible for her to breathe. The Saturday night bar crowd was going home.

Just after 3:00 A.M., when she had finally fallen asleep, she was jolted awake by the sound of deep and painful retching. She got up and went to the window. The cap of the moon protruded from the side of the building across the street like an ephemeral ear. A woman was in the alley, on her knees, vomiting up her night's consumption. Her black strapless dress had fallen around her ribs, and she clutched it with her left hand, tugging up on the straps between heaves that threw her shoulders up around her ears. Jerking, chicken-pecking retches. Two other women, also wearing small black dresses, stood swaying, waiting on the sidewalk for their friend to finish. The reeking ferment of booze and chips, mingled with perfume and smoke, rose from the pavement. Despite the repulsive stench, a longing rose in Daphne's chest. *The breath of the west wind bore her.*

When she'd first moved to Montreal, Daphne had gone to the bars in her neighbourhood, wanting to talk to everyone, to touch them all, men and women. She had wanted to coil herself around the women and have them wrap her in their tiny white arms. From the men she had wanted hands — hands that would hold her buttocks, one in each, and rock her on the dance floor.

But compared to the bubbling and giggling exotic beer women she felt flaccid. Their glow was one of certainty: their bones fit comfortably into every angle of their lives. She was enticed by them, as she had been by Jeremy, who had seduced her with the crimson streaks that feathered his cheeks. Even when living with Jeremy, for over three years, she had felt forever estranged. His jokes had flown by her; his references to his trips abroad, to his summers in Europe on language exchange programmes, to the house he wanted to own on the outskirts of Toronto, all of these – his dam of confidence – had blocked her flooding need for him, had pushed Daphne back into herself. Their shared moments had somehow made her feel absent.

She shut the window and threw herself back into bed. Feeling her pubis she detected stubble, so she grabbed the tweezers and flashlight and dove under the sheet. She shone the light on the dotted field of her labia and began to pluck. Once she fell back into sleep, it was undisturbed until late in the day as the heat was reaching its climax.

The sound of Sunday was a drum. The rap of flesh on skin, the echo of an empty chamber, the pounding of a skipping heart through the whole neighbourhood. Daphne could hear it coming from Mount Royal, entering through her opened balcony door. The afternoon was in full swing; still she lay stretched out on the bed, no clothes, no sheet, sticky with sweat. She remained in that position for some time, gazing at a crack in the ceiling, with the rap of drums wafting in with the breeze. From her night table she picked up a book.

> *The Amazons invaded Lycia and were repulsed by Bellerophon. . . . A maiden, Clytie, fell in love with the sun god and, unrequited, followed him across the sky until she was transformed into a sunflower to stare at him each day. . . . And Sisyphus was punished with the plight of futility, his rock forever rolling back down the hill.*

The tedium appalled her. *Bear and forebear* said the new voice with the accent. She got up.

The idleness of Sunday dilated as the sun travelled to the back of Daphne's building, and its saffron spray deepened toward pink. Daphne roamed her apartment purposelessly, then stepped out onto the balcony. The temperature had not dropped, but a gentle breeze tickled her skin, and the rhythm from the park beckoned her. Returning inside, she searched her desk for the Audubon bird guide. Among the papers scattered over the old oak door that served as her desk she came across the slip of paper with the name *Sheila Eyre* written on it, along with a phone number. For a split second she couldn't remember who the name belonged to, then the feeling of stepping and missing caught up with her, and she remembered her aunt. Another of the voices with the rhythms. *The breath of the west wind . . .* The sound of the voice now had Surefoot's lips behind it. Would her aunt have flapping, warm folds of skin Daphne could curl into? She folded the piece of paper up into a triangle and balanced it on the receiver of the telephone. It stood, tent-like, waiting for the next call. When she found *Eastern Birds*, she went out, cradling the book under her arm.

> *Black-capped Chickadee:*
> *Tame and inquisitive.*
> *Call a dry, chick-a-de-de or -dee-dee. Song a simple, clear*
> *whistled dee-dee, first note higher.*

*Chick-a-dee, dee*, she repeated to herself, but some of it slipped out as she walked toward the park.

Reaching the concrete square at the foot of the mountain where bronze lions guarded the towering statue of an angel, Daphne joined the massive crowd gathered around the drummers. There were twelve musicians: eight men on congas, bongos, timpani, boxes, and cartons; one played a marimba; one a washboard; and one woman was blowing quietly on a saxophone next to a man playing clappers. The music was without measure, the varying pulses of a protracted afternoon. No one orchestrated the event; it was a Sunday improvisation, as unpredictable as its audience, which varied, though many in the crowd were regulars. It was simply known as "the drumming" to the residents in the area. Some afternoons it was wild and frenetic, on others it was subdued and forced – the mood governed by something intangible. But in the heat that Sunday there was genuine abandon in the arms of the shirtless men who, with palms pounding on stretched leather, carved out the afternoon, giving shape to the day's leisure.

"You never want to dance," a woman said to the man beside Daphne.

"That's not true," he countered, "I just don't do it in public."

Daphne tried to overhear the rest of the couple's exchange, looking for vileness – having learned it was always lurking yet unpredictable – but the words got garbled in the noise of the crowd.

Many people were dancing to the drumming. A young woman in a long print dress, her hair reaching her waist the way her mother's had twenty years before, waved her arms in the air, undulating and heaving her belly in and out, around and around like a harem star. Beside her a tall, skinny teenager with long hair falling from the centre of his head tossed the bushy tuft from his eyes on the downbeat, wrenching his neck about to his own rhythm.

Daphne pushed her way through the crowd to the other side of the square. The whole area at the foot of Mount Royal throbbed like an Eastern bazaar. Billowy clouds shied away from the sun – not a single one filtered its spray – and the air was heavy, coating the skin. The crowd was a mixture of young and old who spilled out from the centre of the dancing to the sidewalk on avenue du Parc and the grassy picnic area. Children rode the lion statues like carousel beasts. Families gathered, some just listening, others dancing, along with a few solitary older men moving with Tai chi arms. Children and cyclists collided. Men who regularly slept in the park gathered discarded cans and bottles. People who had brunched in downtown cafés and those who barely ate at all were at the same party. The sound enticed everyone; the comfort of the crowd held them.

Daphne began to bounce on the spot, although she wasn't aware of it. Her busy eyes scanned the area. She wasn't surprised when she spotted Joanne dancing at the front of the crowd. Gyrating her hips as she pushed up on to tiptoes, Joanne's body was an instrument played by the twelve musicians. A child danced beside her, and occasionally she joined the child's rhythm and took him by the hand. Daphne smiled to see Joanne unbridled, her lips pressed together in a serene smile. Making her way through the crowd and up into the woods, Daphne's own step was light and in tempo with the receding beat.

The sound of Sundays was a drum, or at least it had been for the last three Sundays, but that was unusual for Châteauguay. Daniel was the first to arrive. He stood by a brown vinyl folding chair at a card table set up in the middle of the garage watching Lucie Marchand arrange nuts, pretzels, and *biscuits au beurre* on the table. The Marchands had decided to hold the meeting in the garage instead of indoors because of the heat, and in the hope that more neighbours would drop by when they saw the meeting in progress. Some of the neighbours needed coaxing to participate in this protest.

On Saturday, Gaston Marchand had knocked on Daniel's door to let him know about the neighbourhood meeting he and his wife had planned in order to organize a counter-protest at the Mercier Bridge. "It's time we took action," Gaston had said to him, emphasizing the last word. Before Gaston's visit Daniel had focused his indignation on time – his loss of it – and had tried to harness his moments of frustration productively, so as not to be pricked by the thwarted sense of entitlement that had already spurred his neighbours to anger. But with Gaston's words his bucking awareness of his own ineffectiveness had been released, and his daily nightmare of trying to make it into the city prompted him to show up, curious to gauge the reaction of others. Now he wasn't so sure he wanted to be here.

Gaston held out a soft drink in one hand, a beer in the other, nodding at each to indicate that Daniel had a choice. Daniel declined both, twitching and nervously adjusting his belt.

"How long is it taking you to get into work, Danny?"

"Daniel. Sometimes three hours."

"Yep, same as most of the rest of us. I'm no manager; I can't be late. I'm losing sleep. Gotta leave here at 5:00 in the morning. And everyone's just mad as hell, you know, and they're out for themselves, won't give you a break and let you in the lane, nothing. Lucie was cut off, almost ended up in a ditch, in a big accident, eh, and that was around 7:30, before the real stuff starts to happen. We called the MP, the MNA, and the city guy, but everyone says we gotta hold off and see what the feds are gonna do. Shit, I'm 'fed' up. *He he.* My brother-in-law says that all the time! It's all part of the same federal problem. If this had happened in Toronto someone woulda done something by now."

"You're probably right. They don't like to miss work in Toronto."

"Yeah," said Gaston, oblivious to Daniel's attempt at humour, "but instead we got everyone sitting on their butt waiting to see what everyone else is going to do. Walter down the street says – he's comin' today – as he says – and he's English – this is our land too."

Daniel pulled out the chair and sat down. He arranged his shirt collar and picked a speck of thread from the short sleeve. A teenager with buzz cut wearing a denim jacket emerged from the house talking on a cordless phone. "Yeah, get over here now," Daniel heard him say as he headed down the driveway. Daniel saw Lucie and Gaston exchange a quick look. As the garage filled up, Lucie busied herself with finding chairs and welcoming people, too distracted to offer refreshments. People stood around talking, in French and occasionally in English. They were waiting for something to happen. Daniel crossed his arms and looked down into his lap, listening.

"I'm losing money every day; the reserve gives me good business . . ."

"We should boycott that grocery store if they keep sellin' to the Indians. Let them run outta food, then they'll come out . . ."

"These Indians think they're above the law . . . this has

nothing to do with a graveyard . . . they can't take the goddamn bridge everytime they're mad about something . . ."

A woman recounted how in Oka residents's property had been destroyed, stores had been looted, and garbage was not being collected. It was rotting on the sidewalks and attracting vermin.

"Soon it's gonna be like that in Châteauguay," said the man next to her.

Native bands all over the country were starting to block major routes in support of the Kanesatake Mohawks.

"It will all get outta control; we'll be the losers if we don't do something now."

Daniel could smell the smoke of a *fait accompli*. A decision had already been made. This meeting was just a forum for justification, not the discussion he thought it would be. Someone had brought a placard that read: CHÂTEAUGUAY POW WOW – YOU WOW AND I'LL POW. Another sign bore the head of an old-coin-styled Indian chief inside a red circle bisected by a red line that mocked the no smoking symbol. Underneath were the words: NO PROBLEM.

Finally, Lucie Marchand stood up in front of the crowd, her turgid pink cheeks going in and out as she spoke. "Thank you all for coming. It's good to see such a turnout and to know that there are so many of us willing to fight for our rights. It's time we stopped waiting for politicians to do what we know has to be done. And they'd just botch it anyway, so why don't we take our chances."

There was a brief, muffled wave of laughter. Daniel looked around and noticed several restless-looking teenagers at the back of the garage. Among them was the Marchand boy, who was drawing something on the back of a friend's denim jacket with a black marker. The teenagers' jackets bore various symbols, none of which Daniel could read, but he could feel the leeching wildness of their caged pacing. He turned his gaze nervously back to his tennis shoes.

Lucie continued. "If we all went to the bridge and made ourselves heard, got the attention of the press, we'd get a lot farther than by making phone calls that are a waste of time. I know that some of you have other things to say, and I want to give everyone a chance, so I'll just say thanks again for coming, and let's not let this thing tear us down."

After sporadic clapping faded to silence, Walter Harris, a tall, grey-haired man with a slow dignified walk, made his way to the front of the garage.

"I've been living here for twenty years. We survived the seventies. We stayed when everyone else was leaving. We survived high taxes and slow business. We survived it all, but I've never been as mad as I am today. I'm not going to be the pawn of political games. I intend to be up there on the bridge to fight like I've always done for the place I come from. I hope you'll all join me. *Merci.*"

Again, scattered applause. An elderly man spoke from the back: "I've been up at the bridge every day, but there's nothin' we can do –"

"Like hell we can't," a young man in tight T-shirt and jeans interrupted, "If it's up to us to do the police's job, I've got a few ideas of my own – tear gas . . ."

The applause was louder this time, with some whoops and whistles, and the sound of baseball bats pounding the pavement. One of the teenagers let off a firecracker. The talk grew louder.

One woman sided with the Natives and their demands but said she felt used and ignored by the politicians, and it was the politicians who should be made to pay. A short man holding one of the placards at chest level sidled up to the front and faced the crowd. "We've worked and lived side by side with these Indians for years. Some of them we know. They're taking advantage of us. We gotta do something. We shouldn't stand for the break-down of law and order in this country any longer."

His speech was greeted by a chorus of grunted agreements punctuated by approving whistles and a smattering of ob-scenities. This was the fuel the group needed. Vengeance shined in their faces. Lucie was moved to tears and dabbed her eyes with her sleeve. The crowd started to break into smaller groups and the discussion took on a feverish edge. Many knew this was a watershed event.

Daniel sat quietly in his chair, one of the few who had remained seated. A vein along his forearm began to twitch. His head was a stew, simmering the way it did late at night in the heat, the sensation rising in him the way sex did. He hadn't been able to sleep, even after drinking the hot brew made from the flowers he cultivated in his garden. The tea wasn't working; the thing continued to creep in each night. Futility: it slithered toward him like a viper. The futility of every step forward, every notch in his belt of progress blocked by some stupidity. Futility was worse than violence. He was reminded of his sister's boyfriend and his gang. They stuck together – similar blood through similar veins – but with a kind of violence Daniel had never before imagined. It surged through their bodies and they used it to get their way. Blood against futility. The gang was made up of young men from the same small town. "We kick ass," her boyfriend said. "Just evenin' up the score." Daniel knew that the town had made them what they were. Moulded by a population of vexed, swearing, nervous adults. Especially the older men. If you were quiet they left you alone, but if you had any kind of opinion or passion, they'd beat it out of you. Their children hated for a reason. Rage was an inheritance, and they believed in balancing the numbers, spreading the blows around a bit. It was their turn on the heavy end of the teeter-totter. Daniel straightened up in his chair and gripped the seat tightly with both hands, feeling as if he was about to lose his balance.

An explosion. Daniel turned toward the driveway in time to see the smoke from a sulphur bomb drift down the street watched and cheered by a group of teenagers congregated around the Marchand's boy. As they moved off in a pack, Daniel noticed the back of one torn-cloth jacket. On it he could see a felt-marker swastika fading into the denim.

"Jesus, they're going," Gaston said as he grabbed his own placard and headed toward his car. The crowd was incited. A few of the younger men pushed over chairs as they scrambled out of the garage. Daniel watched Walter Harris walk, in his long firm stride, to the Marchand's car and get in the back seat. A tingling travelled up from Daniel's pelvis to his shoulders. He shuddered and moved quickly out of the garage, reaching into his pocket for his keys.

In the distance, on the Mercier Bridge, the steady, singular beat of a Mohawk drum began as the sun started to fall beyond the river. Bonfires were being built behind the barricade, as they had been every night of the past few weeks. The drum and lights were taken as an invitation, and the crowd from Marchand's garage dispersed, got into their cars and drove, as though it were inevitable, toward the plaza parking lot, toward the pulse: a rumbling, beckoning thunder.

As Daphne made her way up the mountain, away from the drumming, Sunday strollers were making their way down. The smaller paths up the side of the mountain were of dirt, with stones and roots torn up by the wheels of mountain bikes; others had steps, built to encourage visitors to explore inside the arms of the woods. She chose the torn paths where she knew the birds would not have been frightened away by the crowds, and where she'd be able to hear their calls, to learn them, and call back to them. She had almost assimilated the rich, liquid twitterings and gurglings of the Purple Martin: *tyu, swee swuh, tyu, swee swuh.*

The climb was steep in sections. *Qoit, qoit, qoit.* She paused and heard it again . . . *qoit, qoit* . . . Then she saw it. Brown, with a mottled breast. Flipping through her book, she found its match: *Wood Thrush.* The sound had been its call, not its song, which the book stated was completely different. *Quoi, quoi* . . . The ending didn't sound right when Daphne tried it. She moved on, effortlessly passing the few people on the path who were headed to the summit from where the expanse of the city could be seen.

From the eastern lookout, the waving arm of the Olympic Stadium monster – always looking somewhat wounded, unfinished – was the most prominent sight. On clear days at the central lookout in front of the stone pavilion you could see out to the hills of the Townships, Mount Orford, and even Vermont. And lately tourists were witnesses to the activity on the South

Shore. Through the 25-cent mounted binoculars they could see the fires, overturned vehicles, and spectators of the Mercier Bridge blockade. When she reached the top, Daphne stopped for a few minutes and stood among the crowd. A muted purple light spread through the sky, highlighting the distinctive loops of the westernmost bridge to the island. The scene at the south end of the Mercier Bridge was bustling. Daphne didn't linger. Continuing to the very top, passing the vigilant steel cross that surveyed the city, she headed toward the western view overlooking Mount Royal cemetery. By the time she reached her destination, the waning sun had tinged with gold the clouds that perched on the horizon like outrageously shaped children's cut-outs.

She remembered a game she and her friends used to play as children, lying in the High Park grass guessing what was figured in the clouds. The girls all called out outrageous animal images and human dramas being played out in the sky: *Look there! A snake with a knapsack tied around it. Look! It's two people sucking on each other – they call that a 69er. There: a man yawning* . . . Sometimes all Daphne could think of, all she could see, were fluffy cotton beds for birds to lie in when they were tired. Or amorphous islands of smoke; or giant cotton continents where things of the sky went after they died, the blue sky like the deep seas that separate nations. She tried to see what her friends saw, to beat them to a clever thought, but was always astonished by the sophistication of what they said. Who had given them these words they sucked on and spit out like candy? Who had doused their eyes in sex? She had felt dry and stupid, and she searched for something in the heavens that was hers, something she could name and belong to with a clever phrase.

They would be lying on the ground, one head on another's belly, forming a zigzag link of *T*'s. The trick was not to laugh. You could say the most outrageous things – *look, flying lips* – but you couldn't laugh, because if one person gave way, the whole venture degenerated into the dreaded "chucklebelly": the barely detectable vibrations of suppressed laughter that would make each head bob slightly, followed by infectious, uncontrollable outbursts – stomachs heaving in and out until every head was bobbing, every stomach heaving, all mouths gaping open and choking on giggles, until even the clouds above were infected. The day would dissolve and the clouds disappear behind a storm of cackles, and the sun would be drowned in the intoxication of little girls.

One day the giggling had given way to tears. One of her friends, her head resting on Daphne's belly remarked on a vision in the sky: "Look, here comes a dark cloud up against the fluffy white ones over there. Two white ones and a little black one." Another girl lifted up her head slightly and spurted out: "Yeah, just like Daphne and her parents." Stomachs heaved, even Daphne's, but while the others giggled she merely let the air go quietly in and out of her lungs, holding on to breathing. No wind, western or otherwise, had risen up to rescue her.

Now on Mount Royal she watched until the clouds faded into the sky and the cemetery grew dark. Thirst sucked at her throat, so she headed home. On her way down, she was sure she heard the deep and rheumy sound of sex coming from the darkness of the wooded mountain. She accelerated, sticking to the path. A Whippoorwill announced itself in the distance.

# Gibbous

## 1

There's no mistaking the rolling *coo* of the common pigeon. Daphne was comforted by the call. But it was interrupted by the high squeaky chirp of another bird, perhaps a sparrow. She threw off the bedsheet, sprang into her living room and opened the balcony door. Workday traffic was beginning to build on St. Urbain, but she could still hear the sounds of the early birds. The songs were no longer cheerful. What once had seemed happy-to-be-alive-in-the-morning chirps had become enigmatic – what were they signalling to their mates? Recently she was finding them menacing. Alarms of hunger, battles over morsels, a stressful urban war? Several brown and white birds, small enough to cup in her palms, skipped between the trees around her balcony. Sparrows, but what kind? She flipped through *Eastern Birds* to the section describing sparrows. Eurasian Tree Sparrows? Impossible, of course, no matter how much she wanted them to be so. They were mere House Sparrows, *Passer domesticus*, and she was disappointed by the mediocrity of their name. *Noisy, highly sociable, feisty. Often nests on buildings.* She wanted a different book, one with gilded words that would save these poor brown squabs from banality. *Sing cuckooo, sing cuckooo.* Like the song about the cuckoo, the bird that lays its eggs in other birds' nests. *Summer is a comin' in. Sing cuckoo, sing cuckoo.*

She decided to phone her mother in Toronto, who would no doubt have a bird book she could send. The tent-like paper with that other woman's phone number still rested on the telephone receiver. She unfolded it and stared at the name of Sheila Eyre. Her aunt. Her real aunt. She touched her breasts, one then the other. She pinched the nipple of each, giving them a slight tug. Sheila Eyre was her real mother's sister. As a girl, Daphne had prayed for a sister, prayed with all her might while her fingers pinched so hard on her growing nipples that she'd almost cried. She had resorted to *National Geographic* magazines to help her compare her mosquito-bite bumps to the breasts of the women on those pages – breasts that were full, oblong, and hung to their waists. She longed for the comfort of a sister's voice to confirm or toss aside her fears. Her best friend, Bev Campbell, had a sister who had told Bev that her breasts were stunted, that she'd never be normal. "My sister knows everything," Bev used to say. Sisters were endless sources of wisdom. Her friends' sisters had told them only the truth, they were sure: *Never wipe your bottom from the back to the front, always from the front to the back – never towards the crotch, that causes diseases, VD . . . Fucking is the thing that a man does to a woman the day before they go to the hospital to have their baby. My sister told me – she's 13.*

Daphne had watched her own body become rounder, with dumpling buttocks and a tapering waist, and each day she cupped her hand over her left breast which was swelling while her right breast remained dormant, flat. She would throw herself face down on her bed hoping that either the left one would puncture and empty out, or the right one would wake up and grow. She had been taught the biology of it all, but the map is not the territory. When the topic of the body came up, her mother changed the subject or began singing or doing the dishes. Her averted face became a sign to Daphne that the body was a shield to protect something far more delicate inside. She avoided discussion of sex as though Daphne had been a queasy reminder of its ultimate failure. The day Daphne started to menstruate Jennifer fainted and stayed in her room while Daphne accused her own armour of betraying her by springing a leak. It was her father who finally took her to the drugstore, where he waited outside for her to return with a box of pads that turned out to be far too bulky for her tiny flow. She had worn the diaper-sized pads all day at school before Bev asked her why she was walking so funny and took her home to fix her up.

Her father, Bill, was even less equipped than her mother to

deal with delicate subjects, but was forced to do so by default. As the ringmaster of their family, the gracious pink-cheeked jester, he would always defuse tension with jokes, distracting Daphne with play and laughter. A teacher at the rival high school to the one Daphne attended, Bill taught Canadian History, along with World Religions, his real love. When Daphne was in high school, Bill was known as "History-is-not-the-only-mystery Bill." He played tough, emphasizing discipline and rigour, but the students had him wrapped around their fingers by mid-term. They saw through his pedagogy to the vulnerable and meek man Daphne knew as father: at sad movies he'd cry until he couldn't breathe; when he skated, his ankles buckled as he pushed himself around the rink holding onto the boards. She loved every tear that fell, every smile that wrinkled his pink face. Her friends told her that his students chanted when he left the room: *Bill Baird, Bill Baird, Oh you make me soooo scared.*

But that was a long time ago, long before McIntyre and the passage over the first threshold of guilt, the betrayal of Bill and Jennifer. She picked up the receiver and dialled not the number of her parents in Toronto, the one she knew by heart, but the number on the folded paper, this new direct line to her blood.

The voice she'd heard once before answered.

Daphne remained silent for a few deep breaths. "Um, hello. They gave me your number . . . at the agency . . . I'm . . . my name is Daphne. Daphne Baird." She heard her own voice change as she pronounced her name. Accented. On the other end of the receiver she heard only breathing, a shallow breath in which she could smell spice. She knew Sheila Eyre didn't understand. "I mean, the adoption registry agency. I'm related to . . . well . . ."

More silence as a volt of absurdity shot through Daphne.

"Pardon?"

"They told me you were the contact . . ."

"Who did you say? . . . Ooh, goodness, it's you chile . . . I didn't know who at first, but, yes, goodness gracious, yes."

The voice of her aunt was welcoming. The tongue turned up in wide vowels, swallowed *r*s, and didn't seem that surprised.

"I'm so glad you called. Where are you?"

"Montreal."

"You live here?"

"Yes."

"Which part?"

"The Plateau."

"Not so far . . . my God. I'm relieved you found me. You know, I wondered if you would, and I prayed I wouldn't die first."

Daphne gulped; her throat was choked. The voice asked her if she'd lived there for a long time.

"No, eight months."

"And before that?"

"Toronto."

"My goodness, and now you're here," she said emphatically.

Daphne managed to form the words that told the woman how her parents had moved from Montreal to Toronto when she was a baby, but that she had recently moved back.

"Good gracious," said the singing voice, "You're somethin'. Can we see each other? Soon?"

Daphne had no answer. Her hand began to shake holding the receiver, and it rattled the woman's words. *So . . . oo . . . oo . . . on?*

"Hello? Are you there?"

"Yes."

"What about Friday?"

That would be in three days. Before Daphne could answer, the voice went on and on in a melodious accent, "isn't it amazing that we're both in Montreal . . . it means we can really get to know each other . . ."

"Yes," said Daphne automatically. She took down the address and directions on how to get to the voice's home on the west end of Montreal. Sheila Eyre lived near the river. Daphne thought of Surefoot's proclamation about water and limbs and knew that her aunt was well-proportioned. But something else was lurking in the rhythm of her speech. When Daphne repeated the directions to verify them, the other accented voice, which had become a constant, if irregular companion, hissed in her ear *. . . You can hear the backoo crying in the yard . . . old hyge 'gon suck* *ya blood out* . . . Daphne had no idea what it meant. Saying goodbye to Sheila Eyre, she hung up the phone and tapped her ears repeatedly with her fingers. She left for work.

The humid air caught her in its filaments again, and she struggled to walk down the sidewalk until she reached the library and gave in. She manufactured excuses for being late as she pushed through the turnstile, headed for the aisle of *B*s, then found *Jane*. She sought her place and began to drink in each word, finding herself in the draughty Thornfield Hall. Mr. Rochester. Could his eyebrows be as thick as Daniel's, only darker, his face chiseled and unhappy? But it is Jane's physiognomy that Rochester reads while disguised as a gypsy and tells of the *unconscious lassitude* that weighs on Jane's sad eyelids, the strain, which Daphne herself would have recognized, that signifies *melancholy resulting from loneliness* and the *brow that professes to say — "I can live alone."* Dear, dear Rochester . . . and Daphne could feel the sheath of trust grow a layer at a time.

She read on.

Jane's wedding day arrives, but this can't be all, for there are many pages left to read. Suddenly, *good God, what a cry*. The locked-up first woman*, tall and large, with thick and dark hair hanging long down her back* is revealed and trust is lanced like a clawed pelt. Daphne shivered. Touching her cool fingers to her forehead she remembered where she was. She was jolted out of England into the fact that she had forgotten Copie Copie. Dashing out of the library, she placed the book on the returns cart near the door.

A clock on a building at the corner told her it was already lunch time. Her stomach rumbled. She needed coffee. At the café two blocks from Copie Copie she spotted Marc in the lineup. Although embarrassed by her lateness, she knew that Marc was the only one in the store who'd never chastise her. She liked him for that.

Marc greeted her with a smile, saying nothing about her absence. They walked back together to the store, chatting. Marc was perfectly medium: medium height, medium complexion, medium intelligence. His movements and speech were fluid, and Daphne always found herself gliding comfortably into conversation with him. He made her think of what it might have been like to have had a little brother, someone with whom to giggle and to conspire. She wanted to be soft and calm like him, gentle in both languages and with everyone. She tried to make light of events at the store.

"Bit of a mad-hatter's tea party in there these days, don't you think?"

He didn't understand at first, but when she translated in her awkward French, he smiled and agreed.

"Joanne, she tries too hard . . . she should relax a bit."

Daphne agreed with a sisterly nod. Marc pointed to a record store on the corner.

"A new one. Not bad, small but has good imports." He went on to point out other things, signs in windows, a few other stores that had closed. Things Daphne would never have noticed.

"How was the concert last night?" she asked.

"Oh, *vraiment bon*. It was wild, nothing polite, people on their feet the whole time."

"Isn't that your second concert this week?"

"Third, actually."

"So Copie Copie's just a way to feed your habit?"

"Oh no," he smiled. "The tickets are free, from my cousin. He's a promoter."

She caught his eye and a laugh shrank the space between them. She was less timid with Marc than with most other people she'd met so far. Her connection to others seemed like a tightrope on which she teetered, surrounded by empty space, no ground in sight. Gaps everywhere: stepping and missing. Leaving Toronto abruptly, she'd hoped to be absorbed into a foreign, cosmopolitan city, but she felt more and more as if she had marooned herself in an island village. Here, islanders, and villagers from other parts of the country, other parts of the world, met, mingled, and yet remained strangers, isolated from each other. The city was draped in veils. Behind the first, the languages of two empires were still fighting a colonial war. Her life seemed to be developing behind the second veil, where there was a calm, free space, as in the eye of a tornado, which asked for nothing except her imagination for survival. Life in her neighbourhood seemed suspended from politics as played out in the media, relieved of language and culture in the specific. Her neighbours belonged nowhere and everywhere simultaneously. Language was not an issue: they spoke both and more. They met in bars; they took picnics to the mountain; they decorated their churches with coloured streamers and *piñatas*; they wore traditional clothes; they drove taxis; they worked and didn't work; and their children ran together in the streets. The open faucet of a gene pool streaming full-force, unnoticed, toward the future.

She looked up at Marc and watched his eyes dart. She wondered what he saw.

He changed the subject: "Plans are set for the cabin. Last weekend in August."

"God, I won't last till then. This heat's killing me."

"Me too. I used to go to the pool a few streets over from me, but there are all those kids, you know. What they do in there worries me."

"I know. In Toronto, I used to take the streetcar all the way to one of the biggest pools – one by the lake – thinking that because it was so big the pee might be diluted. No such luck. More kids, more pee."

They looked at each other seriously for a moment and then collided in another giggle.

"And the screaming," Marc added. "I don't remember screaming so much when I was having fun."

"The worst thing is that you spend a day at a pool like that and then you have to get back on the streetcar and go home with all the hot and sweaty people, and by the time you get home you're hot and sweaty too. And you smell like chlorine *and* pee."

Her mind jump-cut to a picture of herself last summer. She had arrived home from the pool at their west-end apartment to find Jeremy spread out on the couch, staring at the ceiling. He had seemed depressed, and she was feeling responsible for not giving enough, so she avoided him. She'd been absorbed in her own problems, bored with the year of temp work that she had made do with since failing miserably as a copywriter at a small ad agency. She had turned on the television and – *click* – the moment was eclipsed. They had both remained slouched on the couch naked, but fathoms apart, too hot to touch each other.

She had longed to swim in the ocean, or in a lake, but while she was a child her family had always stayed in the city during the short, hot summers. And now she wanted the woods, the woods by the lake in the way Marc had described his cottage. *People don' belong in de bush, dat's for monkeys.* Daphne looked over her shoulder, searching for the voice just behind her ear. She scratched her neck.

"Well, day's half over."

Marc's interruption was startling. Daphne entered the store feeling mutable, as though emerging from sleep.

Thursday evening. One more night to pass, then she would meet Sheila Eyre. Daphne wondered what this woman might possibly have in common with Rochester's faithful and true companion. She searched the shelf and found the novel. The library was crowded, the hours just before closing its busiest time. She cracked the spine a little farther. Jane is on the moors, confronting the elements and hearing the birds singing. *Birds were faithful to their mates; birds were emblems of love.* It is yet another unfamiliar landscape, a journey away from the unhinged secrets of Thornfield Hall into the dangerous unknown. Daphne feels the *vulture, hunger, thus sink beak and talons in her side.* The hours passed. Feeling the number of pages left to read slowly diminish between her fingers, Daphne knew the inevitability of a journey's conclusion, the possibility of rest at the end of a long road.

*Ping, ping, ping.*

*Ping, ping, ping.*

The electronic bell signalled the library's closing. Daphne read quickly, trying to finish. Jane returns to fire-ravaged Thornfield Hall . . .

"Excuse me, we're closing. You'll have to go."

The librarian pointed to the returns cart as Daphne closed the book and looked for the spot to replace it. She promised herself that tomorrow she'd return to finish the last few pages.

When she got home she stood in the centre of her apartment staring at the room, demanding it to back down, expecting it to disappear. The walls and spare furnishing stared back, indifferent to her anxiety. With a push of her finger she turned on the television to fill the dead air between the couch and the walls.

The news again. More images of the standoff. "The mounds of earth of the original barricade, reinforced by overturned vehicles, have become a normal sight here in the Pines . . ." The reporter was speaking with his back to a jumble of twisted cars and rows of men in camouflage. His tone was reverential, stirring, as though he were speaking from the last moments of time. Replayed footage of the Native men and women over the last few weeks accumulated into a chronicle.

Each day more came; men who had never held a gun in their lives were lining up just beyond the headstones of their great-grandmothers wedged between the golf course and its parking lot, clutching hunting rifles and AK-47s to their chests, and occasionally, once accustomed to the firearms, spinning them like a baton. A jerky, nervous twitch. Dressed in army fatigues that blended them into the trees, they pulled black scarves up over their faces, covering the last bit of visible flesh; only their eyes identified them as human. Chameleon men among the pines.

The reporter held his microphone to a woman's lips: "It's not just us, the two-legged that are here. The trees are here. Look how long they've been here. Now we're going to stand up and protect them."

The golf course would be stopped, but now, each day, there was more and more at stake. A tidal wave of First Nations support was spreading across the country and a growing sense of Mohawk nationhood permeated the Pines. The people of the Kanesatake reserve closed ranks, fearing police retaliation for the death of their comrade by a bullet from a gun that had yet to be identified. And each day the streets of Oka grew more and more deserted. Barricades around Kanesatake stopped anyone from coming or going. The ferry service across the Lake of Two Mountains from Hudson to Oka stopped for the first time in seventy-nine years, and whites and Mohawks in the town of Oka walked on opposite sides of the street. The weight of three hundred years of history kindled the road between them – asphalt that could burn a bare foot, boil water, fry an egg. And each day the people in the woods were getting hungrier. Bags of groceries intended for the warriors were dumped out onto the highway in front of the Pines. Nothing was going in. The Red Cross had been allowed in once with provisions, but the next delivery was barred. The Salvation Army was turned away. warriors, after being awake for days on end patrolling the barricades, travelled in aluminum speedboats across the Lake of Two Mountains to Hudson, sneaking past police patrols in the dark night to pick up supplies under the stars. There was no electricity, but the sacred fire burned day and night.

Warriors from Kahnawake, off duty from the Mercier blockade, replaced their exhausted brothers at the Pines. Micmacs came, Six Nations people sent gas and stoves, and a Buddhist monk sneaked into the Kanesatake Treatment Centre. Each morning he chanted and banged his drum and gong, reaching the ears of tired warriors. Some were grateful for his spiritual presence, others were annoyed at the disturbance. And at the Main Gate, a circle of women danced and chanted for hours, night after night, under the swelling oblong moon.

Negotiations continued.

Daphne found it all difficult to watch. It was far removed – a circus, a fantasy. These weren't the Indians she knew. *Wakonda deydo wapahdene a-t-on ai. Wakonda deydo wapahdene a-t-on ai.* Something she'd memorized as a child; a poem that had ossified in her mind.

Her eyes methodically scanned the shelves of the bookcase. They stopped at three schoolbooks grouped together on the bottom shelf, which she had brought with her from Toronto, even though none had been opened in twenty years. She pried the pocket-sized hardcover edition from between its larger companions. *The King's Treasuries of Literature,* edited by Sir A.T. Quiller-Couch. The green case cracked as she opened it to Longfellow's *Hiawatha.* An introduction by Edith Kimpton, MA, preceded the long poem that was then followed by a section of commentary and content questions. When she turned to the very end, a small piece of paper with a note in her father's handwriting fell out. *To my own little Hiawatha, don't forget your homework.* She smiled. It had been from her days of trying on cultures, her Indian days, and Bill had always been concerned about her homework.

> *All the Indian "writing" is in pictures. A very good idea of the way in which primitive peoples express their ideas may be gained by reading Rudyard Kipling's "How the Alphabet was Made," in* Just-So Stories. *The native dress is elaborate and often beautiful, for Indians make much use of feathers and porcupine quills gaily coloured. Although silent as a rule, the Indian is wonderfully eloquent on special occasions, and can make speeches of which any orator might be proud. He generally controls his feelings well, and this gives additional weight and dignity to his words when he speaks.*

She was stepping around the crack, comforted by the second-hand telling of a second-hand tale of a sixteenth-century Indian. The eloquent Indian, his prayers for strength, his courage against the wrath of nature – the familiarity of the image massaged her. These were the quiet people she knew, not those defiantly boisterous others on the television behind her.

"...And on the Mercier Bridge, tensions remain high, with residents in Châteauguay trying to block volunteers from buying food at the local IGA to take behind the barricade to Kahnawake ... Details from our special correspondent ..."

The growing unrest on the Mercier Bridge mirrored events in the Pines. The reporter described how the Mohawks had established work shifts. The sound of drums was constant, but especially loud on nights like the previous one, when Châteauguay demonstrators had accosted a Native woman in the parking lot of the grocery store. Food was hard to get, snuck in only by non-Mohawks to whom the police turned a blind eye. The scene jump-cut to a group on the bridge that was said to be wired with explosives. A masked warrior bluntly reiterated the warning: "If my people are hurt the bridge will fall."

A special report from a Native journalist took the scene behind the barricade. The stalemate had grown staler, and warriors roamed the woods along the highway. The reporter talked about what he had seen, the booby traps – holes covered by branches, and deep inside the holes, long spikes – intended to impale police prey foolish enough to walk in foreign territory. He described the warriors' long days, the end of which would be marked by a return to the fire in the centre of the bridge where the older women would feed them what they'd been given from the outside: macaroni, bread, milk, and donuts from the owner of Country Place. Everyone worked to break the tedium of the wait.

> *Should you ask where Nawadaha*
> *Found these songs, so wild and wayward,*
> *Found these legends and traditions,*
> *I should answer, I should tell you,*
> *"In the birds-nest of the forests,*
> *In the lodges of the beaver,*
> *In the hoof-prints of the bison,*
> *In the eyrie of the eagle!"*

Daphne remembered the immense freedom she had felt on first reading these words. She had run about High Park with her friend Bev, with whom she'd invented an additional verse: "*Wakonda deydo wapahdene a-t-on ai.*" (*Father, a needy one stands before thee and that needy one am I.*) They had vowed to become like the noble Hiawatha and befriend the animals and shout to the sky for thanks. *By the shores of Gitchee Gumee, By the Shining Big-Sea-Water.* They had given each other names. Bev became Chibiabos, the musician, and Daphne was self-dubbed Nokomis, Mother of Hiawatha. They had invented names for others based on their physical characteristics. Boys at school had been transformed to "Metal on Teeth" or "Walks with a Skip." And the poet himself was surely a proud, dignified, and tall man. Longfellow. In her naivety Daphne had imagined the writer, this long fellow, as a convivial and placid Indian reciting a story of his people.

"...in Kahnewake, an emergency team of Mohawk women has set up a food bank and medical centre for elderly..."

Daphne resisted the television's intrusion, lingering in the warm innocence of the past, but the voices dragged her back to the reality of the apartment and the kaleidoscopic images on the screen. The camera panned over a crowd of onlookers in a plaza parking lot near the bridge. They sat in lawn chairs watching police, support groups, and Natives come and go. Even the children were allowed turns with the binoculars. The camera panned away from the commentator, and Daphne spotted an overweight Native woman approaching the warrior lines. Her arms were balanced at her side, weighed down with food-filled plastic grocery bags. Surefoot. The camera moved in on her, following her movements in much the same way as the spectators with their binoculars. The reporter described her as one of the few people sanctioned to walk up to the front line to hand off supplies and messages to the Mohawks at the Mercier blockade as long as she was willing to endure the long identification checks, searches, and the harassment of the watching mob. Surefoot's flesh overwhelmed her scanty singlet and shorts. Moving close to the set, Daphne thought she could see one of the scars she'd memorized from the photographs. She watched Surefoot briefly lift up both arms; she could almost smell the sweat as the breeze blew through. Then the camera moved in on a hole in Surefoot's singlet from which dirty sweat dripped like mascara tears. Daphne's heart sank. *Daughter of the moooooooon, Nakomis.*

Surefoot passed the first group of onlookers and police checks before reaching the smashed vehicles of the Mohawk blockade. Many in the crowd were yelling obscenities, some directed at the police, some not. *Give 'em a case of beer and they'll get out.* A young man, sounding drunk, yet barely of drinking age, was yelling something at her. It was a poem. He screamed out static verses. On the last line, his voice appeared to walk up Surefoot's spine and settle on her shoulders, where the extra flesh accumulated like jewellery in fold after fold. *Don't you worry, the army is coming.*

Daphne turned off the TV. She made herself some pasta.

Later that night, sleep again impossible, Daphne returned to the TV; the news repeated itself. Now that it was past midnight the helicopters that had surveyed the bridge all evening had withdrawn. The city had quietened. In the late evening there had been confrontations at the Mercier blockade on the Châteauguay side of the bridge. Placards carrying the residents's message filled the TV screen, the camera cutting from sign to sign. One depicted a defecating bull bison labelled OTTAWA with the caption: CHÂTEAUGUAY SHOULDN'T PAY FOR 300 YEARS OF CANADIAN HISTORY. She flipped to another station. The same news (*stood the wigwam of Nokomis, daughter of the moon Nokomis*). *Click.*

The bathroom mirror revealed an unmarked face, neutral, pre-pubescent. Taking a black eyeliner pencil from the shelf, Daphne deliberately framed her eyes with dark rings, outlining the sockets, then began to put exaggerated freckles over her cheeks, moving to her neck and then onto the cleavage revealed by her light dress. For a few minutes she stared at the minefield mapped onto her features then ran the tap, filled her hands and washed the spots down the sink.

Slipping out into the night she could feel the restless grating of the endless days of heat. People hissed the sound of electric lives. They came out of cafés and walked together with a common destination. She walked quickly, feigning purpose, first passing the pizzeria where everything was striped green, red, and white, and where teenagers sat on the curb eating slices whose cheesy orange smell wafted up, unappetizing after the goopy pasta she'd eaten. The laundromat was empty except for a couple folding their clothes into a grocery buggy. Crossing St. Laurent quickly to get away from the swarms of night strollers and bar-hoppers, she turned up avenue des Pins towards the three-storey walkups of the Portuguese neighbourhood. Heading north, she walked past men in white singlets and shorts sitting on their front stoops next to sprawling gardens of tomato plants and herbs. Each house was different, some painted clapboard, others brick with wrought-iron staircases winding up the wall to the second and third floors. The materials clashed and knotted, all the decades since they'd been built layered on one another like the siltstone of a mosaic city. At the next corner she slowed down to read the street sign, repeating it in her head like a chant, with a rhythm that matched her walking: *Na - po - lé - on . . . Na - po - lé - on*. She turned right, moving deeper into the moraine of the neighbourhood. At avenue Laval she turned right again and walked past rows of greystones, old mansions converted into small apartment buildings.

The street was asleep except for its flowers. Untamed blossoms adorned balconies. Fully opened, falling-petalled pink roses leaned over a wooden fence. Petunias, geraniums, impatiens, and snapdragons filled the boxes and glistened even in the darkness, moistened by the thick hot air. Passing a corner she heard music, a rhythmic bass and piano coming from the side window of a basement unit. She stuck close to the wall as she snuck toward the open window. She bent down to look in, trying to focus in the dark, and then she could smell it – the frowsty smell of skin on skin, friction belaboured, sweat not fire. The slap of fatigued flesh was arrhythmic, one body pounding into the other, the other silent, patient. She turned away, still squatting against the wall, and began to caress herself under her cotton shift. Closing her eyes she tried to improve on the smell and sounds of the black room, but her mind couldn't come up with the right blend. She released her breast, stood up, and continued down the street.

A little further on a beacon attracted her attention. She followed the light to the ground-floor apartment, the only one on the street whose yard was unadorned. What should have been a front lawn was bricked over to accommodate a patio, or a car, yet nothing was parked there. Inside was simultaneously lush and stark. She could barely see past the plants on the windowsill: ferns, a rubber plant, jasmine, ivies. Beyond the lush sill the room was empty of furniture but for a few gigantic pillows scattered around the floor. More plants grew in bottles and unlikely pots: silky ferns spilled out of a felt fedora; sprigs of wisteria poked from the holes of a colander; and red-tipped moss choked the glass cylinder of a blender. A greenhouse living room. But on the white walls hung immense grey-on-black images. In large monochromatic prints of snow and ice, snowbanks towered like the mountain ranges of a different planet with their own horizons. These deserts of ice – wasteland accumulations – were stiff with loss.

Daphne moved around to the side window facing the narrow driveway and peered into the bedroom. The bed was unmade, the walls bare; clothes were scattered about the floor. She pressed her face against the glass to see the source of the light she had seen from the street. The huge floor lamp fashioned from a streetlight looked as though it might have been snatched from a busy street corner in the night. Its glass face was ridged to diffuse light and reduce glare for drivers. Here it dominated the room like a giant watchful eye. On the left wall hung a different kind of photograph, a portrait of a big family. It was the kind of family which was full, bursting over, generation into generation of the same faces. Sisters . . . so many. Their faces varied, but each had something that connected it to the others: a line of the chin or a fold over the eye. Daphne lifted her forehead from the pane and moved down the alley toward the next window.

"*Est-ce que je peux vous aider?*"

She leapt, bruising her shoulders as she flattened her back against the wall, her palms pushing at the brick as if enacting a scene of inevitable exposure. Standing a few feet away from her she could make out the form of a man with wildly curly dark hair. He was holding a bulging green garbage bag.

"Oh, no . . . I'm . . . ah, I'm . . . I must be in the wrong place. I'm . . . looking for my friend's place. I thought it was this one, sorry. Is it your . . . ? I'm sorry. I could've sworn it was this one. The number is right. Must be the wrong street. I must've turned down the wrong one. What is the name of this street?"

"Laval."

He was patient, cautious. As he moved forward into the light from the window his walnut eyes swam to the fore – wide, dark, deep – to dominate his face.

"Oh, that's right, of course, it's the one after this. Sorry again."

She turned. Quick steps became long strides by the time she reached the corner. She saw herself in his eyes all the way home: *caught, caught, caught.* When she passed the pizzeria, the teenagers were gone, but she had to dodge customers coming out of the store. Breathless. Heart pounding. Cheek quivering. *Shit shit shit . . .* She tried to steady herself. Her hands shook as she put the key in the lock. *Turn, come on, turn . . .* Finally back in her room, she threw herself onto the bed, still clothed, and even in the heat began to shiver.

Caught. *Stupid.* She hit her temples with her hands. Humiliation. Taking deep breaths, she pressed her palm to her quivering cheek. Then she reached for the pillows, one of which she placed between her legs, the other over her head. *Idiot, idiot.* The deep breathing calmed her, but each time she replayed the event in her mind her cheek started its staccato tick. Now hot once more, she fumbled with her clothes, stripped, and wriggled them down around her legs before bringing the sheet back over her head. She clutched the pillow again, and after a few minutes it became a distraction. Using it to take herself out of time she began the slow movement that forced its rub against the inside of her thighs. She began riding on the soft down. It was pacifying – immediate. For several minutes it lulled her. Then her movements picked up speed, became urgent and frenzied as she rocked, grinding over the pillow with fierce intent. In time she came, melting into the bed. Entwined in clothes and bedsheets, silk and cotton arms, vined and floral legs, she eventually slept without dreaming.

Friday afternoon. Airport anxiety flowed in: that wiry anticipation that accompanies the greeting of passengers, the one that flips the stomach and moistens the palms. It stayed all morning, teasing Daphne with the familiarity of a face glimpsed on the other side of a sliding door. The excitement of coming home. She dressed carefully, changing three times before deciding on the high-necked lemon-yellow dress. The pattern of thin black lines in the fabric made her hornet-like as she fussed with her hair, pinning it down at the sides, shaping it with gel. Holding tightly onto Sheila Eyre's address, she left her building and hurried down the street. Every few minutes she glanced to her right and caught her reflection in the store windows en route to the library. A wisp of her bangs had curled up like a fishhook, and she flattened it with her palm again and again.

The library was cool and quiet. Daphne flitted to the aisle with *Jane*. She read enrapt, swallowing regularly to push back the emotion that engulfed her, innocently, fully, like the trick passion had always played on her. Had Rochester's cry across the moors been just another trick? Finally, Daphne finished the novel, and she and the blind Rochester *entered the wood and wended homeward.*

Despite the broad daylight and the wide avenues of Notre-Dame-de-Grâce, Daphne moved stealthily along the unbroken sidewalks to her destination in the far-west end of the neighbourhood. But here, unlike in the congested districts of the Plateau, she was exposed in the gaps between the houses that sported gracious lawns and spacious driveways. When she reached the small semi-detached home that corresponded to the number written on the paper, she hovered at the front door, unconsciously holding her stomach. She touched her cheek to shush it, palmed her bangs, then rang the doorbell. A tall, dark woman with a thick flat nose and almond eyes appeared on the other side of the door. *The breath of the west wind bore her.* The woman's face was worn, the rails of her worry lines crossed by a junction of hesitant eyebrows, but she smiled when she saw Daphne.

"Hello chile, come in, come in."

Sheila led her into a living room draped in Victorian loops of fabric and fringe. The French Provincial couch was covered in plastic, and the lamp beside it dangled plastic crystals. Daphne sat on the edge of the couch feeling lost in the foreign room.

Sheila had prepared tea and immediately set about serving her guest. Meek but stubborn-looking, she had hands too big for the teacup she held up to the steaming pot, but Daphne noticed that they were in proportion to the rest of her. Her aunt was all big bones and angular chin, softened only by the flow of her long patterned skirt and the dark-green silk blouse with thin pointed collars. As she spoke, Daphne watched her lips part and shirr and meet, and could see her own there, full and pleated like a skirt. Sheila's accent came and went with the up and down of memory.

"I don't get to see many people from home anymore," she said, passing Daphne her tea.

Daphne bristled slightly at the reference to herself, resenting the idea that this woman had anything to do with the things she knew.

"In Guyana we saw people all the time, people jus' droppin' in and stayin' for a drink . . . Mummy liked that, your grand-mother, Mary, . . . but here is very different."

Daphne saw the lips almost pout as Sheila sat down beside her with her own teacup in hand. Those lips delivered the high-lights of a long sentimental journey that Sheila undertook to tell her about Guyana. She cooly described the country as a slab

of land with mud and jungle. "Too many mosquitoes," she pronounced, with a wave of her long hand in her front of her face
– chasing away a swarm – making her set of gold bangles tinkle
gently. But when she described the town, her tone grew hotter.
Georgetown. Sheila said the name came from King George of
England, and even though she was talking about South America,
the place had the sound of England – Princess Street, Regent
Street, walks in the Promenade Gardens with her parents. Guyana,
she said, was a rich country, lots of gold in the interior, as well
as bauxite, which made all the aluminum in England.

"But after independence, it all fell apart, just became about
colour, nothin' else. My Daddy was never in favour of independence. The President stole all a' the people's money, and now
people jus' fight and steal from each otha. It would mek him cry
to see it now."

"I've never been anywhere like that."

Sheila patted Daphne's cheek. "But your folks were good to
you, chile?"

"Yes." (*Bill Baird, Bill Baird, ohh, you . . .*)

Daphne moved her face away from the hand.

"That's all that matters. I came far in my life, chile . . . here."

*Here*, Sheila said, with the relief of landing.

"But, you know, in Guyana I never went anywhere. Even
Kaiteur Falls – they say it has the sheerest drop in the world. No
roads to the interior then; you had to hike, then go by a dugout
with the Amerindians."

Daphne tried to picture this place that had spawned her,
with England in its town, jungle on its border. A seething place
with the rushing sound of water and the buzz of mosquitoes like
the tinkling of gold. Something was missing. She was waiting to
hear the sound of her mother from Sheila's pleated mouth. It
was a long while before Sheila mentioned her sister, Muriel,
and when she did it was abrupt, final. She got up from the
couch and walked to a mahogany cabinet, opened it and took
out a photo album, which she placed open on Daphne's lap
before sitting back down.

"Your mother killed herself."

No, not this, not now. Daphne had just begun to picture the bush, to imagine the jungle of her mother's hair. No. Looking down at the photos in the album, as she was expected to do, she saw two young women in their Sunday best, gloves and pillbox hats, standing on a cement wall, beyond which flowed a dark body of water. The older, Sheila, doesn't smile, but looks toward the camera with suspicion. The other girl is tall, slim, her eyes catching something off camera, her smiling teeth as white as her dress. Muriel. Just a name now.

Daphne tried to find the expected tears, to feel something sad, but all she could say was, "Those are my arms."

Sheila sipped her tea delicately, but with strength and endurance far beyond that of the china. Daphne waded through the album, seeing wooden houses on stilts, couples embracing on the long wall with the sea behind them, and fashionable young people of all colours at cricket matches and picnics. She was about to open her mouth when Sheila preempted her.

"I know it's not what you expected to hear."

"I had no 'expect' . . ."

"I don't know if she'd have wanted me to tell you. Dear God, have I done right? But she wasn't in control then. Her edge was steep, poor chile. She's gone. It's better you know, isn't it?"

Daphne was waking up from a dream, not a nightmare, just something experienced through a hazy lens. Her mother, Muriel Eyre, sat on her lap, smiling up at her. Her arms and Sheila's face were a part of her body's reawakening, like the tingling of pins and needles.

"I did that to her?"

"Well, chile, we can never really know the inside of someone's pain. She wasn't a strong woman, your mom. She sometimes told me about things . . . about things she thought. Once she told me that trees used to threaten her, the shadows of them movin' over the floor in our house in Georgetown. She was sensitive. Loved to write, like our Daddy. He was a poet, was writin' all the time while he worked in a department store, and your mom, she might 'a been a poet given a chance. Guyana had some good poets . . . men though . . ."

"How?"

Sheila looked at her, not understanding the question.

"How did she do it. What did she do?"

Sheila paused for a long time, looking straight into Daphne's face until Daphne had to look away.

"She drown' herself, just after we came here. I think water was the one thing that neva' made her frighten'. She was lost for weeks. They found a body in the river . . . near here, near the canal. It was hard to tell if it was really her, but it was . . . You were a tiny, tiny thing."

"Did she leave anything? A note? Anything?"

Sheila's eyes dipped toward her teacup, avoiding contact for the first time during the visit. She shook her head as she lifted her spoon to stir the tea again.

Daphne turned her head away from Sheila, digging her chin into her own shoulder and asked, almost to the shoulder itself, "What am I supposed to think?"

"You think about your life, dear, to live it good . . . and I'm here . . ."

Daphne could feel her impulse to click out coming on, but she fought it, looking around the room, wondering if her mother had ever sat on this couch. She dared not ask.

Sheila picked up the teapot and went out to the kitchen. Daphne heard her filling the kettle, opening a package, and preparing more tea. From the kitchen, Sheila asked Daphne what she used to call herself. Not having received a response, she came back into the room with a fresh pot and continued: "I mean, what was your hyphenation? I have a friend, a lady from home – she makes me laugh. She says, 'In dis country it's important to have de propa' hyphenation.' Funny, makes it sound like havin' the propa papers, but it's just what you call yourself when someone asks you where you're from. 'Where are you from?' 'I'm a Canadian.' 'No, I mean where are you *from*?' I've heard that so many times in thirty years. Now you know your hyphenation. West Indian-Canadian. What did you used to say?"

Daphne's mouth opened slightly. Too fast, too much, all of this. "Nothing. I'd say nothing . . ."

Sheila's hands lifted the pot to pour.

"*Bansimande!*" She put the scalding china down quickly and shook her hand, flicking her fingers to cool them.

"What was that?"

"It was too hot, dear."

"That word . . ."

"Just a word we use at home. It doesn't mean anythin'; just a word when you can't say anything else – a surprise, or a shock – or somethin' hot. It comes from a song . . . you must not know all those words we use."

Daphne started to fidget. She closed the albums then straightened the hem of her dress as she stood up. She had to think.

"I have to go."

Sheila's face drooped, "But we have so much to – "

"I'll come again, another time . . . I have to go now."

Daphne got up, not knowing how to leave, what kind of goodbye to offer this woman who shared her lips. What would those lips feel like pressed to her cheek? Blood to blood. No, it would be too much. She moved toward the door as she said goodbye and thanks. She went out and was almost to the street before Sheila called to her from the stoop. She was holding two leatherbound notebooks.

"She might have wanted you to see these. They were our father's, from Guyana. The last of him. Go in peace, chile, and remember that some words hide truth just like fat hides bone."

Daphne took the books, tucked them under her arm and walked, perspiring, all the way home.

Inside her apartment it was even hotter. She put the notebooks down and pulled off her dress. She sat anxiously on the couch in just her panties, avoiding the journals, knowing that each step taken on this journey was irreversible. She picked up a *National Geographic* and browsed through it, stopping at an article on a tool-using bird, the Egyptian vulture. It had been written by Jane Goodall in 1968.

*The midday heat seemed intensified by the blackened*
*ground and smell of smoke, aftermath of one of the periodic*

*grass fires that sweep east Africa's plains. . . . we were headed*
*for country we had never seen before.*

*Suddenly Hugo noticed vultures plummeting down in the*
*far distance, and we swerved to see what had attracted them.*
*How well Hugo's sharp eyesight would be rewarded! . . .*

*Amazed, we watched an Egyptian vulture, a white,*
*yellow-cheeked bird about the size of a raven, pick up in his*
*beak the stone he had just thrown down. The bird raised his*
*head and once more threw the stone at the ostrich egg lying*
*on the ground before him.*

*It was true! We were watching that seldom recorded*
*phenomenon — the use of a tool by an animal. And we were,*
*as far as we know, the first scientifically qualified witnesses to*
*this extraordinary talent of the Egyptian vulture.*

She flipped to a page with a picture of a giant otter curled
over a tree trunk that was suspended across a river. In another,
the otter stretched out like a starlet on a divan. Pictures, good.
More pictures, no more words or names. Flip, flip, more photos,
wild animals and bushes. Flip, villages in southeast Asia. Unable
to hold out any longer, she tossed aside the magazine and
grabbed the burgundy notebook, identical, except in colour, to
its black mate. Its binding was well-worn, cracked in some places,
with a thin gold frame etched into the leather cover. Jagged-
edged pages were sallow with age and some were dog-eared as
if to spotlight their significance. The book smelled of mould
with a leathery tang. The dated entries on each page were all
written in the same hand. Diaries. On the inside cover she read:

*Gerald Eyre*
*born in the year of the new century, 06.*
*when the sun was in conjunction with Neptune.*
*and*
*and*
*what then?*

Turning to the middle, she read a sample from among entry
after entry written in the inconsistent scrawl of a blotting
fountain pen.

*January 30, 1960*

    *Telephones, like gossamers, connect me to dead voices. Last night I had three calls from people I used to know. One was my wife. The other two didn't tell me their names, but they must be related to me, since they asked me if I was eating adequately. They always ask you about food if they don't know what to say. It hides their shame like fat hides bone.*

    *The farter was in here last night. I didn't open my eyes; I didn't have to, she left that same lingering sulphur mixed with turd stench she always does. Last week I told her she smelled like a rotting jumbie and should wash her dirty coolie self. She fixed her eyes on me, that's why I haven't had a movement in a week. She's done it before. She does it to the others too, they're always complaining about their aching bloated bellies and she just smiles, gives them medication and turns with a fart out the door. She hates us all, especially me since she's not sure if I'm more white than black. I'll show her cocoa coolie ass what's black. Let her have a look here – my thing, my man, will choke her farting ass.*

    Words were conspiring again . . . *like fat hides bone* . . . Daphne felt for her stomach, heard it churn, then picked up the black notebook and turned its pages quickly. In its raging sentences, she sensed the littered narrative of the time before she was born, a past that had sat in her lap with those photographs just a few hours before. Quickly she closed both diaries, suddenly and remarkably embarrassed and horrified. She got up and placed them on the desk near her other books. Her face was burning with a rush of blood that felt shared for the first time in her life, and she dabbed her cheeks with the cool back of her hand. She picked up the *National Geographic* again and searched for the giant otter. She tried to concentrate on the images, but they dissolved into the fine strands of the word *gossamers,* which kept surfacing in her mind. Finally, a close-up of the drooling jaw of a grizzly bear grabbed her attention and she gazed into its teeth, intrigued by their pointed cusps.

# Full

## 1

Saturday nights were potent, and the pregnant moon rose in the sky as confirmation. Daphne lingered on the streets, looking into store windows, watching people line up for dinner. She had spent the whole day ignoring the notebooks, doing mindless errands, laundry, and cleaning, but had neglected to buy any groceries. Hunger was tearing at her stomach. The Burger King seemed adequate, so she went in, bought herself some fries and a coffee, and sat staring into her cup for a long time, trying not to think about January 1960 and the violent handwriting in the diaries. When she left the restaurant it was dark. Cars were bumper to bumper along Ste. Catherine, their stereos blasting, the decibel level encouraged by the heat. Tourists and residents watched each other from tables at outdoor cafés. People burst out of the doorways of bars, and the bass beat from inside spread to the street.

Inside Moxy's, the brass rail looked cool to the touch, so Daphne sidled up to it. Several men held onto it with one hand and hoisted a beer in the other. Daphne pressed her stomach against the coolness and ordered a vodka. Flickering light caught her attention. The television again, silent under the bar music, but bright with flashes of news, this time of a peaceful demonstration in the city in support of the Mohawks.

The demonstrators marched casually through the streets, a parade of out-of-step chanters, mouthing "justice" in the offbeat of the bar's dance music. Shots of the crowd were spliced with interviews from individual demonstrators. Suddenly Joanne's face filled the screen, her snarl hatching, her eyes bright and passionate. Even in the heat she seemed vibrant. Daphne tried to make out what she was saying, but all she could see in that mouth was what she thought was the word *water* – two syllables formed by the puckering of Joanne's thin lips. She concentrated; there it was again . . . *ww* . . . *aa* . . . rounding out then closing again. What was it? Without considering other options – *waver*, or *warrior*, *weather*, *whatever* – Daphne felt content to believe that Joanne was acknowledging a longing: *water*. The segment ended and the scene jumped to the white-haired newscaster. Daphne focused back on the dim bar. Blood rushed into her cheeks; she had been lingering at the male corral. Men of various ages were spread along the bar as though at a giant urinal, talking to each other but not catching another's eye, not looking down. Instead they fixed their eyes across the dance floor to the tables near the window. Tables of women. Women in waiting, holding anxious cigarettes like dainty fans.

Daphne picked up her drink and moved quickly away from the bar looking for a table. Snippets of conversations floated by: *Moi, je peux dire "margarita" en trois langues . . . You know what they say about unmarried women over thirty? Lower your standards . . . Single men have a short shelf-life . . .* She found a spot of wall against which to lean, and she closed her eyes, remembering Toronto bars and Jeremy. She had handled things so badly. After three years with him, she had packed her things and moved, not even leaving a note, while Jeremy had been away in Calgary. When he finally tracked her down in Montreal he had little else to say to her other than "Your part of the phone bill comes to $68.97." She felt ashamed, never having considered herself brave enough to simply walk out. Once she had been intent on dissolving into him, on uncovering and then becoming his secret, but the more she became him, the more he disappointed her. At his sister's wedding, dancing slowly to the wedding couple's first song, Jeremy had whispered to her that they should start to consider *their* song, and it had been a slap of ordinariness that so shocked her that she'd pushed him away and stared into his eyes, but saw nothing of herself there. After that she had slowly retreated, finding everything lacking. Her departure had been an automatic gesture, as though pre-programmed; one day she found herself packing. She was only beginning to understand –

this summer and relatively late in her life – how the effects of actions rippled like a stone dropped in a pond.

She returned to the bar, ordered a margarita, and licked all the salt from around the rim before gulping it back. A man resembling a cartoon animal – the same frightened-deer stare – asked her to dance. She declined politely, but when he winked at her, she abruptly turned her back to him. The music turned rigid and angry as she gazed into her empty glass and ordered yet another.

*The fifty daughters of Danaus were obliged to marry their fifty cousins. All of the maidens were opposed to the forced wedding and had fled to another village with their father, where the villagers protected them from the pursuing cousins, maintaining that no woman should be forced to marry against her will. But after the cousins' scheming, the marriage feast took place, nonetheless. In defiance, the father gave each of his daughters a dagger as a wedding gift. All the brides, in the dead of night, killed their bridegrooms. All except one, Hypermnestra, who pitied her young man and helped him flee. For that act her father imprisoned her. But the forty-nine others were punished in the underworld for murdering their husbands. Each day at the river's edge they filled their jars with water, but the jars were riddled with holes, so the water poured away, and they had to return to fill them again, see them drained, and return. On and on into eternity.*

The comfort of familiar myth thudded to a halt; other images invaded her imagination. She felt herself slipping away, into choking words like *fart* and *turd*.

She threw back the last margarita and walked out. Wiggling home, she went along the back streets and paused to look into the window of an apartment on Ste. Famille. She peered in. Nothing interesting. Dizzy, she turned and walked away.

"*C'est toi . . . Salut.*"

She whirled around, startled by the voice.

"Remember me?"

"No, I don't."

Daphne stared directly into the deep brown eyes of the man who had caught her peeping the other night. She stepped awkwardly to her left to go around him. This was not his house. She was baffled.

"It's interesting to watch someone when they're certain they're the ones with the view."

Daphne gulped and kept walking, focusing her foggy brain on the sidewalk ahead.

"Wait a minute!" He caught up to her. "Photographs are safer, you know. You can look at them over and over again . . . possess them . . . I do."

She quickened her pace. He followed.

"Okay, I give up, if you want to play that game, but you do owe me something, a gesture at least, to show you know what I'm talking about."

An involuntary grimace was Daphne's only response. She felt her calves tighten and noted the broken cement of the sidewalk beneath her feet. She stepped off the curb at the corner, crossed the street, and with a light skip was back on the sidewalk. Expecting more humiliation, she was surprised at the similarity of their strides and at the absence of any scorn in his voice.

"With me it's photos, places I've never been – which is just about everywhere . . ."

She was wary of a trap.

"I'm Michel. Michel Duchesne."

Daphne didn't answer right away, but when the traffic light forced her to stop, she felt her voice sneaking out, exposing her. "Daphne Bai . . . Eyre. Eyre."

"Nice to meet you – again – Daphne Eyre Eyre."

"Just one Eyre."

"So you must live around here."

"Yep."

The light changed. She kept her eyes down as she crossed the street. His stride matched hers.

"But you've lived somewhere else."

She looked up at him, "How do you know that?"

"Well . . ." He became embarrassed, and Daphne sped up, dipping her chin to her chest, trying to hide her nose, thinking she knew what he meant.

"I mean, the way you look at things . . . comparing . . . Do you want to stop for a drink or something? I won't bring it up again."

She flinched, still feeling the weight of his eyes on her.

"I don't drink."

Her response broke his stride and he started to slow down, giving up, but she slowed to his pace. Stopping outside a brasserie, he looked up at her questioningly. Avoiding any eye contact, she entered and he followed her to a table. As she sat down, Daphne tried to get the attention of the waiter so as not to look across the table at Michel. They ordered beer.

"I thought you didn't drink."

She couldn't hold back a smile, which seemed to put him at ease.

"The light's good in here. I prefer bright bars. You?"

"I guess so . . . this one anyway."

"Where do you usually go?" Michel was direct, digging with an archaeological skill she was unable to sidestep.

"I don't know many places here. You?"

"Rarely go out at night. My days start too early."

"Why's that?" She felt herself slowing down, slackening her usual spin, not outside of herself, above and looking down, but watery deep inside. But she didn't trust the feeling.

"Why?" One eyebrow rose slightly as he took a swig from his beer.

Perhaps he was making fun of her for wanting to know more about him than she could already have guessed from his plants and endless photographs of snow, but he began to tell her about himself. He was the youngest of eight children, his father Québeçois and his mother Italian. Growing up on a farm, his mother had made everything, all the food, all the clothes. By the time his father was ready to retire from his vegetable business in Jean Talon market, he'd been the only one of three sons willing to take it over, so he ran it with one of his cousins. He described her as miserable, a constant complainer who often made days at the market unpleasant. The business didn't leave him much time for photography, except in winter.

"The price of families," he finished gently.

"So that was your family on the wall?"

She forgot to be embarrassed about being caught out, and he let it pass.

"Most of it, still a few missing, some cousins in Italy."

"Lots of women."

"Yeah, mostly. Five sisters. And my father had six."

"Wow. (*the breath of wind, the breath of wind . . .*)

"Wow?" He teased with a straight face, but when he finally smiled, the left side of his upper lip arched toward his eyes in a way that made something flip below her bellybutton. Desire: the trigger for conflicting instincts, the way smell is a trigger for memory. In the years before Daphne had met and moved in with Jeremy, she'd had several brief affairs, most lasting only a few weeks, the longest just over two months. Then there was Jeremy and the testing, the pulling and pushing – a trial of love as a concept. A slow vanishing.

She rubbed her forearm, making the fine hairs on it stand at attention. Across from her, Michel's arm rested on the table like a slumbering beast. She trembled at the ease with which it lounged just a few inches away, and at how the dark hair streaked the tamed skin. With the beer her mind became watery, her eyes soft, her jaw relaxed.

"You've met the ones from Italy?"

"Not yet."

He told her about having wanted to travel his whole life but never having the money, and then with the business, never the time. He supported two of his sisters as well as his parents.

"What about you? Where've you been?" he asked.

"Only here," she answered.

It slowly dawned on her that the question had, for once, not been *where from*, but *where to*, a distinction that loosened something within her. She dropped her guard and found herself telling him about her fascination with the Greeks. When he apologized for his lack of reading, telling her again how much time the market took up, she found a new part of herself aroused.

"Aubergine." She said it almost unconsciously.

"Pardon?"

She looked up into inquisitive eyes.

"Oh, eggplant. My mother . . . used to call it aubergine so that I'd eat it, 'cause she knew I liked the sound of things better than the taste."

Michel smiled. The fact of her spying had been casually dropped. She wanted to run her forefinger around the outline of his eyes to remember their shape in her skin, but an old reminder surfaced just then, one that told her that amidst the longing and the touch, and in the proximity to eyes and bones, to skin and breath, lurked a bottomless loneliness. Lust was a quest, like faith, but after it was sated came an empty, glaring doubt, tired legs, and spent breaths. She lowered her eyes and began tearing small pieces from the napkin under her beer.

"Markets make me nervous," she said deflecting her thoughts.

"But vegetables are neutral. Take tomatoes: good fruit, good vegetable."

She looked up at him. "Can't be both at the same time," she said, trying to joke, but scrutinizing his face.

He dropped his gaze. "Your eyes are sharp," he said, into his beer.

Realizing that she'd been staring, Daphne attempted some distance. "So, that's what you sell? Tomatoes mostly?"

"This time of year, yeah. The best. And I can cook aubergine better than you can say it. Want to try it sometime?"

"I'm pretty busy . . . doing research," she said looking down again.

"On what?"

". . . birds . . . bird . . . movement, migration, habits, stuff like that."

She'd shredded the whole napkin before looking up to see him grinning. They laughed at the same moment, relaxing. But she refused to let go. She listened for the voice, begged it to come. *Eh, eh, girl . . . you don' let no boy tek yu breath away . . . mm, mm, mm . . . not one breath . . .* Her head was getting heavy. She excused herself, saying she was tired. When Michel asked for her phone number she scribbled it on his napkin. Waving for the waitress, he offered to walk her home, but by the time he finally caught the server's attention and signalled for the bill Daphne had slipped out the door.

It was late when she woke the next day, and she lingered in bed, dozing on and off, until she was too hungry to stay there any longer. On the way to the kitchen she spotted the leather-bound journals on her desk. She hesitated a minute, but her curiosity burst. She opened the burgundy journal and forgot her hunger.

*October 3, 1959*

*I heard my hair move this morning. They made me dress and took me out on the sea wall, but my pores prickled and the breeze rustled my scalp and the prickling was too much. I screamed and embarrassed them. They took me home.*

*She's not going to put up with me much longer, this woman. She brought me this book and this blotting fountain pen to write out what I haven't been saying to her. She thinks it's because I'm sick, or angry, but she doesn't know it's because speaking doesn't count — that it vanishes into people's breast pockets. Speech and numbers are the two things that lie. Blast you, Desmond, you damn liar with your Mr. Jones' breast pockets.*

*She accepts me, each night, folding her limbs like a gentle flower around me. She is delicate, has the bones of a small bird and it is she who comforts me. They are all home today, must be Saturday. Mary is trying to clean quietly so she won't disturb me. They all whisper, plotting something. They're trying to make me love them again. They all stare at me, except her, the youngest one, who avoids my eye. She has her mother's skin, almost green, and she has marzipan teeth. I am like chocolate beside her.*

*October 4, 1959*

*Each day that lizard walks the same path across the wall at about the same time. The sun divides the room into then and now and in the blackness of now I rest in the shade. This room is at the back of the house, behind the kitchen where people chatter and gossip. The floorboards creak when I walk to the window, so I don't go to the window any more. Just as well. The squalor. The dogs destroy the yard and their scraping paws pelt our garbage at the house. Chickens run, squawking, and rough brown mud in mad chicken scratches splatters the whitewash in the rain.*

*If I lie still enough I can feel a breeze from the sea and smell salt mixed with cardamom from Mrs. DaSilva's spice shop. Me, as a boy, walking past her shop plugging my nose and mouth tight for fear I'd vomit right there on the road from the choking, chalky smell of powdered flavour. It was she who was responsible for my finally working at Atkinson's. She would see me with my nose plugged as I walked by and cry out: "Hey boy, don' plug up yu face like dat. Y'ain goin' no fuder dan dis block, mista you damn cheeky, too-good-for-the-rest-of-us boy." Even when I was older, she taunted me and teased me, calling me "Spice Fear Boy" every time I passed the shop. She called it out one day as Mr. Atkinson was leaving the shop and he stopped to ask me what she meant and I told him. We talked and I impressed him with my civilized behaviour and I said the right words and he knew I was going somewhere and he gave me my job.*

*October 5, 1959*

*I pretended I was asleep when Mary came so I wouldn't have to shame her with silence. She's starting to hate me. Damn them all. They mourn me as if I'm dead, but I'm as alive as a statue in a square, as dressed for battle as Raleigh, and if my blood is not pure enough for them I'll slice the skin between my toes and mash up skin like grapes and distil – a wine, a blood – a vintage obedient man. I am an obedient man.*

*I stood in the store and stared at the sparkling silver trays and bowls and coffee urns. I could see my long face and bulb nose in* them. The shapes made my face even longer and my nose was grossly out of proportion. The store always smelled of faraway tea and the crates I unpacked were marked with special names that made me dream of flowers and gardens: Waterford, Wedgewood, Limoges, Rockingham, Worcester. Linen smelled of lavender, clothes were heavy and unfamiliar, and I knew we wouldn't have them long, so I rubbed my hands over each garment, over each plate before Atkinson put it on display. I was sure we would sell it all in one month. How could people help but buy these things? I knew because I was civilized for a 16-year-old.

October 6, 1959

To give responsibility is a gesture of hatred. It diminishes the receiver to sycophant, doomed to be grateful for a sip of self-worth, for morsels of freedom. Taking it is another thing altogether.

October 7, 1959

Today it is too hot to be anything but dizzy, and the past is swarming at my head like bees. I took all morning to calculate the number of years it's been since Spice Fear Boy showed them: 37 years, 37 years, 37 years, 37, 37, 37
73, 73 73,
years, years, years, sraey, sraey, y. y. y. y.

Each year with more to do – more people to speak to. Each year with a new task – a new responsibility. First sweeping, then unpacking, then serving, then selling, then counting, then ordering, then hiring, then firing, then expanding, then organizing, then hiring, then Desmond, then holding on, then ducking – now pulling each knife out carefully, careful not to tear arteries in the small of the back. Soaking up the blood as it drips down the back of my legs. Trying to count the spots on the ceiling.

Come to me. Come to me again, just once more.
Just once more.

*October 8, 1959*

I know what to do. A petty executioner speaks in the buzz of these bees. Tempered words like justice and blame. Others obscene and ridiculous, like fairness. I'll speak to young Atkinson and I'll get on my knees and I'll say the sacred 37 at least 37 times and I'll tell him it's Desmond who should go, and I'll assure him that I am an obedient man.

It's rising in me again, and it pours out of my head like an electric current. And the current is wet, changes to tears, salt and water dripping down the side of my face, sticking to it – a balm of penitence. And when it flows like that, I go to her, but if she doesn't accept me the hum increases, it flows from my ears to ignite and light up the room. And you have to take me, you can't deny me, not like this. So I push and she hits her head and she too has the saltwater billows in the eyes, and I try to help, but she thinks it's something else, and I try again, but she doesn't understand. She does not cry out. Not like this, Not like this, she whimpers.

*October 9, 1959*

I bathed and dressed – my best suit and hat – and walked into the kitchen and they were quiet – more quiet than their whispers. I told them I had some letters to post and that I needed the fresh air. They looked at each other, puzzled, and I walked past them, careful not to let them hear the gurgling from my scalp, and I walked out into the bright sun.

I bow my head to view only my feet and the rich and rough broken path, because I know how many steps it takes to get there. I pass children, dogs, donkey carts; people pass me on bicycle and ring bells hello or get out of the way. I can see what I pass without looking up: houses, stilts, whitewash rum shops, the pharmacy, the post office, St. George's Cathedral, Rudee's soda shop – where Mrs. R. is bending over the counter, her massive bosom resting on it like a sack of flour for sale – the betting office, striped awnings on the window at Merle's groceries, a long stretch of hopeless, impotent merchants – the coolie man with his coconut sweets, the jewellery woman, the basket twins black as night, another rum shop . . . sugar and rum, *casreep and rum, paper and rum, this damn country and rum.*

*I stop eleven steps short. Around me the bicycles, people, carts, autos, dogs, are buzzing. The buzzing blends into a single note and the pitch rises, higher and higher, until I can't hear it anymore and all I can hear is a faint tickle behind my ears and the rushing of blood to my face. I raise my head and the scene around me is all too familiar, like any working day, and someone is looking at me, talking to me, but I can't hear her. I think I'm supposed to know her from the store, but I've never seen her before. I look past her to the store and see the wide balding road on young Atkinson's head – the two sidewalks of hair somewhat greyer. And the buzz begins again and the snake crawls up my spine. I pull down my hat, turn on my heels and run clumsily, sweating, back home. It seems to take me forever.*

*Inside the door of my house: big eyes and fallen jaws. The three of them staring at me. There is a crack in Mary's eyes. I see it, it runs across her face and down her neck to her bosom, where it expands and shatters her chest. I put it there. My suit jacket is drenched, my trousers are splattered with mud and in my hatless head there is a throbbing as if the blood were knocking to get out. I refuse it. I won't let it leave. I shut my eyes to stop the noise, but it crawls like a demon through my veins. My knees collapse beneath me and the tears of our Lord fall to the floorboards. Red, bloody tears from his white, white face – our Lord, the white face of a hero – my Lord Nelson, and he is defeated, confined to the tower; he crumples up in a corner, his armour cracking like a skull, and his wife and children surround him as he whispers and curses the name of his opponent: Desmond – but they do not hear. He has to shout it, but they do not understand and pull him up and walk him to the bed. But it's from this they will make a statue – no, not like this – a bronze statue to stand watching, guarding the honour of the square. Our Lord from England, our civilizer, brought to his knees. Not like this. Not like this.*

The words were like dust settling on her chest, covering her in desperation. Daphne put the journal down and lay still on the couch. She had been walking in the mind of a related stranger, his pain running along her shoulders and down her spine. She straightened up and moved to the bathroom, where she ran the water a long time before going under the shower. The water beat down on her as she tried to put Sheila Eyre and the man behind these words together in the same house, but her thoughts were stifled under the repetition – *not like this, not like this* – and by the smells evoked by the handwriting. The shower spray released them and sent them swirling down the drain. The Sunday drumming from the park resonated in the tub. She needed to get some air.

Walking down the busy boulevard, she rubbed her belly, hand over hand, like an expectant mother, hopefully caressing it into growing. *A southern wind, a southern wind.* She tried to imagine the feeling of a southern wind. Pausing before a small épicerie she considered buying some food, then she noticed a bin of green okra displayed among the produce in the sidewalk stall. She looked around, quickly grabbed one of the conical vegetables and slid it into the pocket of her shorts. Continuing down the street on her usual route toward the store, she passed by the diner. On an impulse, she turned around and entered the restaurant, hoping to see the wide brown face that had chastised then forgiven her. There it was. Surefoot looked up from the newspaper spread out on the counter in front of her. Daphne sat on a stool, and Surefoot poured coffee into a cup for her.

"You again."

Not knowing what to say, Daphne looked down at the article Surefoot had been reading: *Life Goes On for Natives and Whites in the Middle of Armed Standoff.*

Daphne looked up again, "I lost a bracelet here the other day, I think. Did you find it?"

Surefoot turned without speaking and went to the cash register, pushed a button, and the drawer shot open. She retrieved the silver bangle and brought it to Daphne.

"I wondered if it was a gift."

Daphne took the bracelet, but then pushed it back across the counter to Surefoot, who looked puzzled and scratched her underarm. Her smell, a combination of bacon and sweat, made Daphne gag.

"I wanted to ask you something," she said after swallowing.

They both paused and measured each other's expectations.

"To ask you what it was like for you, I mean as a kid, in a convent."

"Look, don't do a case study. I've had enough of those."

Daphne looked down shyly into her cup of coffee.

"Okay, what is it?" Surefoot said, giving in.

"It's just that ... did you always feel like an Indian? Like one of them, even when you didn't know where to look?"

"Boy, you are something. How old are you?"

"Thirty."

"Funny, you seem like just a kid." Surefoot saw Daphne flinch, so she continued in a different vein: "Were you ever in a foster home?"

"No."

"Well, I was, lots. You don't have a clue. Other kids who beat the shit out of me, foster parents who fucked me weekly – it's not Hiawatha, girl." Surefoot's words were like a fist in Daphne's stomach, but she restrained herself from reaching for her abdomen. Surefoot continued, "In a convent, it's either bright or dark. White walls and sheets, but the nuns' shadows were black. Reflection and shadow, Heaven and Hell. I snuck behind them down the hall, just to see them walk, to see if they had any legs. I pretended to pray, but when I did it was to be dead. You have a boyfriend?"

"Not anymore."

"I never have."

She paused and took a deep breath, which Daphne felt suck up some of her own oxygen, and went on, "No, belonging is what you give yourself ... Indian summer, Indian rubber, Indian underwear ..."

She mimed the cruel trick children play on each other, pulling underpants up from the inside of jeans to make them outerwear. *Ouch*. Surefoot chuckled silently.

"They're all things that burned eventually . . . and then I burned too. It was inevitable. You just need one thing that's yours. And then again, sometimes it's just about getting up the next day. A Mohawk friend told me it didn't matter what tribe I belonged to. She has a saying, about a wolf . . . oh yeah, 'A wolf disappears into the woods, but on its way it leaves tracks in the snow, and this is the mark of its existence.'" Surefoot fondled a scar on her left wrist. Daphne gave in and touched her belly.

"I have to get back to work," Surefoot said.

"Sorry, I didn't mean to – "

Surefoot raised her hand to avert the apology, "You've got a lot to learn. Come up to the bridge this week. It'll open your eyes."

"What do you do there?"

"Just help out, trying to get food in, medical supplies."

She turned around quickly and pulled a basket of fries out of the bubbling oil, shook off the grease, then flipped them into a tray. She filled two plates, then plopped them on the far end of the counter for the waitress to pick up. Daphne watched her, wanting to say more, not fully understanding what the woman had meant about the bridge, but afraid to ask. The diner was slowly filling up. Supper time. Daphne pushed the bracelet farther along the countertop toward Surefoot, then left.

# Full

# 2

At the stroke of nine o'clock, Marc unlocked Copie Copie for business. When Daniel was late, which he had been for the last few weeks, it was Marc's job to open the store. Daphne was already at work on the large copier, and Sylvie was at her desk, her fingers swiftly punching numbers into the calculator. Marc prepared the front counter for customers, making sure everything was ready, since during the rushes in the last few days he'd found it impossible to keep up. With Daniel away, Joanne was using her mornings to look for another job, and often he was left to work the counter as well as do the computer work piling up on his desk. A few minutes after nine, the first customer entered wearing a disappointed frown.

"I need some business cards printed. Just 100."

Marc started to write down his order. The rumble of the immense copy machine subsided as the final sheet of the job Daphne had programmed flipped into the tray. The room fell silent while she stocked the paper shelf near the front counter. As he finished writing the order, Marc watched his cutomer shift from foot to foot and fret with the promotional flyers on the counter.

"How're things?" Marc asked.

"Slow, pretty slow. Too hot. Too much bad news."

Marc nodded sympathetically. The man's eyes shifted to the front page of the *Montreal Sun* that was sitting on the counter. The photograph was of a front-end loader carrying Mohawk warriors.

"Looks like the Premier has thrown up his hands. He's begging the feds to take over. Ironic."

"About time," Marc returned politely.

Sylvie looked up, her fingers pausing over the calculator keypad, "Oh, this can't be," she complained. "So much fuss, so heated up. We don't even know yet who killed the policeman, right?"

No one answered her immediately. Daphne tore open a package of light-blue paper and placed it neatly on the shelf. The customer was the first to speak.

"The police still say it was the warriors, but the Indians are holding to their story. Must've been caught in the crossfire. There's an old army saying that it's usually the crossfire that proves to be the most dangerous place. Targets can run . . ."

Daphne wandered back to the copier with another package of blue paper and loaded up the machine for the second job of the day – three hundred copies of a single page. A schedule for chamber music concerts at a local church. As the machine started up, she tuned into its whiz and out of the discussion about Oka, her eyes fixed on the pages disgorged onto the tray in front of her. Words flew up like fragments of a secret message.

> Festival de Musique . . .
>> à L'église de la Sainte-Trinité . . .
>>> l'Ensemble Atlantis . . .
> Vendredi . . .
>> Mozart . . .
>>> clavecin . . .
> Mardi . . .
>> violoncelle . . .
>>> J.S. Bach: Suite . . .
> Jeudi . . .
>> pianoforté . . .
> Mardi . . .
>>> Ensemble Hausmusik . . .
>> Schubert . . .
>>>> "La Truite" . . .
>>> Quintette avec piano . . .
> Jeudi . . .
>> piano romantique . . .
> Vendredi . . .
>>> Académie de musique de chambre

*Musique de chambre.* Music of the bedroom. Sleeping music, music to be woken by, music under the sheets, music no one else need hear. She tried to imagine Orpheus animating the room, making the tall, thin, bedside lamps dance and slither, and the pillow covers flap their frills – Orpheus having retired to the *chambre* after a long day of leading the trees over the hillsides and bending the rivers with the sound of his lyre. But the river was wider now, and the hillside denuded, and all she could see was a man on a seawall rubbing his head to quell the prickling of the wind.

*October 13, 1959*

*I think. That's what they told me, but I don't know if I can believe them. They told me that my new address is Berbice Hospital on Princess Elizabeth Road, and I'm to tell people to visit me here, have my mail sent here. People will call me here.*

*Telephones in Bedlam.*

*I must have been asleep for a few days because I've missed some entries, but they've told me I should sleep, that I haven't slept. My wife Mary was here this morning when I came back from breakfast and was asking about my account at the bank. She fidgets when she speaks and can't look me in the eye. It's costing money to keep me here, but she's afraid of me. I can see her lips quiver and the vein throb along her neck. I want to tell her everything is fine, but I can't go near her; I hear the buzz if I get too close, so instead, she suffers from my abandonment.*

*Everyone knows about the ward here where men are chained to their beds because they attack the nurses. I haven't seen it yet, but I can hear the screams. The violent ward. Violence has a special category in the world, like love, but there is no love ward, no place to go if you have forgotten it or if you have never had it. The violent ward is at the other end of the compound. They say it has no roof, just a tarpaulin that drips rain and drenches beds when the season comes. And there are cages, metal bars and small tombs for those who can't be controlled. Mongoloids and the insane in the same cage, the one unable to recognize the absurdity, the other too full of* it. One eats the waste of the other from the floor. The pale and penitent walls of this room do not block out sound or smells. Urine and melancholy, like soup.

There are 24 of us on this floor – I counted the names on the nurse's list. I haven't seen them all, because some reside only in the small and sharp corners of their rooms. I am the farthest from the nurses' station and close to the common room, where three or four sit, conspiring. The nurses are mostly white, but a few are coolies, Chinese, and two are mulatto. They hate each other. There is no love inside these walls. That's why they put me here.

*October 14, 1959*

Two doctors are assigned to speak to me and prod me and ask me about my relationship to the moon. I fool them and tell them that the sadness has gone, that I can leave soon, that my excess of bile has been purged by the rod. I think they must be experimenting on us, since most of us here are not white, although I am the closest to it. Large features are enough to zoo the elephant. Silence will get me out of here sooner than not.

They feed me fried plantain that is shrivelled to the size of a baby's turd. One day it was mashed beef and potato that was so dry it fell off the fork before I could lift it to my mouth. We all sit, staring into our plates and wondering how to tell them that it's food that makes the man, when it is they who control our stomachs.

*October 15, 1959*

Today there is a slow throbbing at the back of my head, but I must not let them hear it, or they will treat me the way they do the others. I detest all of them in here. There's too much screaming and too much fuss – they are polluting my head with their damn fuss. Asking me to remember. Prodding me to remember. "Write down what you remember about the time before you came here," says the nurse who smells of garlic. "Tell me about how you feel about your job," says the doctor who looks like Winston Churchill. Damn *fucking prodders — I'll tell them. I'll tell them about loyalty and faithfulness and devotion and I'll tell them all it amounts to is a knife in the back and a toss aside like a worn-out machine — useless buck mulatto. I'll smash their fucking china, their heavy lace collars and chalky faces — chalk, alabaster, lace, and worn-out machines.*

*October 16, 1959*

*She says: "Here now, Gerald, why so sad today?"*
*He says: nothing.*
*She says: "We'll have to get the doctor to come to talk to you; perhaps he can cheer you up a bit."*
*He says: nothing.*
*She says: "Now look here, why don't you come for a walk with me down to the common room and you can have a bit of tea with the others."*
*He says: nothing*
*She says: "Very well then, suit yourself, but it would be better for you to be more happy. The doctors would like that."*
*He says, quoting the villain: "Even now, now, very now, an old black ram is tupping your white ewe!"*
*She scurries out of the room, her pink ass covered cleverly by a uniform.*

*October 17, 1959*

*If the lizard crawls and stops and speaks of St. Fillian's blessed well and recommends my frenzied dreams be dispelled by a dip there, I will listen. I trust only him.*

Daphne's chest hurt, tight from shallow breaths. The phone was ringing. *Breathe, breathe.* When she answered, it was Michel, shy but not hesitant, asking her out for dinner. Distracted and unable to come up with a suitable excuse, she politely declined his offer claiming a busy schedule of research . . . on birds . . . another time, perhaps. She hung up and looked back into her lap at the notebook.

The handwriting was angled and precise, the pen steady and

deliberate, as exacting as an engraver's burr. But the dated entries broke off, the handwriting becoming erratic and sloppy, spilling off the lines.

The next entries were lost to chronology.

*I am the sacrificial goat to whom the evil spirits have been transferred. They placed the eel on my belly and its shock drove me out from me to me – I have eclipsed even King Saul, whom God has punished. My David's not a harpist but an electrician.*

*I would prefer the leech to the eel. Bleed me of this yellow bile, the coloured man's cursed mix of sand and tea, let the leech rest its puckered, gluttonous lips on my temple – forego the eel, it only contributes.*

*Thus am I bound and imprisoned on this ship, set adrift as part of a medieval circus to search for my home and my destiny, to perform for foreigners at welcoming ports, the ship of fools and a colony of madmen no longer belonging to Britain or to the world.*

*Found in a book given to me by a friend:*
*A thirteenth-century herbarium offers a specific cure "for lunatics who suffer from the course of the moon. If peony herb is bound on the neck of one who is moonstruck, quickly he will rise up healed; if he carries it with him he will suffer no ill." A century later the cure was more drastic: "Incise the top of the head in the shape of a cross and perforate the cranium so as to expel the noxious matter."*

Many blank pages followed these entries, and then:

*November 3, 1959*
*Time is hiding from me again, and I am forced to consult calendars and ask the nurses for dates and days and hours. My treatment continues. It seems I sleep often and for long periods, but I can't remember and am not rested. I'm spending more time in the common room, talking with some of the others who are not as annoying as those on the first floor. Frederick is the best of them. He has given me books, and we talk about things in private; but*

*even he looks at me fiercely, with fiery green eyes, and he provokes all the nurses and most of the other men. He has a way with them. They listen to him, and some are afraid of him, but I think he is decent. He is wise, although he is young. He is a Cockney, a man of London, and has a single protrusion of hair coming from the back of his head in a wide band. He brushes it over his forehead, and it lands in a fringe over his eyes. And he has a mustache that I think he's grown to compensate for the thin head of hair. It's ridiculous, but he is not a ridiculous man. At least that's what I suspect. He is tall yet round, and waddles down the hall like a reigning goose, looking at everyone and silently commanding their obedience. But with me he is guarded, not so menacing.*

*"And you, mate," he said to me, "you might right be behavin' yourself or they'll be puttin you in the tank next time." There is a place called the "tank" but I haven't the nerve to ask what happens there. "She's a pretty one, your youngest. Bit flighty though, ain't she? She don't speak nothin', nor does she really look . . . in the eye an' all . . . Me, I never 'ad no children, although I mighta liked it. They make ya softer, you know, softer in y' touch, in ow y'walk. Yo'ave ta walk slower, move gentle like. Yo'ave ta take smaller steps. I like that."*

*He talks on and on. All the men in the common room talk about independence and the expulsion of the monarchy from the jungle, and I indulge them, but tell them that they are behaving like ungrateful sons. The gift of civilization is like the gift of life, and a man does not turn his back on his father after he has learned to copulate.*

*I told Frederick about the shining red pool behind the road that turns toward the river. It was a secret place that only Manny and I knew about. Manny was the buck boy who lived outside town on the river and whose mother was an obeah woman. But that was before. People used to lower their eyes when they saw her in the street, but later they shook their heads and grinned at her and Manny. On the edge of town there's a path that leads into the bush, beside a gulch. It's the one lined with ferns and hemp bushes. The bushes that shriek as you pass them. The ones that Manny's mother cooked, and the strands of which she twined to make a noose* that people feared. *If you follow the hemp through the palms far enough into the bush, you reach a pool of warm fresh water surrounded by guava trees. Then you have reached the bower of my youth, where I spent sacred days with Manny, swimming, eating, cursing, and singing bad songs. They were my best days. No one knew where to find us, and we pledged secrecy and loyalty, and we never broke it, and it has never been matched.*

*He showed me his thing; it was longer and fatter than mine and not circumcised, and I became ashamed of my thin and wiry member. We had a game. We took turns being High Man and Low Man. We would bathe in the pool and before drying off would roll our entire bodies in the red brown mud we dug from the side of the pool. The sun dried it into an armour of mud and we couldn't smile or scratch without it cracking and falling off. Next we broke berries and scraped leaves and mashed them for colour and High Man was painted with as much extravagance as we found materials for. When he was finished, he had the power to rule the bush and could command obedience from Low Man. Sometimes it meant fetching sticks for a fire to boil plantain in the pot Manny had stolen from his mother. But most of the time High Man ordered Low Man to rub his thing and to pull on it until the hot white scum shot out into the pool. Low Man was not allowed to refuse. That's how many hours in the afternoon were spent. We took equal turns.*

*One day Manny's sister came to the pool and spied on us and ran home to tell her mother, who set out cursing and swearing to my father's house and threatened to work obeah on him. My father whipped me and forbid me to go back there, threatening me that I would get expelled from school if the headmaster found out. I often sneaked back to the pool with Manny, but we never played our game again.*

*November 4, 1959*

*Frederick used to be a sailor and he speaks all the time about the sea. His breath is the foulest I have ever smelled, but he speaks more sense than most of them here. He says I'm civilized for a coloured man, and he thinks I may not really be one. If I were to*

*tell anyone about my relation to Lord Nelson, it would be him.
But not yet.*

*Frederick is fixed and focused when he speaks:*

*"There's a chap down'the end of the corridor who says ee's been
in an' outa 'ere for the last twenty years. God! If I 'ave to stay 'ere
another month I'll really lose my mind. It's my captain who
suggested I come 'ere, thinks I been causin' too much trouble, but I
tell 'im, and you know mate, I just keep tellin' 'im that it's not the
way to do it − yo'ave ta 'ave a little order about it, or the whole
thing just goes up in smoke, I say. It's really I'm just a bit tired . . .
Yea, tired, I guess, is the word you could say. You see lotta things on
a ship. A lotta things in the ocean that are there and aren't there.
And it makes you tired. Yea, I'm tired." When he perceives his
mind drift and feels like he's being too serious with me, he
regurgitates bad jokes and slaps me on the shoulder. When he
laughs he is a different man, and he looks ten years younger and
twenty pounds lighter.*

*"God, this place'll really do it you, won't it mate."*

*When he says "God," it's longer than that, almost GOOD, and
sometimes I'm not sure which one he means.*

*November 5, 1959*

*My family was here to visit − embarrassed, looking at their feet,
not at me, and me not looking at them and me sinking further and
further away from them, and when I open my eyes they're still there
shuffling and not looking and when I pretend I'm asleep they go
and we are all relieved.*

*November 6, 1959*

*The wet scaly belly of the snake along the spine is rising once
again, but I have to fool them. Quiet . . . shhh, quiet, or they will
know and they will cut off your hiss with their own electric current
and skin you alive.*

*November 7, 1959*

Frederick and the Chinese nurse are fighting. He refuses to co-operate with all the nurses and he must know that they will make him pay for it, because he steadies himself before he argues, and rubs his temples slightly while she speaks her soft and subtle agitations. He taunts them, and each time they take him for treatment he calls to us, wants us to watch him, unjacketed, hands at his side, being forced down the hall by the huge monkeys in white coats to their laboratory.

He spent ten years sailing between here and England on grand cargo ships. He might have even crewed the ships that brought supplies for Atkinson's department store. He had a wife, but she died in an accident a year after they were married. He says his father was a rich British merchant, but I don't believe him. He's poorer than I. No one else believes him either, especially Lucy, the nurse who torments him. And she, she's not worth spitting at. She'll get her fair share in hell where she'll be tied in a straitjacket and forced to taste the urine of the inmates and be buggered nightly by the doctors with electrical eel members.


*November 8, 1959*

Often I wake in the middle of the night and there is a horrific smell around me in the room and I hear the loud stomping and clumsy heels of that blasted coolie nurse and I know she has come in here to fart at me and curse me with her bowels. Some days I cannot breathe and I call out for air and they think I am sick again and I tell them it is her curse on me, but they don't believe me, and she gives me wicked glares and she knows she is choking me.


*November 9, 1959*

They're prodding me again – preparing me – and as much as I say I am better, they don't believe me. They use me like an animal. Their names float by me when they come in and I don't remember to write them down once they've left – or I'd report them to the government. They're prodding, poking, bloody ditch dogs.

*November 10, 1959*

*I can't lift my arm from the bed higher than this page. I have searched up and down the wall for some sign of life, but no lizards dare enter this ward for fear of being confined, but I, chameleon, now belong.*

*November 12, 1959*

*And High Man and Low Man trampled through the bush – painted and patterned with the gifts of civilization – and they felled trees and brought animals into their service and together they protected the bush from ennui.*

No dates identified the next entries.

*When the eel and the goat mated they bred me and I jumped out of the goat womb with my four thumbs and hooves and long screaming member and I roamed the earth and pounded the faces of devils and drank the milk of maidens. One day I was a bastard and all of that stopped.*

*Capitulation*

Daphne closed the journal, her stomach in knots. She placed the diaries gently into the desk drawer as if they might splinter or shatter on impact. Outside, helicopters were circling again. She tried to hold on to the words, but the noise reverberated through the images conjured in her mind, scattering them into meaninglessness. She stood up to open the sliding door to her balcony. The whir became a boom of rotating motors, of mon-strous flapping mechanical insects. She followed the sounds out the door, down the stairs, and outside into the humid night. The light had faded. The air was softer, safer. The sundried armour of mud, the pool lined with fruit-bearing trees, the wily lizard: all of these were new, yet not unknown. The busy street in front of her was in the present, the here and now, no walls, nothing climbing them. *This is mine*, she thought, then repeated it to convince herself.

The bus took her to the West End, to NDG, and she walked through the placid neighbourhood until she reached Sheila Eyre's home. The stickiness returned, and she became strangely out of breath. The idea of speaking to Sheila had seemed compelling back on the Plateau, but in the middle of this wide, open street, she felt herself backing down.

Lights were on in the living room and Sheila, sitting straight and tall at a card table, was playing solitaire. Her dress was fashioned from chiffon and lace, with a high Victorian collar and a tapered, ribbed bodice. Daphne imagined the heat trapped inside its piping and tatting, and she pulled the neck of her T-shirt away from her throat. Speaking to her would be impossible tonight. Sheila's face was blank, as though made of brown wax, and her long skeletal arms grew out of the puffy, faded white sleeves of her dress like the skinny legs of a chicken. A muscle in her forearm contracted with every deal of cards to herself. One, two, three, and over the card would go, the arm settling back on the edge of the table until the next play. The light from the antique fringed lamp on the sideboard cast a yellow tinge over the room, and Sheila sat before her like a dull, faded photograph of a Dickens character. Daphne raised her hand to the window, tracing Sheila's figure on the glass, from the profile of her flat, paraffin nose, along the laced bodice, under the table, until she reached Sheila's feet. There, she saw that the woman wore one shoe, while the other was kicked off and overturned. The only glitch in her perfect demeanour. Daphne pressed her face up against the window. Her breath quickened. Moisture gathered on the glass, and she wiped a finger streak across the condensation. Her lips quivered in sadness. Sheila looked up, as though having heard, but looked behind her and didn't see Daphne, who ducked down before running back to the street and toward the bus stop.

# Last Gibbous

## 1

Daniel opened his briefcase as he waited for the kettle to boil on the stove. He tossed aside some papers onto the kitchen table, then picked up a stapled booklet he didn't recognize.

*. . . In 1717, the King of France had given the mission of St. Sulpician priests a land grant on the Ottawa River, where they persuaded Nipissings, Algonquins, and Iroquois to relocate from Sault-au-Recollet. Subsequent actions by French and British colonial administrations had enlarged and confirmed the grant, but had left the Indian population in doubt as to their rights to the land, and increasingly in conflict with the Seminary.*

*At the time of Confederation the Oka Indians remained uncertain and apprehensive concerning their tenure to these lands which they had occupied for 150 years. . . .*

*On 31 July 1868, the Algonquins of Oka petitioned the federal government for full control over the domain, and one week later a similar petition from the Iroquois accused the Seminary of tyranny and oppression. The Superintendent General of Indian Affairs, however, was satisfied with the Seminary's account of its dealings with the Indians and with the validity of its title to the land. The bands were warned to respect the law and property rights, and were reminded that in 1853 and 1854 other lands had been set aside for the Algonquins (at Maniwaki) and for the Iroquois (at Doncaster). An Order in Council was passed in 1869, confirming the government's support for the title of the Seminary. Many of the Algonquins subsequently left Oka but the Iroquois,* behind the leadership of Chief Joseph, remained largely defiant, and a number were imprisoned for selling wood or for staking out lots. . . .

Officials of the Department of Indian Affairs had been convinced for some time that a solution to the dispute was less likely to be found in litigation than in a negotiated agreement which would provide the Indians with alternative lands. In 1881, the Department reached an agreement with the Seminary whereby the latter would purchase lands from the Province of Ontario to allow the Indians to relocate in the Township of Gibson. An area of more than 25,000 acres was acquired, and the Seminary consented to erect new houses and to compensate the Indians for improvements abandoned at Oka. Only one third of the Indian population accepted the offer, and several of these later returned to Oka.

While continuing to exhort the Indians to accept the Gibson compromise, the Superintendent General of Indian Affairs decided, early in 1882, to turn to Reverend William Scott for an opinion on the dispute. Scott was undoubtedly seen as being in an uniquely favourable position to win the confidence of both sides. . . .

In January of 1883, Scott persuaded the Department of Indian Affairs to publish his report of the previous February, along with a postscript. The postscript indicated that while he was still convinced of the rightness of the government's position, he had found "from recent personal intercourse with the Chiefs and people of Oka that arguments and persuasion seem to be of no avail," and that the "sense of justice or injustice seems to be wonderfully developed, and it may not be easy to find a way of conciliation in regard to what the Indians consider primary faults in dealing with their interests." It went on to argue that in view of the Indians' rejection of the terms of the Gibson compromise, the Seminary should consider more liberal terms, in recognition of a deep-seated public conviction "that although the Indians may not have legal claim to the lands, as owners thereof, they are nevertheless entitled to compensation for the loss of lands which they had been led to suppose were set apart for their benefit."

*Although the Department of Indian Affairs proceeded with the Gibson resettlement plan, the majority of the Oka Indians rejected it. . . .*

*Finally, in 1912, the case was taken to the Privy Council, where it was held that the land belonged to the Seminary. . . .*

*The Indians of Oka did not easily accept the judgement and continued to write frequent letters of complaint concerning their condition. The Department generally took the position that the 1912 case had settled the issue, and for several decades took no further action to legislate or to negotiate a solution. Indian grievances became more pronounced as the Seminary began to sell parcels of the land to other parties.*

*In 1945, the D.I.A. purchased all lands not already sold by the Seminary except those used for religious purposes, and also acquired an additional 500 acres of woodland in order to insure a fuel supply for the Indians. As part of the purchase agreement, which was intended to be final settlement of the issue, the Department assumed all of the Seminary's obligations towards the Indians, except spiritual care for those of the Roman Catholic faith.*

The kettle whistled loudly and had almost gone dry by the time Daniel reached to turn off the burner. He closed the thin volume from the Department of Indian Affairs Research Branch and threw it back in his briefcase. *Who the hell does she think she is.* He regretted ever hiring Joanne and now even suspected her of cutting mornings when he wasn't in, having caught her one morning sailing in at 11:00 and offering him a lame excuse. He poured the tea and, cup in hand, strolled out to the garage to uncoil the hose.

It was a perfect morning, and he didn't want to miss a chance to work in his garden before the long and irksome drive into Montreal. The flowerbeds surrounded the house like a rampart, patches repeating the motif under the birch tree on the front lawn and in the backyard along the fence. The whole yard emitted a prodigious steel-blue light. It was made up of a single type of flower – Jacob's ladder. The leaves of the plants climbed more than two feet up the brick walls of the house and up the trunk of the birch, while the petals of those flowers that had bloomed flopped drowsily. Daniel was an attentive gardener, nurturing each plant individually, and the Jacobs thrived in the persistent sun.

His neighbours had been curious the first summer after he'd moved in, when he'd begun digging out the shrubs and peonies planted by the previous owner. They watched from their porches as the yard became striped in indigo. It wasn't just the homogeneity of the garden that alarmed them, which was curious enough, but the arrangement of the rows of Jacobs was unique: six tight, perfectly straight rows on each of the beds around the house. He allowed only three of the six to fully flower in one year. Each year an alternate row grew and flowered, and each spring Daniel would dig up the roots of the previous year's flowering row, dry the roots in his basement, pulverize them in his food processor, and store them in airtight containers on a shelf beside the basement sink. He'd been told by his mother's neighbour in Sherbrooke that the dried roots would help his gas. When obstinate cramps and wild, rumbling convulsions in his stomach had begun to embarrass him at work and in meetings with head office, he'd started drinking the tea made from the Jacob's ladder before bed. Until recently, each night he was tranquillized, his stomach quiet. Although the neighbours had been reluctant to speak to Daniel when he first moved in, they finally came to accept the missing-guitar-string look of his flower beds, and even welcomed it as a dash of something irregular but safe in their neighbourhood.

He lingered over the Jacobs, savouring the weeding and watering, delaying his departure for work until deciding, finally, to go inside to telephone. Daphne answered, but forgot to say "Copie Copie."

His irritation sprouted. "Daphne, it's a business." Silence on the other end, but he continued, "I'm working on accounts at home this morning. I won't be coming in until later today, maybe not until after closing. Some sales calls to make this afternoon ... all the traffic ... maybe not until the evening ... Make sure you send the Patterson job out this morning; I promised him . . . Everything all right there? Okay then . . . Yes, bye."

By eleven o'clock, the garden was manicured and the long green leaves of the Jacobs fluttered in the swelling breeze. Daniel sat in his study making notes for his calls but was unable to concentrate, so he got up and paced the room a minute before deciding to complete the task he'd begun on the weekend. He went down to the basement. From his worktable he took the pillowcase he'd soaked in dye. It had dried to madder red. He put the cloth to his face and smelled it; the colour intoxicated him. He began working, possessed.

First he retrieved an old red-and-black-checkered shirt and a pair of faded jeans from a pile in the laundry room. Placing them on the worktable beside the pillowcase, he then searched through a closet filled with clothing, childhood toys, and magazines. From a duffle bag at the back, he pulled out the leather hockey jacket of his boyhood team and placed it on the table with the other clothes. Then scissors. With heavy shears he cut long thin strips of leather from the jacket. The cutting was slow, the leather thick.

As he worked, a phrase dislodged from memory: "*Hold not thy tongue, oh God of my praise: for the mouth of the ungodly, yea, the mouth of the deceitful is opened upon me.*"

Something was not right, some lines missing. They were words from the Psalms he'd learned as a boy, words he'd remembered for the weight of their doom, but his memory was patchy. The words came and went as he continued cutting. When he finished there were more than fifty strips of leather, which he sewed, with the methodical, meticulous care of a tailor, first to the sleeves of the shirt – a long line along the seams from the back of each cuff, up along the elbow and the triceps, to the underarm – then to the outer seams of the pants, each strip placed a few inches apart.

"*. . . they have spoken against me with false tongues . . .*"

The hours passed quickly as each strip was sewn into place, and his fingertips grew sore from poking the needle through the leather. After putting the needle safely into its case, he laid out the clothes on the table and ran the broom handle up the right leg of the fringed jeans and up through the collar of the fully buttoned shirt. Gathering straw and newsprint from beside the table, he stuffed the pillowcase into the shape of a head distinctly rounder than his own, inserted the top of the broom handle and lashed the cotton flaps to the wood. Crunching up newspaper, sheet after sheet, he stuffed it into the shirt to build arms, a chest, and an exaggerated paper abdomen, fat from freshly smoked deer meat, from beer, too much beer. Next he stuffed the jeans, creating heavily muscled lacrosse thighs, and adding an unnaturally large bulge in the crotch. When the form was fully shaped, taped, and secured, he grasped the end of the broom and lifted the mannequin from the table. The leather strips formed a fringe around its body. A Wild West fringe.

*"Rewarded me . . . thus, they have rewarded evil for good; hatred for good will . . ."*

It was almost ready; all that remained was to add the finishing touches to the head. Selecting black wool, he sewed it to the pillowcase and let the long thin strands fall in a light bounce to the shoulders. Next, the face. With a black Magic Marker he drew large, bushy eyebrows, wild, violent eyes, and an O-shaped mouth frozen in a crimson howl.

A sudden idea sent him searching through the closet again. He emptied two boxes, turning out all of their contents, but could not find what he was sure had once been there: the long, delicate falcon feather his father had given him when he was a boy, telling him that the falcon had sharper eyes than an eagle. One more search through the rubble of his keepsakes, but no luck. He resolved to buy feathers to complete the headpiece.

*". . . in the next generation let his name be clean put out."*

December 7, 1959

*Frederick has lost so much weight I can see his shoulder blades through his shirt. It's not that he doesn't eat. I think it's that he doesn't sleep. He is always in the common room when I go there and always willing to talk to someone about his sailing, or about the* nurses, or about his father. He will tell anyone about his father's mistresses and how they sucked on Frederick in locked rooms and made him lift them up to sit on him, to ride him propped up against the door. They don't believe him, and he mocks them, but he's particularly fond of me, because it's only to me that he speaks about what happened on his last ocean trip.

They had been on the ship for months, with only brief stops at ports along the way and they were fed up, hungry, and wanting to return home. He could taste nothing but salt each time he parted his lips. He could smell only salt when he breathed, and a crust formed over his entire body so that he became a pillar – Lot's wife – on the ocean.

One day, some of the men were bringing in a net and drew up alongside the ship an enormous, leathery fan with a flattened head in the middle, from which supple, fleshy horns projected on each side. It struggled and smashed about the deck until they killed it. When they examined the creature, some of the men called it manta ray, others called it devilfish, but they all knew it was harmless. So there was a moment of silent guilt and shared fear – sailor's super-stition. Frederick drew a quick and silent cross before his bowed head.

Without knowing why, they decided to keep the fish in the half-empty storage refrigerator down below and together they dragged it to its cool tomb and splashed it with water and left it folded, like a wallet, in the darkness. Here in his story Frederick stops and stares past my head and for a long while is silent, barely breathing. Then he begins in a much lower tone and returns to the story by describing his skin, making me feel each particle of salt eating away at it, until I become itchy. He tells me of the night he couldn't sleep from the burning of his skin, and how, naked, he sneaked across the corridors to the huge and heavy refrigerator door, dragged it open, and knelt beside the embalmed monster and touched its cold inviting wing. Lifting the folded wing open, he climbed on top of the beast and dragged his body over the entire span, rubbing his face, arms, legs, and feet into the cool fleshy bed, and he let the salt be taken back by the monster – clearing his pores and scratching his inflamed skin. For a few minutes he lay wrapped in its wings, suspended by the quality of touch.

*He went back each night for three nights until the smell in the container started to be unbearable. On the final night, upon leaving, he spotted a button, from a shirt he knew was not his own, lying in the folds of one of the wings. He realized then that they had all been taking turns.*

*December 8, 1959*

*I told Frederick about the 37 years and about how a man can know all the teas, all the silver, crystal and china the way he can know a woman's body — by touching every part, by smelling every crack and fold, by licking every surface.*

*I couldn't describe well how Desmond came to work there, because I can't clearly see it in this foamy matter that now passes for my brain; no messages penetrate the casket heart. But I do know that he came as my friend and I was, once more, proud of my service. And weeks and months passed like the days at the red pool with Manny, and I taught him the secret of numbers and we were both proud. But then Desmond stopped looking me in the eye and he avoided being in the same room as I, and he stopped inviting me to his house, and he treated me like a disease. It was only two months later that Atkinson told me to leave — to leave or be dragged away by the police. At this point in my story Frederick too started to pull away, but then I went on and told him what was true — that Atkinson and Desmond fixed the books, took the money themselves and that I was their damn foot-licking pawn and they used me and that the coloured man must pay for the curse of his birth. And I must have been screaming and crying because Lucy came and tried to give me something, but Frederick stopped her and said I was fine and he held me and rubbed the back of my head with his still-calloused boatman's hand and he whispered over my head: "You're not to worry, chap, you're just like a friend o' mine in London — ee's as white as they come. We'd go to the horses twice a week and ee'd always beat the life outa me. A winna every time. Ee was lucky, ee was, and you're 'nough like 'im. You don't let 'em whip ya, mate, you're more white than many of 'em, to me y'are, don't you mind."*

# Last Gibbous

## 2

Daphne woke up knowing it was the middle of the week and that she'd be beyond suspicion if she phoned in sick. There would be no insinuation of her taking an extended weekend, as there might be on Monday or Friday, and she knew Daniel wouldn't even notice her absence. He hadn't made it into the store at all the day before. The others had left Daphne to close up, and she had stayed late in the coolness of the store reading and re-reading sections from the burgundy journal. When she'd realized how famished she was, she'd searched the desks for food. In Sylvie's there'd been nothing. In Joanne's she'd found a green pepper, which she'd bitten into like an apple, but it was off, and she'd gagged on the taste, the seeds falling on her chest. Finally she'd settled for a bag of tortilla chips found in Marc's drawer, and devoured them along with some cold coffee. Reluctant to be distracted from reading again, she called the store and offered Marc an over-elaborate description of her fabricated symptoms. A stomach flu, certain to last only twenty-four hours, she assured him.

The phone rang a few minutes later. She let the answering machine get it. Michel asked her to call him when she got the chance. Daphne let it click off and the airy pitch of his voice disappeared into the tape.

She lay on the bed with the electric fan at her feet. Helicopters flew above. The world was humming. Taking up the flashlight and slipping under the sheets, she lit up the floral patterns on the cotton that draped over her like a tent. In the surreptitious manner of a child sneaking in a book instead of sleeping, she quietly turned the pages of the black journal, though the only one to hide from was herself.

*December 15, 1959*

*I've lost time. And time was all I had. They take it away from you and then throw it back in your face like a child that has been missing; you have to care for it again.*

*December 16, 1959*

*I remember riding. It was my first bicycle, a gift from my mother who was wise enough to know it would do me good instead of harm, as my father imagined. I rode it all through the compound, ringing the bell as I passed the houses of boys I knew at school, and then past the girl with the hibiscus flower printed a hundred times on her dress. She was a beautiful Negro girl whose Daddy was learning to build motors and was always building himself a machine to do something better than the last machine. One day he designed a motor he believed would run his boat. He spent years building that boat motor. "What's happenin' Simon?" his neighbours would ask and he'd say, "buildin' a motor, man, you should see it, gwan take me round de 'hole a de Caribbean wid it." For three years he told everyone about the motor, and one day it was finished. His daughter got all dressed up in her best hibiscus dress, and his son in his church suit, and his sister and her family were there too, at the dock in the harbour, waiting to see it work. Wife didn't come. Didn't believe him, but he was going to make it right with her. She'd always said he never did anything right. So she wasn't a bit surprised when he didn't come back that night. She barely blinked when they told her that the boat sped out across the water until they couldn't see it. They thought he would have come back then, but he didn't. He came back two days later. Some sailors on a cargo ship brought him in. He couldn't turn the motor off. He'd built it too well; it hadn't run out of gas, because he'd brought extra gas and rigged it specially. He had to signal to a ship for help and they picked him up. He jumped out of the boat as it sped out over the waves and headed out toward the horizon. They had to throw him a line. He almost drowned, or so he tells it. His wife didn't talk to him for a month.*

*That's the feeling I had with my bicycle – it was too good, too*

*fast. It scared me, but I knew it was taking me away from
something – from me and who I'd been.*

*December 17, 1959*
    *Things are getting closer in time, perhaps happening all at once; all
the faces are swarming in front of me, grinning, and making the cluck
cluck sound of a distressed chicken. The futility of hungry, distressed
chickens – scratching their marks into the granite that is my brain.*

*December 18, 1959*
    *He loves poetry. Even though his soul is lost to sea monsters,
he loves the soul of man. Frederick is elusive.*

*December 19, 1959*
    *Shut up, shut up all of you. Shut your damn mouths talking and
talking and talking and talking as if it makes a difference. Shut up.
Shut up. Shut up. And if you come in here again with your white-
coat large-pocket drivel, I'll drown you in the flood of the Orinoco
and slaughter your horses so that you can't return home.*

    *They pester me. They continue today, after saying soon, soon,
you'll stop seeing the moon. To hell with them. Dark buzzards
circle around their heads.*

*December 20, 1959*
    *I await them. They'll come again, today, but this time with their
huge goons to drag me down the hall. I will not fight them. My
temples are rubbed, ready.*

    *The pissing sky left a message in the garden: Take or be taken,
swim or drown at the whim of the arbitrary clouds.*

*December 23, 1959*
    *Back from treatment and there is quiet again. There are fewer of
us on the floor – strangers have taken the others away. There was*

*singing last night, singing as I slept, and in my dreams a goat sang* HALLELUJAH, HALLELUJAH. *Women's voices filled the corridors of the hospital, but I couldn't open my eyes. I think Frederick came to see me, and he left a piece of ginger cake on my pillow. I smelled it and it joined in my dreams and the goat sang* IN EXCELSIS, IN EXCELSIS, *and his breath was spicy and sweet.*

*December 24, 1959*

*They're sending me away, back to town, for just one day. They are trying to fool me, because I know what they're planning, what they're doing. They're all blaming me for the unruly behaviour in this place and they think that a day without me will prove it. They're all against me, because they don't believe me, and they're testing my strength. They're sending my wife to take me outside, where there are people singing and where they're sure I will remember, but they are all idiots.*

*December 25, 1959*

*People I barely know have brought me gifts, and had they been frankincense and myrrh I might have forgotten the century, for they treat me like Christ – like someone who is about to die.*

*The woman who they say is my wife has put me in the second room, the one that used to be her daughter's, because she says it's quieter there, away from the kitchen. But I know it's because she can't stand to look at me or smell me. The beautiful one, the youngest, runs from her room each morning and dashes her guts into the toilet. Her mother runs to her and stands horrified above her, not consoling, not lifting a motherly finger, just glaring at the back of her head shoved in the basin and her poor convulsing shoulders. Then she glares at me, looking for an answer, and I retreat like a crab in the surf. They all hate me, but I forgive them, because I do not know them.*

*I woke this morning to the vinegar smell of garlic pork and the season became real in my nostrils. I remember years and years of happy mornings on this day, as a boy, looking to steal a sip of pink* gin from my father and looking forward to the garlic belch at the end of the morning.

Outside, Mother Sally is dancing on her wooden stilt legs and the music is blasting from the radios and the children are trying to see up her pants to see how it is she could be so tall and dance so.

I will eat till I'm stuffed tonight and sleep when the moon rises, because tomorrow I will have much to tell Frederick and I will describe for him the noises and smells, and we will roar with laughter at the madness of these people.


January 1, 1960

All of the nurses and doctors are sick from drink this morning. Some of them were at parties in town, some were here on duty, but all of them drank until they could no longer stand up. Dr. Curtis, the only one I like, is on duty today and he looks like a painted-face bush man, chalky cracking skin and yellow eyes. I know it's him that keeps them from treating me as often as they do Frederick and the others, but he has to put up a fight. The six nurses I see during the day report me for not speaking to them and tell tales about what I'm writing. I have names for all of them, but if I call them these to their faces they report me, so I restrain myself.

The morning nurse (who is still trying to get here early enough to wake me up, since I am always up before the sun): Miss Priss
The nurse who brings the medication: Pocker
The one in the treatment room: Sphinx
The night nurse: Farter
The head nurse: Martinet
The one who cleans: Lucy, because that is her name and the only one I can remember.


January 2, 1960

Today one of the men down the hall bit Pocker in the arm and drew blood. Serves her right, the cratered black bitch. I don't know what they did with him, but I hear no sounds from the entire floor now; he must have come back from the treatment room. It's always quiet as a cemetery after treatments and all of us stay in our rooms, doors shut and radios low.

*January 3, 1960*
  *Every day Frederick is getting smaller, thinner, and he sits in the lounge looking like a mantis bent over his game of cards. I don't know how his bony legs support his long frame. His neck is disproportionately long and curved.*
  *Today they're all talking about politics and independence — fools. I can't bear to listen, but some words filter through and run around my head. They'll learn, they'll be sorry. In the fables of buck hunters, the son who rejects the authority of his father will blister and swell in the sun like a rotting carcass; that will be this country without Britain.*

*January 4, 1960*
  *The slow crawling snake is like a penis that enters every orifice and ejaculates a foaming, sticking scum. Muscles are limp, my teeth are coated and the foam gurgles in my ear. This is the snake pit and we are flailing, one on top of the other, crawling in and out of our skins.*
  *Frederick told me about a contraption used in hospitals a century ago. Pulling on your thing was said to make you sicker, so they stopped you by putting you in a metal belt. These are the words he read me from his book:*
  *"It was designed to prevent involuntary nocturnal seminal emissions, to control waking thoughts, and to prevent self-abuse. Secured by a belt around the waist, it consisted of a metal plate with an opening through which the penis was to emerge. A sharp metal point attached to the upper part of the rim would jab sharply if the wearer had an erection. The inventor stated: 'If the wearer be irresponsible from any cause, the appliance can be permanently secured to him.'" Frederick finds all of this amusing. He laughs like a hyena, and I go back to bed.*

  Large, scribbled letters covered the whole page under the entry for January 5.

*I can barely open my eyes, they hurt badly. Behind them is a deep, echoing throb that turns my skull into a map of minefields. Pockets of brain matter are inflamed. Martinet said she would force me to go to eat, but has given up and I can only keep the rhythm, back and forth, the back and forth rhythm of my spine, my legs curled in my arms to protect every cell from the slow crawling, skinless reptile.*

The next entries were undated.

*I am a child rolling in the mud and building armour as tight as Raleigh's and as shiny as a copper penny until each night they rub the jelly on my temples and when I awake it is my own shit that I am sitting up in.*

*In the ocean of death there will be a duel between the one lone survivor of the silver army of truth and the last living member of the brotherhood of faith and one will run a javelin made from the snout of a swordfish through the heart of the other. Either way, treachery and transgression will rule.*

*My belly is rotten and shoots green and foul-smelling faeces through my ass and into my coffin – I scream out, but nurse ghosts cannot hear me. The devil has their souls.*

Daphne placed the book down on the bed. She was soaked with sweat. She clicked off the flashlight, threw off the sheet, and headed for the shower. Rubbing hard on her arms, legs, and face, she showered under a cold spray, trying to peel off a layer of something that had begun to grow on her. Real and imagined smells. Vinegar and garlic left her pores. She reclined in the tub, letting the water beat down on her. She reached back into his words, just barely able to imagine the regular throbbing and then, nothing . . . the treatment and the slow and deliberate eradication of memory. The annihilation of personality. After a few minutes she felt drowned under the obliterating spray. She was tempted to stay there, to disappear inside the crack that had opened wider, but she forced her hand to the tap and turned it off, just barely able to catch her breath as the water dripped from her hair over her eyes, down her cheeks. Water trickled from the corners of her mouth. She sat for a long time in the shallow water. Lying on the rim of the tub was a cosmetic facial mask – a green gel, glutinous and cohesive – which she squeezed from its container onto her fingers and spread over her face. It started to dry immediately, pulling the skin of her nose tighter to her cheek, her cheek tighter to her ears, her chin tighter to her neck. It dried into a plastic mould. When the shivers started, she got out of the tub, towelled off, then stood staring into the mirror at her shining, impermeable face. Peeling off the mask, she felt the tingling of opened pores underneath, and the green sheath, this second skin, came off in one long connected layer – a reptilian moulting. Feeling lightheaded, she picked a pear out of the bowl on her kitchen table and took it back with her to the bed. It was the first thing she'd eaten all day. She dived under the sheet again. The stepping and missing was like a pulse.

*January 15, 1960*

*I am an intruder into the lives of strangers who have spent the day with me. My wife and two daughters were here for several hours. One of them is very beautiful; I can't remember which she is, but she has a strong face with sharp cheek bones that run in a delicate line from her mouth to above her ears. Her lips are not wide and flat like the other one's and she smells of jasmine. When I look at her she puts her hands in front of her, as though hiding something, and she looks away. She was speaking, but I couldn't hear her. They all spoke, but I don't know what they were saying.*

*Someone else was speaking, not to me, but to my father, above the roar of wind – me, standing below the wind of their breath. He, he wasn't speaking exactly, was more self-engrossed, but she was making wild gestures with her arms, at times arching up on her toes trying to physically penetrate his thoughts. Her hands would fall on his, and he would squeeze them – a reconciliation – and for a moment all I could hear was the wind; but then the hands came apart. Their disagreement remained and would blow up like spray*

from a waterfall, until later, at home, my mother would cover me
and kiss me gently, wait until I feigned sleep and then sneak off to
their room where her whispers would mend the day, and their
breathing would rise and disappear like scintilla escaping from a fire.

These strangers brought me a lunch of roast chicken and rice
which we ate in my room. They packed up their wares and kissed
me before leaving. I wonder what they came to tell me.

*January 16, 1960*

Lucy bangs and clatters around here like a clumsy cow. She
complained that I have been wetting the floor at night. The nasty
slant-eyed whore has pushed me too far. If I catch her with that high
and mighty grin again I'll box her ears and send her flat face
through the wall . . . but they'd get me for that, you can be sure;
they'd have me jellied and frothing like a mad dog. I am muzzled.

*January 20, 1960*

We were in the common room, Frederick and I, and we played
a hand of cards before starting our usual stories. He came from
treatment yesterday and is not as talkative as usual. The black
half-moons around his eyes are sinking into his bones.

When Sam, a new, fluffy white man in the section entered,
Frederick gave him a slow disapproving nod. Sam is a short, neat
bastard with a natty little Hitler mustache. He bounces and prances
about wearing a cravat. His speech is sprayed with multi-syllabled
words. He asked for a locker when he came here, but soon realized
the absurdity – in this place where everything is shared, where even
my facecloth has been used to wipe up someone's vomit.

Frederick and Sam spent an hour weighted down by each other in
the room and then Frederick told him to leave because he stank like
the pit of a perfumed spinster. Sam came to our table, toppled over
our game and then Frederick stood up and spit in his face. They
started to brawl, and I warned Frederick, told him to stop, that he
must stop, but he couldn't hear me. They were taken away, and all
the while I was sorry I didn't beat the balls out of that uppity prick.
Perhaps they will heal him quickly and send him away from us.

*January 23, 1960*

*These nurses are making my bowels back up. I am bloated like a puffer fish. If I fart, I will fill the room with poison.*

*January 24, 1960*

*Green dung threatens to enter my eyes from my throat. Fuck them all.*

*January 25, 1960*

*No shit yet today*

*January 26, 1960*

*Nothing*

*January 27, 1960*

*And the fat of rams lodged in the bowels of Saul's men could not appease the prophet, so he hewed Agog in pieces before the Lord.*

*January 28, 1960*

*Pissed once every hour in a long, loud running stream. Bowels are petrified. Plantain remains lodged in my gut: fodder for a dinosaur. They ate pebbles to digest ferns, a diet of the earth, a mineral ceremony. In me, human waste accumulates waiting to explode and be forgotten.*

*January 31, 1960*

*Surprising when it finally came. This morning my guts exploded into the toilet on their way to hell, the brown liquid splattered the edges of the seat and echoed through the hall. It's the last of the blackness, the last of the stifling servitude. Frederick was right –
I am a white man.*

*February 1, 1960*

*Frederick returned yesterday after five days of solitary confinement. He looks straight ahead, and if he has to look to the side, he turns his whole body. No more shifting eyes. His coughing interrupts his stories about the ship, and I've noticed he doesn't talk about his father's women or his father's money. Mostly now he speaks about fish and rigging. Backstays and bobstays and crossjack braces mixed with sharks, albacore, barracudas, and groupers — the sea again in his hands and nostrils. He sweats as he speaks, talking as if facing straight into the sun, shouting at it to turn itself off. Then he coughs his engine sputter and continues his card game.*

*February 3, 1960*

*He says: "So, Gerald, how are you feeling?"*

*He says: "Very well."*

*He says: "That's good, that's good. I'm glad to hear that. Mrs. Walker says you've been much more comfortable the last few days."*

*He says (not remembering which one of the fucking bitches he's talking about): "Of course, she's right."*

*He says: "Now, I have a few questions today, do you mind?"*

*He says (cursing him with his eyes): "Of course not, doctor."*

*He says: "Can you tell me how long you've been here?"*

*He says: nothing.*

*He says: "Do you know how long?"*

*He says: "Yes, not very long."*

*He says: "What about this; can you tell me what 25 times 3 is?"*

*He says: "75"*

*He says: "Of course, good. Now can you multiply that by 15?"*

*He says: "Yes"*

*He says: "Okay."*

*He says: nothing.*

*He says: "Well, Gerald?"*

*He says: "I said, yes, I could" (he has to be careful not to seem too irritated, to keep his voice from rising).*

*He says: "Very well, tell me a little about what you did just before you came here – about your life."*

*He says: nothing.*

*He says: "Do you remember what you were doing?"*

*He says: nothing (but he knows he is trying to get him to talk about Manny and the painted days at the shining pool; he thinks he is the kanaima but his skin is no whiter than his, as he wants him to believe, so he answers): "Of course, I'm the manager at Atkinson's, responsible for the inventory, staff, and the bookkeeping. I was feeling a little dizzy at work, so they brought me here."*

*He says: "Did anything happen to you there?"*

*He says: nothing.*

*He says: "Did something happen between you and your employee, what was his name . . . Desmond, was it?"*

*He says: nothing, because he won't be fooled by the test and he won't falter and say Manny's name or tell him how they made the colours or how warm the mud was.*

*He says: "Maybe you're not up to discussing that today. I'll be back in a few days and we'll try again."*

*And He doesn't say: Damn you all to hell for your inquisition of my soul and fuck you in your behind like a poor, groping dog.*


*February 6, 1960*

*Sam and Frederick are in the common room playing chess. Only recently have I noticed what must have driven Frederick to want to annihilate him. I have to leave the room every time he does it. He sniffs himself. When he thinks no one is watching, he scratches himself in his crotch or in the pit of sweat and dirt under his arm, and then he puts his finger to his nose and holds it there like a flower. He's nervous and fidgety and can't keep still. He digs in his crevices, wildly searching out scent, and then sniffs after every sentence he speaks, like punctuation.*

*Frederick seems less affected by it recently. He is almost perpetually elated and flushed, even though he coughs and hacks into the chessboard and his cheekbones protrude from his face. He must be happy to be whipping that dandy mincer at his own game.*

*February 7, 1960*

*I don't know why Frederick puts up with that bastard. He's caused problems in here since the day he came and somehow it's everyone else who suffers from them. He gets away with acting like that, and it's us who pay the price.*

*February 8, 1960*

*They finally showed us a movie last night after many promises and failures. Frank Sinatra played a dealer, turned drummer, then a good-for-nothing. Frederick said he thinks I look a little like Sinatra, and when I pass a mirror the sharp angles of my face surprise me. He may be right.*

*February 9, 1960*

*He says: "Gerald, your wife telephoned me and she's worried because you haven't answered her letters or wanted to speak to her on the phone."*

*He says: nothing.*

*He says: "She told me that the last time she came here she talked to you about going to Canada with your daughters. She wants to know how you feel about this. They'll send for you as soon as you're better, Gerald."*

*He says: nothing, because people around him are lying again, testing him; no one talked about anything of the sort.*

*He says: "You have nothing to keep you here after this, you know."*

*He says: nothing.*

*He says: "And it might be a good break from your associations here and with your former place of employment."*

*He says: "Stop" and the back of his eyes tickles like a numb foot regaining circulation.*

*He says: "You think it over, Gerald, and they'll be coming back to visit you."*

*He says: nothing, but knows that if he could go anywhere, he'd go to England, not Canada, and he'd never go anywhere with people whose names he doesn't know.*

*February 14, 1960*

It was dark, early morning, when I heard his hoarse breathing up beside my ears. Frederick sneaked into my room in the middle of the night and was kneeling at the side of my bed. I jumped and almost cried out for Christ, but he stopped me. I focused slowly on his oval face, a flaming pink skeletal egg. His eyes were bright and runny, as though he were crying, but he made no sound other than his strangled breathing. He had shaved his mustache and looked to me like a wicked child who has been caught mimicking a grownup.

He kept his voice low while telling me they were sending him to another hospital because he is getting sicker and because they don't want the rest of us here to be infected. He said he'd be back and, between gasps and hacking, told me that I was supposed to write down in this book that he believed in Christ, but that Christ couldn't believe in him, or me, or anyone else, because he was dead and the dead don't make myths out of the living.

He said goodbye, he'd see me soon, but before he left he rested his cheek on my hand and I could feel the moist ague, and I held his head until he whispered: "we took turns; we all took turns with the winged creature." Then he left.


*February 15, 1960*

In the common room today it's quiet, the only tangible sign of life having left this morning. Sam is reading a book, sitting on what has become his chair, and the other feeble specimens are churning up their spells, walking on beaten paths, back and forth across the room. The usual ones groan and cry to themselves. They all make me sick.


*February 16, 1960*

Sam came to my room to give me a book of poetry. There was a marker at a page to this:

I wake and feel the fell of dark, not day.
What hours, O What black hours we have spent
This night! What sights you, heart, saw; ways you went!
And more must, in yet longer light's delay.

*With witness I speak this. But where I say*
*Hours I mean years, mean life. And my lament*
*Is cries countless, cries like dead letters sent*
*To dearest him that lives alas! away.*

*I am gall, I am heartburn. God's most deep decree*
*Bitter would have me taste: my taste was me;*
*Bones built in me, flesh filled, blood brimmed the curse.*

*Selfyeast of spirit a dull dough sours. I see*
*The lost are like this, and their scourge to be*
*As I am mine, their sweating selves, but worse.*

*February 17, 1960*
*Outside there is a dry buzzing of wind on the savannah and a*
*smell like dry lime. Inside it is quiet in the common room and*
*Frederick's hoarse laugh is missed.*

*February 19, 1960*
*Another book from Sam, a new book by an invisible man.*
*Reading is slow and quiet. Sheets smell beneath me.*

*February 20, 1960*
*Still reading Ellison.*

*February 21, 1960*
*Finished Ellison. Slept all afternoon.*

*February 22, 1960*
*Dreams and not dreams confused.*

*February 23, 1960*
*Taking me for treatment this afternoon.*

# Last Half

*How long do the amnesias following ECT persist? Do they clear up rapidly or do they continue indefinitely? To obtain some preliminary information on this problem, a follow-up study was carried out on as many of the patients as were available. Altogether, 5 of the 19 ECT patients were re-examined, each of whom had completed ECT from two and one-half to three and one-half months before the follow up interview. The follow-up recall tests were limited to those memories which each patient had failed to recall when tested approximately four weeks after the last treatment. The same questions were repeated as in the preceding post-treatment interview.*

*It was found that most of the experiences which the patients failed to recall in the original post-treatment interview were still unavailable to recall . . . This finding bears out . . . the general conclusion that a series of electrically induced convulsions, as administered in standard psychiatric practice, produces circumscribed amnesias for past experiences which persist beyond the usual period of recovery during which the temporary organic reaction to the treatments clear up.*

Daphne closed the book and tucked it under her arm. Her skin smelled musty although the air conditioning had dried the sweat and dispersed the staleness. She had left the house without taking a shower and hurried through the already sticky morning air in order to make it to the library as soon as it opened. Even so, she was going to be late for work, so she would have to be satisfied with the book in her hand. No time to browse. She moved through the electronic posts towards the exit. Beeping was followed by the turnstile locking, trapping her. The librarian looked up from the check-out counter and called to Daphne, asking her to sign out the book. Daphne stood mute, blinking, unable to comprehend; she wanted to find out about shock therapy, that was all. She blinked again and pushed her hip against the turnstile. Locked.

"Excuse me," the librarian said less politely this time, "but you'll have to sign that book out. Please bring your card over here."

"I don't have one."

"Well, you'll have to fill this out, over here, please."

Daphne's heart started to race. After a few seconds she pushed her hip to the bar again. Suddenly, in the resistance of metal against muscle, she sprang up and over the turnstile and spun through the revolving doors onto the street. Shouting followed her as she ran down the sidewalk and out onto the busy road, dodging the cars. Turning a corner she slowed down to a jog and checked behind her. Safe. Her heart leaped; her face twitched with the pulse of her disarray. The notion of a card had seemed so absurd in that moment with her hip jammed into the metal – what good would it have done, when her name itself had lost its meaning? Daphne, the mythical nymph, Apollo's first love, had abandoned her.

She walked quickly to the store.

Joanne and Marc sat across from each other at the circular meeting table near the coffee machine, waiting for the day's first customers. Daphne arrived out of breath, her shirt soaked with perspiration. Beads of sweat trickled down her forehead onto her nose and hung there. Engrossed in their discussion of the previous day's events, Joanne and Marc paid no attention to her, but as Daphne wiped her face with a Kleenex she saw Sylvie look up from her desk with a glint of suspicion. She kept her eyes lowered and nonchalantly slid the library book into a folded newspaper on her desk. As she sorted through the pile of copy jobs that had been left for her, she tried to forget about the library and concentrated on cooling down.

Joanne was enjoying the sound of her own voice as she wiped up spilled coffee grains from the table, dabbing the last few with her damp index finger, then flicking the grains, one by one, into the ashtray. "It was perfect, like it was out of a Monty Python skit, or that puppet show, you know, *Spitting Image*. He couldn't understand what the fuss was all about. 'I'm willing to negotiate,' he says and then boasts about reneging on the golf course expansion. He's standing in front of the camera, and he says, all earnest and sweet: 'I told the Indians we could work together on this, and that they should create an Indian village on that land. It's well positioned, close to Montreal; many people would drive out to visit. It's good business for everyone, right here, just half an hour from a large consumer market. They would do well, but, you know, they wouldn't go for it, so what more can I say? I've offered one solution. They just aren't listening. I can't understand.' Can you believe it? He wants them to sell toy tomahawks and teepees to tourists. You should have seen his pasty shark face. Hungry."

Marc stirred his coffee. He remained silent, but looked as though he wanted to speak.

Joanne turned to Daphne. "Are you coming to the bridge with us tonight, Daph?"

"Why?"

"I told you a couple of days ago; there's a rally to show support for the Mohawks, to out-yell the Châteauguay Nazis."

"Come on, Joanne, they're not Nazis," Marc defended. "They have their lives to live."

"You can be damn sure that the rednecks that do go down there are out for blood. They've flown in the KKK from Georgia for support . . . I'm not kidding."

"And you can count on your group being perfectly peaceful?"

Joanne thought seriously for a moment, and her silence allowed Marc to continue as a voice of reason.

"There's no point in going; you're just going to make it worse. And people might get hurt."

Joanne shot him a pained look of indulgence. "Not unless

those hothead SQs lose it under pressure and open fire on the whole lot," she said dryly.

Daphne exchanged a look with Marc. Joanne was viperous today, her curled-lip passion teetering her off balance. Daphne looked again at Joanne's thin outstretched arms and ungainly shoulders. Landlocked.

"Maybe it's more complicated than you think, Jo," said Marc.

"Maybe, but I know what I see, and I can't sit out. Daph, you've got to come to the bridge. We need more people who look like you on our side."

Daphne bristled. She touched her belly, responding the only way she knew how these days. "I'm pretty busy . . . I'm doing some research . . . but I'll let you know later."

She picked up a work order and moved to the colour copier. The door swung open and Daniel burst into the store, soaked with sweat and fuming. He said nothing, just walked straight to his desk. Daphne drifted closer, peering over his shoulder as he searched for something at the back of the desk drawer.

"Like a fly on a wall: always there, aren't you."

Daphne backed away silently.

Daniel turned around. "Always watching but not doing anything, for Christ's sake . . ."

She tried to speak, but tripped on her tongue. He continued to rummage in his desk.

"Looking for these?"

Daphne hadn't seen Joanne sneak up from behind. She was holding two eagle feathers which she waved in front of Daniel's face.

"Give me those." He tried to grab them out of her hand, but she pulled them close to her chest, taunting him.

"You know, you gotta wonder about you, Danny. You go on about the law and then you have this little Indian fantasy tucked away in your drawer. Doesn't figure – or is this some kind of weird cross-dressing thing?"

Daniel grabbed her wrist and pried the feathers loose. One broke in her hand, then she let go. He placed the feathers into his briefcase and left quickly. In the instant the door shut,

Joanne was at Daniel's desk ransacking the drawer. From under some papers she pulled out photographs and laid them on the desk. They were photographs of his family: his mother and sister, and one of his father. Next she pulled out two watches from the pencil tray. Marc hurried over to her.

"Joanne, what the hell are you doing? You have no right –"

"Just seeing what else the psycho's got in here."

"It's none of your business."

"Oh relax," Joanne said, examining one of the photos. Marc gently pulled it from her fingers, replaced the photographs and watches, and slid the drawer shut. A customer entered, and Marc moved to the counter to serve her. Daphne looked into Joanne's face which gradually broke into an ear-to-ear grin of victory. *Sing cuckoo, sing cuckoo.*

Daphne retreated to the copier but found herself staring at the wall. She reached inside herself for Jennifer Baird, mother. Reaching and reaching, she couldn't hear her, but that other female voice re-entered her like a germ, and she pictured the teenage face. Then his voice – the man in the diaries, Gerald Eyre. The odours emerged, and she could smell Gerald sitting in his pale hospital room reading, his bowels backed up and the sheets beneath him drenched in the stench. She felt infected with his hatred. The tropical country, the decade, the building full of men on the verge of annihilation were all foreign, but were hers as if she'd dreamt them.

Her dreams had been repeating themselves. She is standing in a large room with whitewashed walls and creaking floors and she is drawn up toward a crack in the ceiling. Then she is released, shot out like a projectile, ricocheting off walls and fixtures, unable to slow herself down, while people below stare horrified and ridiculing until she is sucked up again, into nothingness, as if through a vacuum cleaner hose. Even during the day, a pro-pelling shudder replicated itself in her chest.

Concentrate, concentrate, she told herself, as she picked up a simple copy job: ten photographs of 1930s body tattoos to be enlarged for transparencies, five copies of each. She watched each one flip by: a dragon with brown-and-red fanned wings and a tail of fire . . . *where? on a chest, a hip, a sculpted arm?* . . . next, a bright orange rooster standing on a snake whose mandibles were open, teeth bared, *one, two, three, four, five* . . . then, a woman's head coming out of a rose, with the American flag as a large petal behind her head to the left, the German flag to the right, *one, two, three, four, five* . . . a naked woman wearing a garter and a flapper's headband, sitting in a martini glass, *one, two, three, four, five* . . . a dagger through a rose entwined with a snake . . . *four, five* . . . a dagger through a skull wrapped in a sash that read *Death before Dishonour* . . . *three skulls, four skulls* . . . and a horseshoe adorned with flowers and the name *Maria* written across it . . . *Maria times four, Maria times five.* Counting replaced trying to imagine them on her foreign body.

*Tick, tick, tick*: the day edged slowly toward closing time. Daphne checked her watch over and over. She'd drifted through her day's work, taking a few breaks to read the library book on ECT. All day long she'd thought of nothing else but Surefoot, wanting the assurance of flesh as she continued to lose her own. The air in Copie Copie was cool, but sticky with attitude; Daniel and Joanne's confrontation had left them all guarded. Daphne checked her watch: 5:47. She was fed up with trying to manipulate a résumé to fit onto a single page. Having moved the headings closer and used smaller type, she was now tempted to delete the experiences she found useless, without telling the owner. Instead, she powered off. Marc sat staring at a sandwich in front of him. Joanne paced. Sylvie had already left, saying she had a doctor's appointment. Finally, Marc wrapped up his sandwich and threw it in the garbage.

"That's it; I'm out of here."

"Me too," said Joanne, taking his cue. She grabbed her knapsack and bolted out the door.

"I'll lock up," Daphne said, watching them both leave. She put the library book in the drawer of her desk and locked it.

Suddenly Joanne came bursting back into the store. "Hey, don't forget about tonight: 8:30, right at the bridge, the front line. We need the ethnics."

The hair stood up on Daphne's arms. "Well, I'll see . . ." she said, forcing an insincere smile.

Joanne took that for a yes and gave her a thumbs up signal before rushing out again.

The sun was still high, the breeze absent. At the base of the mountain the air was noticeably cooler. Joggers and cyclists congested the widest path, so she climbed along the cool, shaded trails toward the lookout. Nuthatches were bounding upside down along branches, poking into crevices for insects. *Tea-kettle, tea-kettle, teedle teedle* . . . a wren sang busily.

Now what? How would she find her now? Daphne took each step up the wooden stairs winding through the poplars slowly, wondering what to do. After leaving Copie Copie, she'd hurried down the street to the diner. "Fired, missed too much work," said the thin young man frying eggs at the stove in response to her query, sparing no sympathy for Surefoot. Daphne closed her eyes and tried to see the folds around Surefoot's neck, but when she opened them again she saw a man in army fatigues hugging an elaborate gun a few steps ahead of her. His baseball cap had an official, ornate emblem. He didn't see her scurry back down the steps and change her path for the wider, populated one. Joggers passed her, mountain bikes sped toward her, forcing her onto the shoulder. The climb was long and steady, but not steep.

At the top, just behind the lookout, jeeps, police cars, and large utility trucks were parked with engines idling. More SWAT-uniformed men were unravelling barbed wire from a mammoth spool, erecting a fence around a new communications tower and generator. Helicopters circled directly above, obviously in touch with men on duty at the generator. The noise obliterated the coddling of the woods. She looked around, left, right – people everywhere. She walked past them all on her way to her spot overlooking the cemetery.

Around the bend in the path, she saw him, a camera strung

across his chest and tucked under his arm.

"See, it's meant to be." Michel's eyes danced as he spoke.

She felt the push/pull in her groin. He was entering dangerous territory – had he realized that? The tests, the pushing, pulling, the fear of abandonment, the self-fulfilling prophesy. *Not again* . . . She shook the hand that he held out so calmly and surely. Maybe it would be different. With the touch of his hand she could see herself on a wall, photographed, framed, smiling among cousins, aunts . . . She breathed deeply. They walked for a while silently, unable to make themselves heard over the chopping blades above them, but when the noise faded into the distance, Michel touched her shoulder to speak to her.

"It's just too hot. It should snow and all of this would go away."

She knew he was expecting her to understand, and she did, but she couldn't let on.

"What do you mean?"

"This would never happen in snow; it covers everything. We're all the same underneath it."

She felt her belly flip again. She tried to sound casual. "Well, thank God, snow's unlikely."

"Maybe so, but it is a great leveller. Better than death."

"Why?"

"Cause we get to watch it."

She looked at his feet – solid – and wished for a snowstorm. He started to talk about how he took his photographs facing directly into the sun, so that snowbanks sparkled like stars in a different sky. "The best would be in the Arctic . . . always wanted to photograph there."

They reached the cemetery, where Daphne stopped to stare up at the shapes in the clouds.

"Looking for something in particular?"

She didn't hear him at first, so he bent closer, his mouth almost to her ear.

"You said you were doing research."

She blushed. "Just thinking."

"About what?"

"It's silly, really . . . manta rays . . ."

"What about them?"

"They manage to fly through water . . ."

He put his arm around her, bent her head back, and kissed her – a deep, hard kiss. She didn't resist, but the longing rose so high that she pushed him away.

"Sorry, I can't." She looked away, "I gotta go . . . sorry."

She walked away unsteadily, then ran. Down the path. Past the cyclists. Dodging joggers. She didn't stop. The manta ray wrapped its wings around her and flew her home.

A wood pole was pressed against her knee. Daphne twisted on the vinyl seat to free her leg from under the woman's placard. It was turned away from her, so she couldn't read what it said. Other people carried signs, some with symbols, others with protest slogans. They filled the bus, but Daphne was lucky to have got on long before, securing a window seat near the back. The black journal lay on her thigh, which was stiff from the run down the mountain. At home, she'd thrown herself onto her bed in confusion, thinking about Michel, even reaching down between her legs. But her fingers had failed her as her mind kept skipping back to the asylum and Guyana, so she'd stopped. She'd flicked on the television, but in the instant of knowing what she'd see there, flicked it off again. Surefoot's whereabouts had finally occurred to her

Night was falling as the bus wound past the downtown core in the heavy traffic bound toward the South Shore. Daphne opened the journal to the few remaining pages left to read. Her jaw grew sore from tension as she completed the last group of entries. At her destination she looked up, distracted, and was drawn into the sure and steady flow of bodies and placards inching out of the idling bus onto the shopping mall parking lot. They pushed her aside as they headed to the barricade. Daphne followed, the words of Gerald Eyre accompanying her, narrating, punctuating, underlining events throughout the evening.

Some residents of the South Shore had decided to strike back with a blockade of their own and had blocked a bridge just west of Châteauguay. Their cars were parked in rows all along the bridge, and a hundred-odd windshields passively reflected the lights from the street lamps. There were half that number of police officers in riot gear, but they marched toward the chain of demonstrators trying to push them back from the approach to the bridge. A few of the men held up baseball bats to counter the nightsticks and shields of the police. Children were among the crowd, some holding stones as though ready to skip them across a flat lake. One man ran past the approaching line and jumped on top of a police car, cracking the windshield and tearing off the light bar, which he threw into the cheering crowd. Another threw his tire iron into the air randomly, and it landed on the shoulder of a man just a few metres away. The police continued to advance and managed to arrest some of the crowd and chase others down the streets, where more police vehicles were parked, where more were smashed. In front of Quincaillerie Boucher a group of men wrenched open a fire hydrant, letting the water shoot across the road. Shop windows were shattered by teenagers who accompanied the rioters. A family affair. Someone started a fire in the street, and a group of men fed it with furniture and paper from a ransacked office. The officers raised their arms, preparing to launch the tear gas.

*March 4, 1960*
*Chicken is not enough . . .*

*not enough to satisfy a deep red hunger that tears at the back*
*of my ribs*
*not a flesh that's human*
*enough*
*when need makes everything human*

*when want makes my own flesh prey*

*still, they feed me chicken.*

At the Mercier Bridge, a large crowd of spectators had gathered at the intersection point of the police and the Mohawk blockade. For the most part they were peaceful, watching as negotiations took place between the police and the Native representatives. Surefoot walked purposefully back and forth between the men at the barricade and the police at the approach to the bridge. Both sides had heard of the riots and the blockade of the second bridge. They were afraid of what would happen if the rioters showed up at their front line. Already, fires had been set and bricks had been thrown at some of the policemen. Earlier in the day, a pickup truck carrying vegetables to the store near the barricade had been overturned, and a few men had thrown onions, potatoes – anything hard they could lay their hands on – at the police. That evening, small home-made explosives were heard in the area. Those who had come to watch were getting nervous.

Surefoot carried a large aluminum pot, filled to the brim with water, toward the fire. The pot's weight forced her to rest after a few minutes and stretch out cramped fingers. She looked into the pot and  brushed her eyebrow as though she'd caught a glimpse of something that needed adjustment. She picked up the pot and walked to the fire, placing it on top of the grill to boil. Daphne arrived in time to see Surefoot move off again toward the barricade. She moved toward her, but was halted by an SQ officer.

*What you have made me do . . .*

"Daphne!"

Joanne's shout came from the right, deep within the crowd. Daphne looked around anxiously and spotted Joanne waving her over toward her and her friends as they moved toward the front. Daphne followed, pushing her way through the dense cluster of bodies. Keeping her head down, she concentrated on the feet of those she tried to pass, placing hers in front of theirs, feeling lost amid the arms and chests she pushed aside.

*March 6, 1960*
*What you have made me do is piss the shape of a fish*
*in the sand,*
*like a signpost of Christ:*
*a sacred message of forbearance*
*You believe it is a symbol of capitulation; that this thin spineless*
*fish twitches its way toward, but just short of,*
*the shore*
*But what I have mastered is the gluttony of Jehovah,*
*the hunger of generations in my loins, and when I reach you I'll*
*crush your skull in my jaws and carry you to ossify*
*in the Leviathan's tomb.*

When she reached Joanne's side Daphne realized they had pushed their way right to the front of the crowd, into the outstretched arms of the police holding back the bulging mass of protesters and observers. Joanne looked confident, her sense of right embossed on her cool face.

"Watch those fuckers, Daphne."

Daphne peered underneath the arm of the policeman across to the barricade. Frenetic. Urgent movements. Something ticking.

Her lips slid into a smile. She saw the corpulence of Surefoot, who had just run back from the police line and was shouting something to the Mohawks. Surefoot's round, jiggling face was tempered and sober, yet something undermined her authority. Something cracked the certainty. Her body, rooted and abundant, seemed at the same time ready to cleave. Something subterranean, existing in the infinite memory of granite, in the cleft between vegetable and rock, seeped from her. Her T-shirt, stained with sweat, clung to her fleshy back. Her whole elbow, Daphne noticed, was a scab.

After she had delivered her message, Surefoot stood off to

the side of the resulting activity, taking a moment to compose herself. Her back was to Daphne, and she stared toward the river in the distance. A few minutes passed. Far away in her thoughts, Surefoot raised her hand to the scab on the elbow. The injury was many days old and the crust that had formed over the wound was dry and dark brown. She began to pick away at the scab. A few small pieces flew off into the air. Then she raised and bent the wounded arm so the elbow was at eye-level and, calmly, purposefully, tore off the dried blood and skin until the scab was almost gone; underneath the revealed pink flesh, blood welled up to pour again. Each fragment of old skin was tossed onto the pavement of the bridge. Daphne was repulsed. *Father a needy one stands before you . . . By the shores of Gitchee Gumee.* Then she recognized the unnamed something she had sensed, the thing they shared that kept them adrift from others, seeming laden and ridiculous. They were creatures that made sense only in the imagination, that had to be invented like the improbable animals formed by clouds in a childhood game. Animals that floated against all odds. That belonged nowhere else. Like an awkward llama in the clouds.

Daphne watched Surefoot walk to the line of women at the barricade, where she took the hand of one woman in both of hers for a few seconds, then broke away. She walked toward the police messenger who stood near Daphne and in doing so noticed her. With a sudden pivot, Surefoot turned back to the fire. Daphne's heart sank; she had been snubbed.

Surefoot dipped a cup into the steaming pot of water over the fire and drew out enough for a warm drink. She added a teabag then walked to the officer and said something to him, pointing to Daphne. The man shook his head, refusing to bring Daphne the tea. Surefoot raised her palm and shoulders in a why-not stance, but the officer simply walked away. Looking over at Daphne, Surefoot acknowledged her with a nod. Before turning away, she called out to the officer: "You know, if you take all the laws, lay them out under the sun, and let the snow and rain work on them for awhile, there'll be nothing left of them but the earth they've become."

In the distance there was the continuous sound of a single drum.

*March 10, 1960*
*I am on the edge of a red orange world – the screams ting tanging*
*in the far left corner of my head like a distant steel band threatening*
*joue vey.*
*But the screams are from men I have known in the school of*
*obedience – these white walls drip with saliva from the spray of*
*silent hollers.*
*When they release me, the spring from the precipice will be a plunge*
*into the bright crimson fire of silence in the world beyond the*
*dripping walls, in the time beyond the drums*
*where each night I am dancing out of my skin.*

Just behind the first wave of spectators others arrived. They came in a torrent of shouts and whistles, pushing the spectators aside. The mob held high the now familiar placards, and above them they raised stuffed mannequins – the flopping bodies and wild feathers of puppet Indians. Dozens of men and a handful of women formed a pack that pushed through the crowd to the sound of mock war cries. The spectators parted to let them through, afraid to stand in their way.

Daphne felt an elbow nudge her ribs. Joanne pointed and led Daphne's gaze over to Daniel among the mob. He moved determinedly through the crowd carrying a huge Indian effigy. The spring in Daniel's step made the puppet dance. The lengths of black wool bounced up from the puppet's shoulders, leather tassels flapped around its body, and the eagle feathers bobbed on its head like the crest of a peacock. Daphne watched Daniel take his place in the centre of the circle of his neighbours, stop to prop up the effigy on his shoulder, then look about at the crowd. With ceremony, he struck a match and held it high in the air. The group around him urged him on, their voices coming in a low gurgle from the back of their throats. He lit a fringe on the shirt. Slowly the flame caught, but then sputtered to a smoky halt. He lit another match, this time not bothering with the ceremony, and applied it directly to the shirt fabric. He raised the effigy. The fire walked up its sleeve, then ran. The gurgling of the crowd got progressively louder, higher, until one of them cheered, "This fucker dies!" and they all yelled, filling the hot night with savage whooping that carried over the river. Daphne backed up slowly, forcing her body between the people pushing forward. A woman beside her screamed a spirit-revival, evangelical howl. She swayed and tumbled into the arms of her husband who tried to pull her out of the crowd. The drum beat faltered slightly, off beat for a split second, but soon picked up. Communal fever. Screams circled each other, making the whole crowd dizzy; demonstrators and spectators alike started to sway as they all moved closer to the Mohawk line, forcing the police line back. The mass of people swelled, enveloping the night.

*March 15, 1960*
*An ancient verse by a Romantic poet entered me like a mirror and*
*green orchards and diving swans appear on the savannah. Each of*
*my sobs is "self-folding, like a flower" and I am a blinded lover in*
*a gated city, with only England as my home.*
*White-coated healers perform an orange surgery to rescue the looking*
*glass from my throat, extracting the symmetry of conquerors and*
*hoping that my soul retreats to the blackness of the bush.*
*But on lifting the blood-stained glass to their faces they will see me*
*looking back at them and wonder which of us imagined the other.*

Daphne pushed away someone who had begun to cough and choke at her neck, and suddenly her own throat was constricted and her eyes itched and watered. She gasped for air and knocked over a teenager who had doubled over. More coughing and choking all around her. Struggling to breathe, she broke from the crowd.

She was running again, in the direction of the highway, toward even more groups of people coming on foot and in cars. A cramp in her side slowed her down, and the noise confused her. She headed toward one sound, stopped, headed toward another, not knowing which one to trust, which direction to run. Pivoting away from a family coming toward her, she was certain she heard a little girl singing, repeating a line of a song.

*Summer is a comin' in. Summer is a comin' in. Summer is a comin' in.*

By the time she arrived at the shopping mall, the stitch in her side was so bad she had to hang her chest over the bus shelter bench to ease the pain. She rested there, panting and sweating, her temples throbbing wildly with the rushing blood.

*March 23, 1960*
*They say they will "send for me" as though I am a package they will order from a catalogue. These three female ghosts, from a time before I died, have come to say goodbye and are weeping like sad trees; I do not speak and even more they weep.*
*As if going to the cold might contract time and in doing so obliterate huge chunks of it. As if the touch of snow on a cheek might awaken the last trace of familiarity like a drowsy kiss. As if sending for me is a gift.*
*So to reciprocate, to silence them and drive them away, I mutter: "Fine, send for me then."*


*March 29, 1960*
*I live in the eye of the lizard that crawls across my white stucco wall.*


*I live in its tail*
*in its tongue*
*and in the tiny spot in its brain where it knows it is no ordinary gecko.*

*Becoming transparent like wind across the earth, it sneaks towards*
*its chameleon home; just as I,*
*when I leave here,*
*will become the world.*

She walked the interminable stretch of highway and bridges
back to the centre of the city, back to her apartment. The night
no longer existed. She was propelled along the sidewalks and
across streets, hypnotized.

*April 1, 1960*

    *Early morning, before the sun was up: a penetrating scream from*
*down the hall. The scream turned into a succession of hollers from*
*the back of a man's throat. All of us were woken by it and several*
*ran into the hall to see what had happened. Sounded like the cry of*
*someone murdered, but it continued. Nurses came, told us to go back*
*to our rooms. Later, S told me what had happened: A man in the*
*section woke because he felt something strange beside him. Lumpy*
*and warm. He reached down to examine it. Felt a hairy, warm,*
*fleshy object and then pulled off the sheet to see a man's leg lying in*
*his bed. Started to holler, claiming that someone had placed in his bed*
*body parts from the corpses that never left the hospital. Nurses could*
*not convince him that the leg was his own.*

*April 2, 1960*

    *S was up most of the night waiting for F to come back, but F*
*didn't arrive until early this morning and has been asleep all day. I*
*peeked into his room and watched his heavy breathing, but couldn't*
*see his face. He looks like a collection of child's bones heaped under*
*bedclothes. S and I sit here, waiting for him to wake.*

    *Doctors bother me less these days. Morons. They like to see you*
*foaming at the lips and crying out like a mad dog and then they*
*feel they're doing their job. They decide what's wrong with you, set*
*out to correct it, and you become what they see in order to avoid the*

convulsions that rattle your soul like God's marbles. But my plan is working – I'm fooling them. They want me to be a coloured man and that's what I tell them I am. Only the mirror does not lie. They want me to be grateful and I drip with thanks. They want me to kiss their asses and I willingly bend and lick.

*April 4, 1960*

S takes F for walks around the building since F is too weak to go by himself. They spend more time together now than F and I do. I can't afford to be seen with them; doctors will think nothing's changed. F doesn't seem to mind my lack of attention; that part of his soul is gone. Sometimes he is animated, flushed and aflame with excitement. He doesn't hack as he used to, but he has no strength.

*April 6, 1960*

Food is getting worse; I am always hungry but no one is giving me the right food. They are trying to make sure I don't leave – that I look as thin as a sick man so that I won't be allowed to leave. I must eat . . . I will show them.

*April 10, 1960*

S reads two books a day. I've never seen anyone read a book the way he does. He sits and reads until he finishes it; takes a break for a chat, a walk with F, and a meal, and then reads another one. He gets his pretensions from them. His world is an epic poem.

*April 11, 1960*

Got up, ate, slept, ate, and am on my way to sleep again.

*April 12, 1960*

Feel him slipping away and taking me with him. Have to fight it – have to hold on.

*April 14, 1960*

F came to look at me. Stood, just staring as if across water, but into my eyes. Taking me with him, but I'm not ready to go.

*April 15, 1960*

He has stopped speaking. I will ignore him or they will never release me.

*April 20, 1960*

F is dead. Came to me in the night, his clothes hanging from him like the wings of a manta ray, looking already like a ghost. Didn't say anything just floated in and floated out again. This morning his door was shut and nurses whispered their evil-breath whispers. Making plans to bury him, but they want to contact family in England. They do not consult me or S. He precedes me to a kinder place; I am trapped by the barbarians of sanity. His soul left an angry corpse behind. The look on its face was a smirk of betrayal.

*April 21, 1960*

Today the silence is loneliness.

*April 22, 1960*

I am traipsing around like a healed coloured man – friendly and obedient, stoic and proud. That's what they want to see – my white soul masked in their portrait of me. F is watching from heaven, rolling on his ass, laughing.

*April 24, 1960*

Eating is torture, but I stuff myself with everything they offer, as a gesture of health.

*April 26, 1960*
*Talk of my going home.*


*April 27, 1960*
*Doctors prowling to catch a glimpse of what I'm writing. No use.*


*April 29, 1960*
*Leaving here tomorrow.*

# Last Quarter

It was running late. Nothing to look at but pastures and the same cows as the train crawled between small Ontario towns. It felt as if the cars would pile on top of each other as the train accelerated and almost immediately geared down to a halt. The passengers' impatience, revealed in sighs and the sucking of teeth, followed the ebb and flow of the locomotive. Restless children ran up and down the aisles. Their shrill voices jabbed at the nerves between the shoulders. Slumped in her window seat, Daphne stared out at the cows – *one cow, two cow, red cow* – clubs of cows lying orderly, facing the same way, expecting something. The train inched passed the next cow.

Daphne shifted in her seat and felt something squish in her shorts. She straightened up and reached into the pocket. It was oozy and warm – the small okra she'd taken from the Caribbean épicerie. The one she'd imagined learning how to prepare with the expertise of her ancestors. Her fingers gently gripped what they could, and with her other hand she reached for the paper garbage bag at her feet. She shoved in the pale pulp, then checked her knapsack and touched the diaries to ensure they were there.

Finally, west of Kingston, the engine geared up to a consistent speed. The rest of the landscape passed quickly. As the train pulled into Toronto, Daphne was struck by the rich sheen of the city's buildings. She'd forgotten its scale, which diminished cars, people, her own feelings. Towers gleamed, looking freshly scrubbed. Someone had turned up the brightness knob on the urban image. After the cocoon of Montreal's Plateau, Toronto sprawled before her. She hadn't been back since she'd moved, having even avoided returning for Christmas.

Daphne made her way through the underground passage from Union Station to the subway. On the northbound car, she took a seat close to the door. She looked around, feeling like a tourist. *That exit . . . shopping tomorrow . . . my uncle said . . .* She realized that she understood everything being said around her. Words came at her like arrows: *They're moving to Burlington, bought a new house . . . I can't save money . . . Cannon printer, it's faster . . . I don't like kissing him anymore . . .* She dodged them. In Montreal it was easy to live in her head, to block out chatter, because there was so much of it she couldn't understand. But here she heard intimacies and banalities that made the slow, rambling, metallic movements of the subway bulky and be-laboured. She hummed to herself to drown out the sounds. At High Park station she left the subway, relieved to be free of the noise, and walked the familiar path to her parents' home. Home – the word made her knees weak. It had been a lie. Who had whispered it to her for so long? She was embarrassed when Jennifer Baird opened the door and found her staring out into the street contemplating a quick escape.

She brushed her mother's cheek with a light kiss. "Hi," she said quietly.

"Dear me! Daphne, why didn't you tell us you were coming? Look at you! Come in."

Jennifer Baird was a tall and slender woman of fifty-seven. Her curly hair was cut short at the back, but hung over her forehead like a mop, with grey gradually usurping strawberry-blonde. Her skin was very fair, almost pearlescent, her angular features accentuated by a long straight nose, a combination that gave her an ethereal appearance. Daphne had always thought of her mother as beautiful and felt cheated by the odd combi-nation of her own face. Bill's features were less sharp, but not as sloppy as Daphne's, although his lips were full. He too was very handsome. Shorter than his wife, he was stout and stalwart, with beautiful legs – sturdy and sculpted like the base of a piano stool – made for a kilt. His skin was almost pink, translucent along the neck. He was the same age as his wife, and they had known each other since the age of sixteen. Neither had ever made love to anyone else. Daphne could never imagine one without the other, but she had come to notice their distinctly separate existence. Her mother had a few friends from the bank where she had worked for more than fifteen years, but she kept to herself most of the time. She wasn't unfriendly, only encased, with a crab's withdrawal from the world, not unlike Daphne. Her father was more gregarious and played golf with his friends every day he could during the summer. Jennifer and Bill seemed like visitors at a guesthouse, meeting for meals, always cordial and pleasant. Daphne had never heard them argue, but neither had she ever witnessed any displays of passion.

Daphne scrutinized Jennifer's form as it fussed with the overnight bag. She called to her husband while carting it up the stairs. "Bill! Daphne's home! Bill, come! She's here. Do you believe it? All the way here without telling us. Goodness, Daphne, you could have called."

Home. For just a moment it rang true inside Jennifer's double-edged comment – a warm welcome accompanied by subtle scolding.

Bill came down the stairs, took Daphne's hand, her waist, then spun and hugged her, starting to tease: "You need to eat, little girl. *Manges, manges . . .* that's about it for my French."

He pulled her to the kitchen, and when Jennifer came back down the three of them sat together for a late lunch. Daphne was swept up into the reticent intimacy that defined their family. The courtesy and joviality kept them safely distant from one another.

"So, how's your French?"

"Not great, but getting better. What I learned in high school seems useless now. It's not what I remember."

"Nothing is . . . no, nothing." Bill shook his head gravely, but still managed a curious smile, somehow always sidestepping solemnity.

*Bill Baird, Bill Baird, Oh you make me soooo scared.* Daphne never fully understood him but always melted into his affection. In contrast, she felt challenged by her mother, by the rightness in her walk, by the comfort in her clothes, by the creamy smell of her skin that Daphne always wanted to touch.

She looked up from her plate to sneak a look at Jennifer, who was calmly and delicately trimming the crusts from the toasted sandwich Bill had made and served her. Shifting to Bill, Daphne watched him noisily chewing, intent on his meal. She remembered his quirky eating habits, his refusal to eat and drink at the same time: he ate everything on his plate without taking even a single sip from the glass of juice until he was finished. She studied his face looking for a sign of herself in him. Nothing. What had she expected? She looked back to her own plate and felt her cheeks begin to burn.

"How's your game, dad?"

"Not bad . . . not good either. Haven't been out much."

"That's a good one! Don't listen to him, dear, he's on the course more than he's in the house. The air conditioning was broken for a week and he used that as an excuse to be gone for most of those days." Jennifer gently teased her husband, raising her eyebrows at him even as she spoke to Daphne. Bill tried to suppress a grin and then downed his glass of juice.

After lunch, as the three of them were cleaning up, Daphne could no longer hold back. "I met my mother's sister."

Jennifer, her arm outstretched as she wiped the top of the table, froze. She looked up first at Daphne, then at Bill, her eyes wide in fear. One part of Daphne wanted to protect them, but the other was pushing her, tempting her to taunt this beautiful woman, this woman with the fair smell she'd clung to desperately so many times in fear and pain, this woman who'd held her tightly and soothed her. She tried to suppress the horrifying compulsion to throw those moments of despair back at the blue eyes that had loved so honestly. A perverse desire to punish someone for the trust that had been yanked from her at birth.

"You must've expected it some day," she said instead.

"Feared it more than anything," Jennifer said in a weak voice as she pulled a chair out and sat at the table.

Bill put down a plate in the middle of drying it. Daphne was overcome with guilt for her impulse to torture. She sat down beside her mother and put her hand on hers.

"She's very nice."

Jennifer remained silent, her mouth beginning to tremble. Bill put the last of the dried plates into the cupboard above the counter. The flush in Daphne's cheek moved to her eyes.

"My mother committed suicide . . . after she had me."

Bill put the towels away. He took Jennifer by the shoulder, kissed her on the head, then sat down beside her, looking to Daphne. They all sat breathing the pregnant air.

"And your father?" Bill asked in a very low voice.

Daphne hesitated, the whispering voices in her brain suggesting several answers, none of which she was able to utter. "Not mentioned on the birth certificate." Suddenly she had nothing else to say to them. As soon as the details had been revealed they became strangers. The desire to hurt returned. "You could've told me a long time ago."

"We didn't know," Jennifer said, her blue eyes filling with tears.

"We wanted to support you in whatever you chose to do, and since you never mentioned it . . ." Bill stood up. Daphne watched his face toughen.

"But you could have encouraged me to find out."

Jennifer's tears flowed quickly. "Everybody warned us about this . . . I'm sorry, dear. We wanted to keep us all together. Will you see her again?"

"Whatever for?"

"I just thought —"

Daphne threw Jennifer a spiteful look that cut her off.

"Are you all right, dear?" Bill stuttered out gently, trying to maintain harmony.

Daphne didn't answer. She was remembering how Jennifer had tried to brush her daughter's wild, frizzy hair to match her own, but then had given up and permed her own to match Daphne's; how she had tried to make Daphne as beautiful as she had been when she was a teenager, all pink cheeks, red lips, and plucked brows. Daphne felt ashamed for all of them. They sat looking into and out of each other's eyes for a few minutes. The guilt returned. Why had she started all this? What was she doing to them? She saw the chasm in Jennifer's blue eyes and felt it in Bill's breathing. What had she done?

"I need a walk."

At the door, she turned around to look at them holding each other. She loved them.

By the time she reached the park the grass was rushing up to meet her pounding feet. There was high-pitched screaming, which she thought must be coming from toddlers. Weaving past groups of children in the playground on swings and jungle gyms, she tripped over an abandoned tricycle. As she flew up and over, she reached out to stop the oncoming pavement and scraped open her palms on landing. The skin was torn back like a pealed peach and blood dripped onto her wrist. She got up but didn't go to the fountain to clean herself off, just shoved her hands into her pockets, letting the blood soak into the fabric of her khaki shorts where it formed blotch figures and faces hiding in her pockets. People around her asking if she was all right, if she needed help, went unnoticed. The sun was on fire, and the leafy arms of the trees loomed menacingly. She walked steadily on, her eyes fixed on the pond.

It was there when she arrived: the swan with the neck bent in a *Z* shape as if it had swallowed a hanger. It was the one Bill had taken her to see a few years before when he'd forgotten her birthday, saying that the swan had swallowed her present. They had laughed and laughed, and bent over and laughed even more, and she'd hugged him, *Bill Baird, you don't make me at all scared,* and loved him for the bad joke about his bad memory. The swan bent its crooked neck to sip. The *Z* became an *N*.

When she returned to the house, she gently eased the door open, entered, and closed it, making sure to wipe her feet on the mat, which she then dutifully straightened. Faint sobs were coming from the kitchen, but she was incapable of listening to them. Once upstairs in her old room, she locked the door and turned on the radio very softly. She stayed in her room all evening going through the things that had been preserved there: primary school photos, Barbie dolls, adolescent drawings. They smelled of forgery – some other child's things planted in her room as decoys. Sitting on the floor, her hands stinging and tender from her fall, she could see out the window, but the only view was the brick wall of the neighbour's house. She sat and watched as the sinking sun turned the red brick to plum.

Bill and Jennifer ate their late dinner in the small sunroom off the kitchen that looked out over their tiny backyard. They were quiet, mostly silent. One strand of a delicate and intricate web woven over thirty years had torn and now all the fibres hung loose. Bill was gentle, passing potatoes and peas as though they had liquified and were about to spill from the dishes. Jennifer had retreated completely behind lobes of memory. The sound of the cutlery scraping the china underscored their silence. It was Jennifer who finally spoke.

"We should go up, see if she's okay. She needs –"

"Leave her alone for now," Bill interjected. "She has a lot to think about. We'll take her out tomorrow."

"I'll just check on her; I'll be right back."

Jennifer made her way up the stairs with enough noise to warn of her approach, so Daphne threw herself on her bed, her face away from the door, and faked the heavy breath of sleep, exaggerating the up and down of her shoulders when Jennifer pushed the door open gently. When the door shut again, she turned over and listened to Jennifer's descending steps.

She got up and moved to her childhood desk, where she picked up a self-portrait, aged 12, of her sitting on a bright orange horse, a horse she'd never ridden but which she'd drawn as if from perfect recollection. She tore the drawing down the middle. There was nothing stopping her now. Climbing into her single bed, she covered herself with the sheet. She tried the pillow . . . ride, ride, ride. Nothing. She dragged it back to her head and flung it under her neck. An hour of tossing passed. The telltale swish of water and brushes signalled that her parents were getting ready for bed. All too familiar. When she finally dozed off, she dreamt that Bill and Jennifer were standing at her door peering into the room, staring at her. She tried to talk to them, to tell them something, but in doing so kicked off the sheet and woke herself up. She lay quietly, staring at the ceiling, knowing there was little point in trying to sleep again. She got out of bed and dressed, packing her small overnight bag and making sure, once again, that the diaries were there.

Down the stairs and out of the house without waking Jennifer or Bill, Daphne soon found herself on Bloor Street in the starless night. Layers of clouds eclipsed the shrinking moon and the breeze coming up from the lake was strong. Few cars passed. The whistle of wind through alleyways, the skittering of litter along the sidewalk, and the flapping of store awnings along the now slightly unfamiliar street made her journey unsettling. She walked for nearly a half an hour before she saw a bus approaching. She ran to the nearest stop, waving her arm to flag it down and rode to Yonge Street. From there she walked the long, sometimes neon-lit strip to Union Station and arrived just as the yolky light appeared on the horizon.

# Last Crescent

The train staggered groggily out of the city. Daphne was facing the wrong way, toward the back of the train, so she watched Toronto gradually disappear from sight. As the train picked up speed, she hid behind the protective blackness of her sunglasses, impervious to the chatter of the crowded passenger car. She was glad that the woman beside her had quickly become absorbed in her magazine. The woman was dressed in a dark suit, its wool out of season, its colour suitable for a funeral. Her perfume infected the air and her heavy bracelets clanged every time she turned the pages of her *Maclean's,* which featured a photo of the barricade at Oka on its front cover. Daphne looked out the window. A few minutes later, when the woman sat up straight and tense to read an article near the end of the magazine, out of the limelight of events, Daphne turned toward her and strained her neck to read along. The photo was of Mubarak and Hussein and the caption read: *Attempting to defuse tensions in the Persian Gulf.*

*The 13 member nations of the world's most powerful oil cartel, the Organization of Petroleum Exporting Countries (OPEC), traditionally dispute production quotas and oil prices. But, for 30 years, they have settled their differences in the conference room. Even when Iran and Iraq were at war in the Persian Gulf, their oil ministers conducted business as usual. But Iraqi President Saddam Hussein changed the rules last week, dispatching 30,000 troops to his country's badly defined border with Kuwait. Although few observers expected him to invade his much weaker neighbour, many oil industry analysts described the action as extortion. And it* *achieved Hussein's objective. Kuwait and other Gulf states agreed to curb oil production to raise prices—as Iraq had been demanding. The new target price: $21 (U.S.) a barrel (about $24 Can.), up $3 from the $18-a-barrel benchmark that OPEC set in 1986. . . .*

The woman turned the page and nestled back in her seat.

"A-barrel benchmark," Daphne muttered to herself. The woman looked up, surprised. Daphne pretended not to notice as the woman angled the article from view and went on reading.

The clanging of the jewellery grated on Daphne's nerves. She was irritated by having to travel backwards. Everything was laden, heavy, and comically symbolic. She felt like the brunt of a joke.

Arriving in Montreal she took the bus straight to NDG, walked boldly up the street, and banged at Sheila's door. *Auntie Sheila.* She tried to say it out loud but couldn't. She didn't wait to be invited in, just barged past Sheila and flopped onto the plastic-covered couch.

"What kind of place was that?" She looked into Sheila's face, watching her lips part slightly in surprise.

"What do you mean, chile?"

"The place he was in."

"You finished the books —"

"Of course, you intended me to, didn't you?"

"Yes, well —"

"Why?"

"Well, for you to know . . . part of you . . ." Sheila stood still in the middle of the room where Daphne's first question had stopped her. Her hand moved up to her neck and nervously gathered together the bands of her collar. "You have to understand that Guyana was not modern, its hospitals not like here, they didn't know any better, dear."

A muscle started to twitch in Daphne's shoulders, striking flint to her anger. "And was she like him? My mother?"

Where did that word belong? Surely not to this odd woman's sister; surely it was only the name for a voice Daphne had invented. Sheila came toward Daphne and reached for her hand, but Daphne pulled back.

"Your mom was a happy girl, always smiling, and very good, helpin' Mummy all the time. Everyone liked her . . . she was so popular. Not like me . . . "

Intrusion. Daphne didn't want Sheila to infiltrate the discussion. "How did he, your father, die?"

Sheila looked around as if expecting to see someone who would help her with this, this whirlwind that had blown into her home.

"Would you like some tea?"

"No tea. What happened to him?"

Sheila sat on the couch and adjusted her blouse again. She began to speak, her voice controlled and calculated as though she had rehearsed for this very moment. "He had lots of pressure at work, too much pressure, of course, we all knew it and we saw it comin', but we really couldn't do anything about it. He was bein' very stubborn and wouldn't rest, poor soul, wouldn't relax when we told him he was workin' himself too hard. He felt betrayed by his best friend at work and it was the stress on his nerves. In those days there was a lot of stress, but we didn't know to call it that. He had a breakdown. Mummy had to take him to hospital, and they said it would be just for awhile, so we left him there because he needed the rest."

She paused, looking around her again as though she had never expected to have to do this by herself. Daphne could see that she longed for company, for help, for something from that jungle place to make it all easier.

"I know that much, you gave me the books. But how did he die?"

"He was a poet, you know . . . those books. He wrote a lot of poetry – words that made things betta, and sometimes worse."

Daphne continued to glare at her aunt, not allowing her to deflect the question. She had only a few left to ask, and Sheila's answers would vindicate her disgust. Everything else was formed in her mind like a private fossil. Sheila's face was sympathetic, yet wary. The silence forced her to continue.

"He'd gotten himself too fired up, you know how people can be sometimes. He needed rest. He got better there too. It was when he was in hospital that Mummy thought it would be a good idea if we all came to Canada. With Muriel's condition . . . well, Mummy's brother was here, and he said he would sponsor us. So she thought it would be betta for us here, because your mom was just sixteen and I was doing A Levels. We'd have a better chance here, for education, so it was a wonderful opportunity . . . and we told Daddy we'd send passage for him after he was well."

"But he never came."

"He was supposed to join us, but when he got out of the hospital no one could find him. He just disappeared. Mummy tried to find him, called everybody she knew back home, but no one could tell her where he was. She didn't want to go back to look for him, because it would affect her immigration status, you see . . . then with us losing your mom and all . . . Then about a year later we got a letter and package from one a his friends, a man he knew in hospital . . . a Sam Petrie . . . He told us that Daddy had been livin' in the interior, in the bush, and he had cut up his foot on some rocks in a river. The cuts got infected and his foot was gangrene."

"So he died of gangrene poisoning?"

Sheila paused, moving into a reverie, sorting things out for herself as she said them. "You know, I never knew what was gangrene. I always thought it was a colour. And then after I heard about Daddy, it was even more of a colour, a light green and black, like mouldy cheese. But this was travellin' up a leg. It wasn't gangrene he died of, really, you see . . . well . . . mostly that, yes, but he had tried to . . . he cut it off himself, the gangrene, that is, . . . he cut off his foot and it never healed. That's how he died."

Daphne searched for words to reply to the sound of gangrene, the image of gangrene, the smell of gangrene. She found nothing but the word itself.

"He died without sayin' anythin'. He didn't tell anyone about the pain. And when Mummy heard about it, she was silent too, never spoke another word and didn't come out of her room much after that. I'm surprised the poor woman lived as long as she did, even though she wasn't very old when her heart stopped. It just stopped."

She said the last sentence as if it were a relief; she'd fulfilled a duty, all there was to say.

"The day of his breakdown . . . he wrote about it. He saw it happening. It was October, wasn't it?"

Sheila nodded, resigning herself to the next inevitable set of questions.

"He talks about forcing someone . . . about sex. Was it you?" Daphne braced herself, sitting up straight.

Sheila looked into her lap, then shook her head. "No, chile, not me."

Daphne held on. She began to count in her head, months, days, her mind always arriving at a date she didn't want to acknowledge. Sheila interrupted the silent count.

"It was about a week . . . just a week . . . his nerves were so bad. He was shaken . . . so small and helpless, and he went to her and he cried so much she thought he would simply stop breathing. Every night for a week before they came to take him to hospital, he went to her, cryin' . . . it was sudden, but he didn't force. He cried and cried and his tears dropped on her face and she cried his tears and she hated him . . . was disgusted . . . but she let him do it. She told only me." Sheila moved closer to Daphne on the couch. She touched her face, as she had the first time, trying to comfort her. Trembling, Daphne let her without meaning to. "You resemble him, dear."

Daphne bolted off the couch to escape Sheila's thin hand. Back and forth across the pale carpet she paced to keep in line with her thoughts, back and forth, back and forth. Sheila went on, answering questions she hadn't yet thought to ask.

"I wanted to keep you myself, but Mummy . . . she couldn't face it, and Muriel had already made up her mind . . ."

But all of that was beside the point, the point being that someone had made a mistake. McIntyre. He had confused the files. That pile on his desk from which he had never looked up except to tell her to leave. He hadn't searched the right file. It was simple. She looked at Sheila, who had gotten up and walked to the mahogany cabinet in the dining room and was taking out the photo album again. No. No more arms. No more bush. Daphne went to her bag for ammunition and pulled out the diaries to counterstrike the photos.

"There's nothing of me here. They gave me the wrong file. I want the right file. These have nothing to do with me."

Sheila moved back, frightened by Daphne's blazing eyes. Daphne thought she could see a suspicion rise in Sheila's brow, a doubt that linked Daphne to Gerald in the creases of her aunt's forehead.

"But dear —"

"No, don't call me that again. I don't know you. This isn't fair. It's not fair of you to try to trick me —"

"Please calm down —"

"He's not my father!" Daphne bawled. With the diaries held at pistol height in her raised hand, she backed out of the room like an escaping thief, turned quickly at the front door, and sped out of the house.

The phone was ringing when Daphne entered her apartment. Throwing down her bag in the hallway, she headed to the bedroom. She unplugged her answering machine and let the phone ring until it stopped, but it started again a few minutes later and continued to ring until she unplugged it too. She crawled under the sheets and stayed there, even though the heat was suffocating and she could breathe only with difficulty.

When the alarm went off the next morning, she was curled up in the same position, stiff and caked in dried sweat. She felt cold. Dizziness washed over her as she got up and pulled the cord of the alarm clock out of the wall. In the bathroom she contemplated a shower, but felt such a deep fatigue that she was unable to lift herself over the porcelain rim of the tub. She walked to the kitchen. Standing in front of the open refrigerator she lifted the orange juice carton to her lips. The liquid was rancid, stuck to her tongue and nettled the roof of her mouth. She spit the juice at the wall and tossed the carton onto the counter. In the living room she lay down on the couch and dozed off again.

She woke well into the day and realized that her body had made the decision not to go to the store. The TV's remote control was at her feet but even that exertion strained her. *Click.* A talk show: a man with thick white hair was interviewing women whose husbands were homosexual and men whose wives were lesbians. The couples talked candidly about how they coped with their partnerships. Underneath their faces on the screen came the identifying subtitles: "Joey: wife loves another woman," while Joey talked meekly about care and respect. She changed the station. A children's show: singing bears; a cooking show: stir-frying in a wok; and a program about alligators in the Gulf of Mexico. She turned off the TV, floated back to the bedroom, and opened a book of mythology.

*Persephone sprang into her arms and was held fast there.*
*All day they talked of what had happened to them both,*
*and Demeter grieved when she heard of the pomegranate*
*seed, fearing that she could not keep her daughter with her.*

Nothing sustained her. She couldn't concentrate. The disinterest was immediate. Step, miss, step, miss, again and again. She had instant access to every moment in time: moments in someone's private life in Chicago; the cracking-eggshell moment of an alligator birth; Persephone's enforced season in the underworld. Amnesia: everything in the present, all accessible; no distance, no cause, no effect, no responsibility. Like the amnesia of her own birth that had landed her a stranger in someone else's family. None of it was hers. Step, miss. Invention was no longer possible. She retreated once again under the covers.

Hunger dragged her out of bed to the kitchen that evening. No food. Nothing. A bottle of red wine, nearly full, winked at her as she reached for it. Sucking urgently, she gulped down almost half of what was there. She shuddered and winced, suppressed a choke, and waited. Soon she felt the slow easing behind her eyeballs. She drank the rest in great swigs, and in a half an hour was feeling formless and indistinct.

"Still hunting me?"

She could barely see through the smoke in the bar, but Daphne followed the voice to a booth in the corner. Surefoot sat alone at a table with a pot of tea and a cup in front of her, *La Presse* spread out beside her. Daphne felt the stir from the ceiling fan on the hem of her loose T-shirt dress. She slipped onto the facing bench, ducking under the smoke that hung at shoulder height throughout the room. She held her breath, then let it out slowly, trying to get used to the air. Pulling the newspaper toward herself, Surefoot made room on the table for Daphne's elbows.

"What do you want from me? You don't even know who I am. You looked a little freaked on the bridge the other night. Still do. What's with you?"

"I'm sorry. I haven't been following . . ."

It had been impulse alone that had drawn her to the diner. After downing the wine she had gone searching for food; it wasn't until she'd entered the diner that she remembered that Surefoot had been fired. The cashier had directed her to this bar on St. Laurent, saying it was the likely place to find Surefoot during the day, and Daphne had come away without eating.

"Look, what's up?"

"Stuff about my parents."

Daphne proceeded to unfurl for Surefoot the inventory of her search, the direct questions and oblique answers of the last month. She stopped to order a shot of vodka, continued, stopped again to order another two, and then told of electric shock and manta rays in a voice that was weighed down by a numbed cerebral cortex. Surefoot sat back on the bench, patient, her face expressionless but for the corners of her eyes, which twitched in sympathy, encouraging Daphne to continue. Daphne ordered two more shots.

"Here's lookin' at you, as they say."

Surefoot stopped Daphne's hand as it raised the shotglass to her mouth. "Grow up. You don't know what you're doing with that stuff. It soaks in, stays. This stuff you just found out, like I said, it's about blood. Blood is thicker than water until it gets thinned by alcohol. Then the demons take over."

Daphne pushed Surefoot's hand aside and swallowed the clear, fiery liquid. Her voice was hot with booze. "Well something sure took him over, demons or whatever. He was taken, but he also took."

"That's not surprising. People take turns."

"Where did you hear that?"

"It's just something I know. Maybe this thing with your mother was all he could feel for himself."

"And my turn?"

"It's only a seed; you don't have to plant it. Animals make tracks. You choose the ones you want to follow."

"I look like him." Her head dropped involuntarily to the side.

Surefoot looked off into the distance and then said softly, in a sad, drawn voice, "They're sending the army in. It's coming to an end."

Daphne heard her through a haze, but she wasn't listening. "There's a boy I was wondering if you knew. Manny . . . He rolls his body in mud and it dries and cakes and then he paints on it with berries. He's someone I'm looking for. Seen him?"

"Like I said – watch that stuff." Surefoot spilled change for the tip onto the table and folded up the newspaper to leave.

Her head was cotton, her mouth a clogged drain when she woke the next afternoon. On her way back from the bar Daphne had stopped at her neighbourhood épicerie. She'd slid a carrying basket with five bottles of red wine along the floor toward the cashier and laid out the last of her cash. Two of the bottles were now empty. Walking to the kitchen was difficult. The cork popped easily out of the next bottle, and she drank again, not out of any real need or desire for obliteration, but because she remembered that this was what was done. She had seen, on television and in movies, that this was what people did when their world had fallen apart; it was the only model for action she had. She tipped the bottle back and gulped, watching herself drink in the mirror. Her face danced in the glass, skirting any real examination, as if it knew better, as if it knew that what she wanted to see wasn't there: the face she wanted to feel sorry for had not materialized, and all that was to be seen were the rounded cheeks she'd examined every morning of her life, not the face of a stranger.

She felt foolish and began to distil a sallow hatred for the mind of the man holding the obstinate pen – the hand that had written flagrant *S*s in the diary, perfect and menacing *T*s, the hand that had created a hieroglyphic to pierce her heart in the dotting of an *i*.

She dozed on and off, and to still her throbbing head she drank more – *what colour is the hair of the dog?* – but just on the edge of oblivion, about to do herself serious injury, she stopped. Incapable of functioning, she entered a sleep close to annihilation, a relief from thought, but with her memory mercifully intact. For memory, she sensed, was what made her life.

A stream of vomit had dried on her pillow and her clothes smelled of the shit that had escaped her bowels during the night. She made her way to the tub where she soaked herself in the hottest water she could bear and scrubbed her skin until it was raw and red. When she was finished, she felt a new wave of dizziness and nausea. She vomited gobs of saffron and yellow bile into the toilet.

Moving carefully through her bedroom, Daphne gathered up her sheets and threw them into a large green garbage bag, along with the empty bottles around the bed. Every movement stabbed into her brain. She took down prints from her wall, threw out souvenirs and postcards. Out went the Greek myths, book after book. *Eastern Birds* was tossed into the green plastic bag.

A pounding at the door sent the muscles of her neck into spasm. She walked gingerly down the hall trying to minimize the pain of movement. The rap of panicked knuckles on wood vibrated through the walls and her head. When she finally reached the door, she opened it to confront Joanne's flushed and relieved face and was at once embarrassed.

"Jesus Christ, what's going on?" Joanne let out, entering the apartment without waiting to be asked. "Daphne, I thought you were dead. We lost you at the bridge, and I've been phoning you for two days. God, it reeks in here. Are you alright?"

"Yes, I'm alright. I was just sick, that's all, I'm better . . . fine."

Joanne rested her pack on the couch, surveyed the room, then approached Daphne, carefully examining her face.

"Shit, you wouldn't know it to look at you. You wouldn't believe what I've imagined. I mean I'm glad you're all right and everything, but I imagined walking in here, well actually, having to break the door down, to find you gassed or floating in the tub."

"Oh, please . . ."

"I know, sorry, but you've been pretty strange the last couple of weeks."

"Just preoccupied."

Joanne looked sceptical. "You've done some number on yourself to get this sick."

"I suppose so."

Blackness washed over Daphne for a second. Joanne caught her arm to steady her. "Here, sit down. You really look like shit."

Joanne's solicitousness was disconcerting; Daphne checked to make sure it was really her, glancing quickly at her hands.

Joanne continued, "I've been neglecting my friends, caught up in all the Mohawk stuff." She paused and took an elastic from her pocket. In a graceful sweep she gathered up her hair and tied it back. "But that's coming to a head soon . . ."

Daphne's mind jumped to Daniel's face watching the fire climb up the sleeve of his puppet Indian. Then it skipped to Surefoot. *By the shining Big-Sea-Water, stood the lodge of Pau-Puk-Keewis.* The words were false. It had all been a ridiculous lie. Then, like a burst of rain, Daphne laughed loudly, an awkward, jarring laugh. Joanne looked mortified. To stop the cackle she threw out other news.

"Bourassa gave the Mohawks an ultimatum yesterday. If

they can't negotiate a settlement in the next few hours, he's sending the army in."

They both fell silent, and for a brief moment they shared the same bare confusion. Joanne looked at Daphne, who stared into her lap, her mind filled with the image of black-wool hair bouncing on the shoulders of a stuffed doll. The nausea came back. A sigh escaped from her lips, shifting the mood again.

"Here, put your head back. I'll get you some water."

When Joanne came back from the kitchen she guided the glass of water into Daphne's hand and encouraged her to drink.

"Do you think you'll be able to come with us to the cabin tomorrow?"

"Sure . . . sure," Daphne said, not knowing why she was still determined to go, other than it had been the one promise of the summer that had seemed to make the heat tolerable. She now felt she would enter nature like an alien, wearing skin that stretched out over unfamiliar blood.

"By the way," Joanne said as she was going out the door, "I'm quitting Copie Copie. I've given my notice. I might have a desktopping job with a small publisher. Not sure yet. Money's not as good, but it's important stuff, political."

She left. Daphne watched her head down the stairs then followed as far as the mailbox. She opened it and separated the promotion flyers from the letters. Dropping the flyers on the floor near the steps, she examined the envelopes in her hand. Three from Toronto. Two were in the light and careful handwriting of Bill, one was from Jennifer. All were special delivery. Urgent. She put them back into the mailbox, climbed back up the stairs to her apartment and picked up the diaries to examine them anew.

In the early entries the references to her mother were oblique but undeniable. But her disgust was gone, as if voided with the bile, leaving her only weary and hollow. Daphne sought a fissure in the armour of hatred that surrounded this man which would open into a place she knew in herself.

Re-reading the entries, she was holding on, struggling to keep Gerald's past in place for him, hoping that the next day

wasn't a denial of his identity, an obliteration of herself. She felt
every electric shock that penetrated his cortex, and she tried to
hold on through the known consequence of a jellied temple,
hold on through the thick tasting salve on the lips, the gauze in
the mouth, hold on while the bowels exploded, hold on during
the screams.

As the hours passed, her exhaustion deepened, and her lids
began to droop; the books nodded in her hands, falling a few
inches and jerking up again as she fought sleep. Finally, she gave
in and the slow, deep breathing took over. Her arms collapsed
and all that she possessed of her father fell softly on her chest,
resting there the night.

# New

# 1

Wide awake. Long before dawn. The sound of helicopters grew to an annoying intensity. Daphne slid out of bed and closed the balcony door, only slightly muffling the spinning sky. The darkness was eerie. She got dressed. Hugging the diaries to herself, she went out into the black morning. The air was soft, less humid, but loud with vibration. Heading nowhere in particular, she traced the familiar path toward Copie Copie, arriving at its doors as a thought struck her. She put her key in the lock, turned it, and entered.

Leaving the lights off, she walked to the back of the store to the colour copier. Power ON. The placid hum replaced the chopping of the helicopters. The lights on the panel glowed in the dark room. She took the diaries out of her bag and looked through them, searching for the right page. Finally she found the word, just a single word in Gerald's scrawl. She adjusted the size button to 150% and placed the journal on the glass. The handwriting shot out enlarged. She cut the word out, placed it back on the glass, blew it up again. Finally, CHAMELEON shot out of the machine, almost the size of the thing itself. She took the scissors and cut around it in the shape of a lizard. Then with some clear tape she fastened it to her triceps. Patting it and smoothing it down, she was content with her new tattoo.

Suddenly there was the sound of keys in the door. She quickly powered off and crouched beside the machine. Someone entered and turned on another copier. Peeking over the paper feeder she could see Daniel's face in the copier's green light. His hair stood up on end, slept on and not brushed, and his face hadn't been shaved for several days. He threw a newspaper and some pamphlets down and started to copy some flyers. Daphne stood up with Surefoot's words on her tongue.

"It's just a seed . . ."

He jumped, picked up the stapler, and brandished it as a weapon. "What the hell . . ."

She stood firm. "You don't have to plant it."

"Shit, Daphne . . . What are you doing here?"

"I watched you light that match."

He paused, puzzled, but then realized what she was talking about. "And I saw you running away. What are you afraid of? It's not about you . . . It's about building."

Daniel turned back to his copying as cooly as if in his daily routine. He spoke as the flyers flipped through the machine. "We build and build, then someone takes it down. One step forward, three steps back."

"I'm not afraid of you."

He appeared not to hear her as he stared down at the copier, but continued as if addressing an audience. "That was me. It was really me . . . it was the inside . . . the beams, the girders, the foundation . . . it's that part you can't tear down. They think they can; they think that the whole building will go if you rip out the walls, but they're wrong."

He looked up. Words came to her: *not like this, not like this . . .*

"And besides, it worked. The Mercier blockade is down. The army went in a few hours ago. The bridge is free. The Mohawks agreed, and they dismantled the barricades themselves, all cooperating except a few."

He pointed to the day's first edition of the *Montreal Sun*, which he'd thrown on the table beside the copier. Daphne picked it up and saw the large front-page photo. Surefoot. She was being lifted by four soldiers into an awaiting truck. The photograph had caught the moment the leg of one officer had buckled, causing him to almost drop her, the strain of her weight showing in his face. Surefoot wasn't struggling, but from her face Daphne could see she was channelling all the weight of her ancestry into every cell of her body. Her smile was broad as she looked straight ahead, oblivious to anything else, having gained something – her size her final triumph. *A wolf disappears into the woods, but on its way it leaves tracks in the snow, and this is*

Surefoot's smile wasn't one of nation-hood or kinship; it was a simple one of fact – a fact born of essence, the pith of bone, the bulk of immanence. Daphne looked back into Daniel's flash-lit face.

"I watched it. They made a deal and told the Mohawks they'd ignore the guns. What a farce. They even carried out a fake airlift with helicopters to please the Feds. And some of the Indians had to make a point, like that one . . . made themselves rigid and refused to budge. But at least it's free. The army kept their cool. Nobody got hurt. Next they'll get Oka."

"And what do you get?"

He approached her, touched her arm, and felt the chameleon there. He took her elbow and lifted her arm up to read the tattoo, but then let go lightly without saying anything. No jumps in thought, no diversions, he continued, "It's about how you think and where it takes you. And inside that there's order."

"But . . ." She stopped herself. This was his war. She watched his face in the flash of the copier and saw his features expand with each burst of light. Nose, cheek. Flash, flash. Eyebrows. Left, right, one fat caterpillar of an eyebrow over and over. Flash, flash. The nausea returned.

"I don't feel well. I have to go."

He stopped her. His eyes were watery under the brown bug of a brow.

"The stand-off fizzled; the army's in. What does that tell you about who's smart enough in all of this. You have to fight terrorism with terrorism. Blood for blood."

*Then the demons take over . . .* She sat down at Marc's desk.

Daniel gathered his things, turned off the machine, and headed out of the store. He stopped before opening the door and turned back to Daphne. "It's not what it looks like. It's people's lives, their sweat. Without that the building's empty."

He turned and left. After a few minutes Daphne followed suit.

Fish lay on beds of ice, with dashes of lemon like throw cushions along the counters. Slabs of red meat were lined up to show off the bloodiest angle. Daphne walked from one stall to the next amidst the smells and the *Madame . . . ici . . . bonjour . . .* of the eager vendors. She had never been to Jean Talon market before, and only when the bus had poured out the mass of bodies that had been straddling straw bags, shopping carts, and children had she realized they'd reached her destination. Rows of lettuce heads and green onions sparkled under the sprayed water; cucumbers and beets protruded from baskets; basil, rosemary, parsley were neatly tied in bunches that spread along wooden counters. She picked up and smelled some cilantro. Hands of bananas piled on each other; cartons of blueberries, strawberries, and raspberries showed off their best on top. Chicken eggs, goose eggs, large and small, were spread across another counter. At the end of that row, a whole cluster of stalls with flowers of every kind. Tomatoes: she was looking for tomatoes. The biggest, ripest tomatoes at the market. Beefsteak. That's what he'd said. *Perfect fruit, perfect vegetable.* Michel had boasted about selling the best, and she was counting on that to help her recognize his stall.

At the end of one long row of vegetables sat a man whose strong and clear eyes gave away his youth, though his face was that of an old man. He wore a white clinician's coat and a sailor's cap. His face was dark, part dirt, part pigment. Beside him, lined up one row on top of the other were cages of pigeons. Five dollars a pigeon. The sign beside the crates indicated that the price included a free tune on the vendor's harmonica.

Farther on, more music — the plaintive harmony of an unlikely duo. A sad elderly man in worn clothes was playing the accordion, accompanied by a young boy on the fiddle. The boy's expression didn't alter as he drew the long bow over the violin strings. The man followed the boy's lead, drawing out each accordion note by stretching his arm as far as it would go, filling the bellows of the instrument with air.

Two stalls down from the sad couple Daphne spotted a large sign: TOMATOES: $2.00 A BASKET. She picked one up, then another, then approached the young woman who was collecting money from a customer.

"Do you know Michel Duchesne?"

"He's the owner."

"Is he here?"

"He'll be back in five minutes."

The woman was curt. Two sharp vertical creases over her nose carved out unhappiness on the hardened face. Tension extended across her chest; her collar bones protruded under the tightly stretched skin to form a fragile trench around her neck. Daphne picked up a tomato, pretending to examine the silky fruit in her hands as she looked back at the woman and realized that she must be the cousin Michel had spoken of.

"I'll come back then, when he's here. Thanks."

She wandered around the market picking up fruit, squeezing it, smelling it. She bought some peaches, some cherries, a hand of bananas, some grapes, and a melon. Starting with a fruit salad at the cabin she would start eating properly again. She tried to feel the excitement of the lake, but something else was getting in the way. A wobbly, cumbersome presence within her.

At a fish stall, she stopped and examined the offerings. There it was, in front of her – ribbed and pink, cut into single-serving sizes, ready to cook. She thought her eyes had tricked her, so she checked the sign: RAY: $7.99/lb. She went to touch the flesh, but a voice interrupted her.

"Can I help you?"

"Is that as big as they get?"

"How big you want it? I give you two pounds, three pounds, you make up mind." His functional English was spoken forcefully – survival pitch – with a Portuguese accent.

"No, I mean . . . I mean, in the ocean. Are there bigger ones than those?"

"Sure, sure, bigger ones, five pounds, if you want. You make up mind."

"I mean, could you wrap yourself in one?"

"Of course, I wrap it for you. How big?"

The fishmonger became impatient with her gaping at the ray and moved on to serve someone else. Finally, she drifted away, back to the tomatoes.

When she returned to the stall, again it was his eyes she saw first, radiant, as if anticipating her. Their eyes locked for a second, simultaneously shifted, and rested more comfortably just out of direct contact.

"Hello, I meant to call you."

"Yeah . . . you're busy . . . whatever." Michel's voice was bruised, defensive. Daphne suddenly felt nervous and awkward, not having fully articulated why she had come or what she was going to say.

"I was wondering if you might need me."

"Pardon me?"

"If you had work for me. If I could work here, have a job, that is." As she said it, she knew why she'd come. She was lunging toward solid ground. She couldn't go back to the store, and she realized that Michel had aligned himself with her effortlessly. This was her first step across the crack, the first attempt at filling it in.

"I don't know . . ."

"I can do anything, really, just tell me what there is to do."

She had caught him off guard. He looked around at his cousin. "Let's walk."

They meandered through the market while he explained about the business and his responsibility, and he eventually lead her toward the loading area at the back of the market.

"A guy I hired part-time quit on me, just like that. And my cousin hates getting up so early to be at the food terminal way before dawn." He lifted a crate of tomatoes out of a truck. She watched his shoulder muscles arch with the effort. Putting the crate down on the ground, he continued, "And I'd like to get away sometime . . . We're always looking for someone to help out at the food terminal, but it's part-time, and early work, really early, and I don't pay well . . . I mean you've got lots of other skills . . . I couldn't pay you what you'd get doing computer work. Sometimes it's dirty and cold. I don't think you'd like it. It's very early work."

Daphne felt the picture lock in her mind; she saw herself gritty with soil, lifting crates of vegetables out of the truck. Her back straightened. "That's all right. I don't mind. I need a job."

He wiped his hands on his apron and bent over to lift the crate again. They walked back to the stall. When he had unloaded the contents of the crate, he wiped his hands again and pivoted toward the other end of the stall. Daphne watched the back of his head as he spoke to his cousin. The breeze felt cool. His eyes led the way as he returned to her.

"You can start on Monday; we go back to the terminal then, and I could pick you up, or you could meet me there if you want . . . no, you don't have a car, do you? I could pick you up. If you want. If you want . . . you're doing it again – that watching thing you do."

He smiled and looked down, then up again into her eyes.

"If you'd pick me up, that'd be just fine."

He pulled her toward the stand. "Here," he said, picking up an aubergine and handing it to her.

"Thanks."

"I'll call you on Sunday night to confirm the time. Sometimes it changes."

"I'll be home late . . . in the evening. I'm going away for the weekend."

"But waking up will be – "

"What if you call just before you leave. I'll sleep by the phone. I'll be ready."

"A wake-up call. Good. I'll do that."

"Thanks again."

"Good. See you."

"Yes."

"Bye."

The bus ride home was less crowded, so she could sit. Her legs stuck to the vinyl and sweat trickled down her belly. She touched it. Flat as a pan. She listened for a voice, any voice, but nothing came. Silence.

Joanne had said they'd pick her up by mid-afternoon. Daphne wasn't sure what to pack, how much to depend on the hot weather in the country. So she overpacked and had a large suitcase and a small bag sitting at the top of the stairs long before Marc and the others arrived. Most of the things in her suitcase were insurance against being stranded. Just in case it rained, a raincoat and Wellingtons. Just in case it cooled down, an oversized striped French mariner's sweater. Just in case she couldn't sleep, a bottle of Nytol. Just in case she needed to use the outhouse in the middle of the night, her flashlight. Just in case she felt the weight of the recent weeks pulling her to the bottom of the lake, she packed the diaries. She would continue to excavate them for meaning, for the cause of the brutality that had produced her. They were all she had, so she clung to them as to an amulet.

In the bathroom she caught sight of her face, and for the first time in a week she truly saw it. She was ugly. Generations of submission and rebellion still battled for position there. Were hers the eyes of the victors or of the vanquished? The ears of slaves or masters? Her hair was born of a cruel passion that sprang up kinky and horny in the moist heat. And her nose was a sculpture: a monument to the history of bones pounding other bones, mixing up dry marrow to unveil the post-historic shape that was displayed like a museum piece in the centre of her face. She turned from the mirror to wait by the door, hoping the presence of her friends would quell the hum that was creeping along her neck behind her left ear.

Finally everything was ready. Marc had heaved Daphne's suitcase into the trunk with a groan, but made no remark on its bulk. They were all slightly deferential with her. Traffic on the way out of the city was almost at a standstill. The bridge blockades were coming down, but the army still occupied the highway around Oka, where the warriors maintained their increasingly skittish standoff. Nevertheless, Montrealers were determined to leave the city for the weekend. Exhaust filled the humid air and helicopters circled in the thick grey stew overhead. There was talk of mobilization in the Gulf: Saddam Hussein was calling for a Holy War.

Irritated, Sylvie sat up and gripped the back of Marc's seat. "If I hear just one more report," she said with her accent getting thicker, "I will split in my head. It's been nothing but bad news for weeks. Let's try to have a weekend without it, okay?"

Marc obligingly switched off the radio, and there was silence for a few minutes until Joanne, unable to bear the evasion, launched them back into the usual debate.

"Just when the only international news of the summer is Oka, and just when the UN is finally about to deal with how this country treats its Native people, we get upstaged. Good ol' America swooping in for a media kill. This whole fucking world pisses me off."

Sylvie threw up her hands and slouched in the back seat beside Daphne. Marc, checking his rear-view mirror before changing into the passing lane, made his usual attempt to calm Joanne. "People don't give a shit, Joanne. We're spoiled. Never had an invasion in this country . . . except everytime the army comes to Quebec." He laughed at his own insight and continued. "People are afraid."

It was fuel for Joanne. "Don't give me that. It's the opposite. Greed. You think those guys who own everything don't know what they're doing? Here and everywhere else. Starving off the weak ones, methodically. Eugenic technology, like obliterating bad strains of wheat."

"Oh come on, Joanne, give me a break!" Marc finally erupted.

Sylvie sucked her teeth and grabbed her purse, rummaging through it until she found her brush, which she dragged furiously through her hair. Daphne opened the window and the heat poured in over the air conditioning. *Bad blood stains*, she said to herself, into the wind, then touched the chameleon tattoo on her arm. Her face was tight, her gaze fixed on the passing cars. The others were silenced by the gush of hot air. They changed the subject, stepping around the moment like a mess on the sidewalk.

Sylvie asked whether they had brought enough beer, because this was the last chance they would have to stop. They decided they would risk running out and proceeded in the steady crawl out of the city toward Ottawa and the Gatineau hills.

When they arrived the air was cool but moist. The sun's last moments peppered the clouds, and the softness of the lake was like the inside of a cheek: wet and safe. Daphne was struck by the stillness, to which the lapping of water and the *errk errk* of frogs served as counterpoint. She stood on the dock looking out on the lake and the cliffs on the far shore. She stretched her arms high above her head and bobbed up on her toes, holding herself there a few seconds, stretching as much as possible – high, higher. The slam of the cottage's screen door startled her out of her modest salute to the passing sun. She joined the others inside.

Marc was unpacking, and the others were slowly unwinding, shedding their city bodies. The cabin was modest: three small bedrooms, one with a double bed, one with two twins, and a smaller one with a cedar bunk bed for children. The efficiency of the bunk appealed to Daphne and she dragged her heavy bags over the wooden floor and claimed this room for herself. She opened her suitcase and tucked the diaries into the blankets of the top bunk, then joined Marc in the kitchen.

It was an elaborate kitchen for its size and contained the conveniences of home – toaster, coffeemaker, a blender. Marc had already unpacked the rum for the daiquiris that were a tradition upon arrival at the cottage. Daphne offered him the fruit she'd bought at Jean Talon market. As he cut fruit and assembled the blender, he described the annual rituals to her. "First daiquiris to get loosened up. Then a swim. Tomorrow we have to go across the lake to the trail up the cliffs and watch the sunset from Eagle Point. And one dinner has got to be fish we catch, so I'll wake you up early. I'll have to show you how to handle a canoe."

Daphne felt the eminence of cottages – woodland shrines where rites of the seasons were performed year after year. She was an initiate. This weekend she would be introduced to windsurfing and canoeing, and Marc had promised her a tour of the huge lake and its secluded coves and islands. She watched the fruit become pulverized in the blender. Red berries spun into swirls of pink ice in a few seconds. She gulped with thirst.

Marc lit candles and set them out on the table on the screened porch. When evening and the daiquiris were well underway, the conversation turned back to politics. As soon as it did, Sylvie retreated to the living room with her book, which left Marc and Joanne to sort out their views. Daphne gazed through the screen at the clusters of stars appearing in the sky. She could feel the rum stir up the residue of wine, and her temple began to throb slightly. Marc's patient voice was coaxing the tenderness he knew existed in a sporadically seen part of Joanne. "I know, I know," Daphne heard Joanne say in the distance, while her eyes followed the slow crawl of a spider up the screen toward a sprawling web. As she watched, the spider morphed, sprouted a tail, and became long and thin – a lizard. With a shake of her head it was a spider again. She sipped her drink.

She heard without listening. Elaborate words filled the room. They provided protection the way sound wards off predators. *Like fat hides bone*, she heard her aunt's voice. Words filled up Daphne's head, swaddling her in a momentary calm. She felt old. Over the last month time had accelerated and left her struggling in its wake. Questions to Jennifer and Bill, and to her aunt Sheila about her mother, had all been drowned in litres of red wine. They no longer occupied great spaces in her mind. The real questions were for the man who could no longer answer, the man in the hospital staring at the pale walls marked with the traces of a swift and purposeful lizard.

More daiquiris were consumed quickly. Marc came up with new combinations of fruit, and the conversation on the porch began to lighten, became checkered with laughter and joking. Joanne kidded that when she started her new job she was going to wear suits and pantyhose, to take on a whole new image. "Just to peek over the other side, you know, and to keep every-one guessing."

"Yeah, right," Marc said sarcastically.

The mood buoyed Daphne's thoughts. Sylvie, having grown tired of her isolation, stepped out onto the porch with a fresh drink. "How about cards – bridge or gin, or something." Her eyes sparkled in the flickering candlelight as she flipped her hair back over her shoulder.

"We've got lots of cards, and Trivial Pursuit, Monopoly, whatever you want." Marc looked pleased that the lake had lulled the staccato exchanges of the past month.

In a second of silence, a loon called across the lake – a long, drawn-out *oooooodeeee*. They listened for another, and the lingering, singular sound was followed by a series of short high gobbles, one loon to another.

"Anyone up for skinny dipping?" Marc exclaimed.

"Absolutely," Sylvie agreed, eager to show herself to him.

"Grab a towel. We'll meet down on the dock."

"Oh, I don't know . . . it's probably freezing," Joanne said.

"No way. This time of year the water's warmer than the air."

"Yeah, but the bugs . . ."

"Loosen up, Jo," Sylvie goaded.

"Slimy rocks with leeches, I bet," Joanne grumbled.

"It's a perfectly clean lake," Marc assured them,

Joanne smirked and got up, tapping Daphne on the shoulder as she passed her. "You coming, Daph?"

"Sure."

They each retreated to get undressed. Daphne slipped easily out of her shorts.

"Didn't bring a towel, too bad," Joanne yelled from her room in one last attempt to back out.

"I'll bring you one," Marc said, emerging from the bathroom in a beach-towel skirt.

Within a few minutes they were all wrapped in towels, ready. The porch door rapped out four exits that echoed across the water. Light from the cottage shone a path down to the dock and to the canoe tied up to it.

"And tomorrow morning: canoeing lessons," Marc reminded them, as they picked their way down the path.

"No need; I know how," Joanne said proudly.

"Me too," added Sylvie.

"I guess that leaves me," confessed Daphne.

Marc was the first to go in. He threw off his towel quickly and stood for a few seconds on the dock, sticking out his chest, inhaling the night air before he plunged in ceremoniously. Sylvie dived in after him. Joanne jumped, a cannonball splash that silenced the loons.

Daphne's entry was timid; she waded in from the shore instead of plunging into deeper water from the dock. The soft mud of the lake bottom gushed up through her toes; weeds wrapped around her ankles. The sinking, gooey feeling was unpleasant, so she jumped up and swam awkwardly, breaking the surface now and then with a kick of her feet. Not a graceful swimmer, she gulped for air and swallowed water before deciding just to tread for a while. The first time she had been in a pool with her parents, they had told her to float on her back when she felt tired. She had spent the day in the water alternately walking on the concrete bottom for a few strides and flipping onto her back, having discovered her own buoyancy. She needed to find this lightness again.

Marc swam confidently toward the middle of the lake and was almost silent in his stroke. Sylvie and Joanne splashed about separately, Sylvie's occasional giggle amplified through the silent air. Within a few minutes Joanne had climbed out of the water and sat drying herself on the edge of the dock watching the stars. Sylvie swam out a few feet from the dock, then she too got out.

Daphne turned to float on her back. She gasped at the immensity of the sky, surprised by the density of the stars suspended there, and for a moment she imagined them falling into the lake, a few at a time, in a long stream, like sand slipping from the palm of God. The familiar constellations were easy to pick out. The Big Dipper was hanging to her left. The Lion, Orion's belt, the Great Bear. Jumping from one star to the next, her eyes traced the forms. She didn't feel the chameleon patch on her arm loosen, slide off her skin, and float away. With the lake lapping at her breasts and on the lips between her thighs, she slithered on her back, moving like a reptile. Her right hand moved over her body, down between her legs, and she felt the spiny pad of hair that had sprouted. She emptied her bladder. The lake water dispersed the hot urine, and the release was pleasing. She became acutely aware of what she was hearing, her ears just below the lake surface. It was the silence of nothingness that isolated and heightened the sound of her breathing, the tremor of her own cells.

Ahh, Ahh, Ahh. *eye, eyeooo, eyeoooooooeeoo.*

She tested the water for vibrations, and the sound echoed back, rounded and elongated, with a southern accent: *Ow, Ow, Ow.* Her body in sync with its watery bed, she thought of her real mother. Of the pain that sank her. Treading harder to keep her body afloat, she considered Gerald and what he'd heard in the back of his head. She started to hear it and to feel the fear of being swallowed up by a foreign element so powerful it feels innate. Her mother had loved too deeply, without borders that would stop violations, without the protection of the firm hand of her own will. Her father had been a coloured man who died believing he was white, surrendering to the weight of the asylum, yet finding a way to believe he had outsmarted them. But his own cells had revolted, backed up on him, and stopped reproducing. Blood had stopped visiting his foot. And Frederick had died longing for the touch of the wing of a fish that should have been a bird, that should have been a lover. They were all dead – the inevitable amnesia of all organisms.

The reverberation of her breathing and the caress of water was comfortable, almost too pleasant, as was the sense of being alone with the universe above her. Just then, too timely not to be an acknowledgment of her thoughts, a bright star shot across the sky from left to right and disappeared like a wink. She smiled, laughed, and the *ha ha* reverberated in her ears. Another sound followed. *I live in its tail, in its tongue . . . just as I, when I leave here, will become the world . . .*

She leapt up in the water like a hungry fish, startled by the deep, hoarse voice. Joanne's call came to her out of the dark.

"Coming, Daph? You're going to shrivel! Or are you testing that principle of invisibility again?"

As Daphne waded out of the water she could see Joanne on the path, shaking her head in disbelief. Trailing behind the others, Daphne paused to look back out onto the black lake.

Just before dawn, she stirred, hearing the voice again. *The pissing sky left a message in the garden: take or be taken, swim or drown at the whim of arbitrary clouds* . . . Daphne jumped out of bed to check the bunk above her. No one there. The blanket covered the notebooks. She slid back into sleep.

The smell of frying bacon wafted over Daphne as she lay emerging from sleep, slowly placing herself in the strange room. When she got up she saw Sylvie already on the dock with a coffee and a book. Joanne's door was still closed. Coffee. She stubbed her toe on the leg of the couch as she made her way to the kitchen.

"Morning."

"Morning, Daph."

"Any coffee?"

"Right there, help yourself. Breakfast will be ready in a minute."

"Thanks, but my stomach's not awake yet. I'll save it for later."

"Canoe lesson in half an hour."

Daphne nodded, still groggy, and poured herself coffee. Returning to the bunkroom, she grabbed the diaries, and a romance novel she'd borrowed from a bookcase, before heading to the dock.

While Joanne slept, Marc and Sylvie gorged themselves on bacon and eggs, with Sylvie revelling in their domestic moment. Daphne sat in the lawnchair on the dock, gazing across the lake at the huge cliffs that were turning bronze with the climbing sun. After breakfast Marc joined Daphne and held out a paddle to her. More alert now, she put the diaries down and grabbed the paddle eagerly.

"Slip in gradually, and hold the paddle across the canoe to secure it. Like this." Marc slid gracefully into the stern, balancing the canoe for Daphne's entry. Once she was kneeling in place, he pushed off from the dock and paddled them toward the middle of the lake.

"Cup your palm over the handle. Now keep the right elbow straight . . . pivot your wrist. That's it."

The paddle felt too long in Daphne's awkward grip.

"Stroke deeper – no lily dipping," Marc coached. "There, that's better." They glided to the middle of the lake. "My dad would bring us out here to the middle, tip the canoe, then make us right it and get back in. That was the test, and the only way we'd be able to take it out on our own."

"Sounds impossible."

"It's not, actually, but I'm not sure I could do it now; takes a lot of technique. Haven't done it in years. No motor boats are allowed on this lake, so I don't feel like trying it and getting stranded."

Daphne felt the strain in her shoulder. She stopped paddling to look ahead across the lake. "Who owns all this?"

"Most of it's Crown land, and there's a wildlife reserve over there, around that second inlet."

*A wolf disappears into the woods* . . . She wondered if Surefoot was in jail, whether she had ever seen the vastness of a lake like this, whether she'd ever learned the names of trees in the woods.

"We should head back, see what the others want to do now, maybe go fishing. You're not doing too badly for a beginner," Marc said, interrupting her thoughts.

As they approached the dock, Daphne realized that Joanne was flipping through the burgundy journal. "Leave that alone!"

Joanne quickly shut the journal and backed away as they reached the dock and Daphne jumped out of the canoe – causing it to rock Marc back and forth in the stern – and dashed to pick up the diaries.

"Okay . . . Relax . . . I didn't read it . . . just wondered what the hell you were carrying around all this time."

"Nothing, just some notes."

"Okay, okay, relax."

Daphne felt the tremble in her cheek rise with a fierce maternal instinct to protect the words that were now hers. She wrapped the journals up in her towel and placed them under her chair on the dock.

Later that day, not quite noon and well into the third round of daiquiris, Daphne dragged her lawnchair under the shade of the bent cedar by the dock where she sipped on iced papaya laced heavily with rum. Marc was a generous host, serving drinks and snacks, trying to make their stay memorable, an adventure into summer culture. He roamed around the grassy cottage lot in shorts, shirtless, but with a tie to add a touch of formality. He offered a choice of daiquiris: watermelon, kiwi, papaya, mango, strawberry, or lime. Sylvie lay on her stomach on the dock, her bikini top unhooked, and pushed herself up to sip from a strawberry daiquiri. Covered up in a hat and long-sleeved shirt, Joanne sat beside her reading and sipping a mango concoction. Daphne was relieved to be away from Joanne's intrusions, and her drink was going down like juice – cooling her from the inside. The hot sun faded the trees to olive, and the cedar leaned out over the lake looking as crisp as a brittle branch ready to break and smack into the water.

Marc sat down on the lawn beside Daphne wearing one of the hats that Joanne had brought for the weekend. "This is a day for a rubber mattress, a thermos of daiquiris, and a hat – you float out in the middle of the lake. No wind, so you don't have to feel pressured to windsurf or sail. A day for *ve-ge-ta-bles*." The rum in his accent pronounced the last word as if it was a Latin phylum. Sylvie giggled from her corner of the dock.

Daphne had been pretending to read the romance novel. It sat open on her lap at the first chapter, covering Gerald's two journals, which she kept with her like eyeglasses, afraid to leave them out of her sight.

She felt her bereavement growing under the amber canopy

of rum, propelling her on a grainy interior journey. The family tree: at the top, Gerald Eyre and his wife, Mary; on a branch below them, Muriel Eyre beside Sheila Eyre. And Daphne? Where was she meant to perch? Parallel, cornered, or off to the side? And a branch for Bill and Jennifer? There seemed no spot she could claim for herself, no offshoot to which she could be grafted, to close the gaping hole in her reality once and for all. So many disrupted nests. *Sing cuckoo.*

She longed for Jennifer Baird to wipe out the story of her birth the way she had wiped away tears, wiped out fevers, wiped up those early years before the questions began, but she had shut Jennifer and Bill out steadily since she had known there had been another story – her story. For years she had avoided the question, invented the seed, giving it a shell of her own creation, and Jennifer and Bill had remained porcelain parents, fragile and outside of real time. Now, hoping it was not too late, she realized she wanted to hold them the way they had held her. Hold them and thank them. Born of brutality – she would thank them for rescuing her from that. Thank them for their attempt to revise history. *Bill Baird, Bill Baird, oh . . .*

*Sugar at the door . . . Ting-a-ling-ting, darling . . .* Her real mother spoke from the bottom of the lake. The voice was warped and gurgling. It ripped at her chest, asking Daphne to forgive her, telling her to be stronger than her mother.

"Are you having another?"

Joanne swayed above Daphne, blocking the sun, holding two wide-rimmed glasses in her hand.

"No thanks, not yet, I really shouldn't have much. I'm still recovering from the flu."

"Ah yes, the flu. Very *strange* to get the flu in the middle of summer. Very *strange*. You sure it was the flu?" Joanne's enunciation had slurred, producing the *str* as *schr. Schrange.* She wobbled, as if asking the question had unbalanced her.

"Yes, I went to the doctor; she told me it was the flu."

"Ah, bullshit, Daph, I've never seen anyone as hung over as you were. You reeked of alcohol, man, you had it comin' out of your pores. What's up?"

Daphne looked down into her lap and turned a page of the novel. "Nothing's up. I just had the flu."

"Like hell you did. You know, you are one hell of a *strange* woman. The only time I've actually seen you without this casing you wear is that day, totally blitzed from a long binge. What's your *sch*tick? I mean you walk around the shop as if you're in some kind of daze half the time. Like you float through concrete or something. Think we can't see you? That you're invisible? Is that it? Some black guy said that to me once; I told him he was full of shit. And what are you writing in those books anyway? Is that your writing? Pretty *strange*."

Daphne could feel the hair on her skin rise. Marc got up from the grass and moved toward Joanne, holding his hand out for the glasses. "Here, I'll take those, Joanne. Maybe we've had enough."

Joanne pulled the glasses to her chest. Daphne glanced up at Marc then back at Joanne, and mechanically spilled out words. "*What you have made me do is piss the shape of a fish in the sand . . .*" As soon as the words were out, tears began to blur her vision.

Joanne persisted. "What the hell? Look, why don't you just admit it, you've been juicing and that's why you were away all week. Why don't you just admit one thing, Daph, just one small thing. Take it and hold it and admit it's yours, and snap out of that reverie you're in."

Daphne lurched out of the chair. Joanne, thinking Daphne was going to hit her with the journals, jumped back. "You cunt!"

"Joanne!" Marc interrupted, horrified, as he reached for the glasses.

Daphne struggled to get clear. She felt as if they were encircling her, staring down at her. "Get out of my way." She wanted to vomit but couldn't bear to have them watching, so she forced down huge heaves. The wind had picked up and the breeze splashed her face. She walked to the dock, passing Sylvie, heading toward the edge. Their eyes forced her to feign a light step, a casual stroll. The paddles were still lying on the dock, so she grabbed one. She balanced the shortest paddle across the canoe, loosened the rope from its bow, and glided into the craft feeling already skilled. She pushed off from the dock using the blade of the paddle. Seeing Marc step onto the dock, she started to paddle away.

"Daph, I don't think that's a good idea. I'll come with you."

"She's just picking on someone – it's her habit . . . Daphne, come back." Sylvie's voice was sincere.

"Just leave me alone," Daphne answered.

Daphne paddled on the right but the canoe swivelled back toward the dock, so she switched to the left. Then it arced too far in the opposite direction, almost in a circle, so she switched sides again. Same thing, almost a full circle. She was getting nowhere, except where the drift of the lake was taking her, downwind from the cottage. In a brief glance back at the dock she saw Marc and Sylvie looking worried, guilty. Joanne had disappeared into the cabin. Daphne decided to float for a while to see where she might end up, but there was not enough current to carry her away as quickly as she wished, so she dipped the paddle into the water once more. One stroke left, one stroke right, one stroke left, one stroke right. Her left stroke was much stronger than her right, so she had to compensate by forcing the right stroke. She achieved a relatively straight course and began to put some distance between the canoe and Marc and Sylvie. Her nausea subsided. She breathed deeply, feeling she had mastered the canoe. Her arms were already tired, but she showed off to herself.

A few minutes later she felt a rush of panic, but then realized that she had faithfully carted the diaries with her. They lay on the bottom of the canoe, looking faded and foreign in the noonday sun. The heat was intense, even on the water. The ripples on the lake surface reflected the sun into her eyes. She pulled her T-shirt over her head and continued to paddle in bra and shorts. A large, desolate lake – there was little chance of running into anyone. The whole western shore in front of her was the wooded wildlife reserve Marc had pointed out, and only a few other canoes in the distance, headed away from her, shared what she could see of the thirty-one-mile expanse of the lake.

The water was glassy and clean, clear almost to the bottom

twenty feet below. Happily alternating her stroke from side to side, she paddled until she was beyond a point, out of sight of the dock and cabin. Sudden freedom – being able to float and paddle indefinitely in the loyal tranquillity of the canoe. She surveyed the lake and noticed the reflected sunshine shimmering on the leaves of trees lining the shore. Across a small bay several large smooth rocks jutted out from the shore, perfectly positioned for swimming and sunbathing. The water was soft on her hands as they dipped into the lake with the paddle. Every few minutes she rested, wetting her brow with water.

It took longer to reach the rocks than she had anticipated, and by the time she arrived she was starting to worry about finding the energy to get back. She hadn't yet eaten, and the daiquiris were losing their hold on her. Hunger had gathered her stomach into a tight pellet under her ribs. Her head was feeling light, almost disconnected from her neck and shoulders. Manoeuvring the canoe between two whale-shaped rocks, she stepped out, dragged the bow onto a flat surface, and secured the bow-rope to the branch of the tree that extended over the rocks. She rescued the diaries from the floor of the canoe and reached down to place them carefully in a crevice at the tip of the bow. As she bent over, Daphne glimpsed the lake from between her legs, and in the inverted panorama the lake became the sky, the blue sky a body of water studded with whitecaps of clouds. A rush of dizziness made her straighten and sit on the rock.

Fish gathered in the shallows at the base of the rock, lingering in her shadow as if seeking refuge from the sun. A little farther out, hundreds of minnows swarmed the water. Raising her arm, Daphne discovered that she could control them, frighten them; in unison they would swim away from the rock, stopping a few feet away. Trusting one more time, they would return. She raised her arm again; they fled. The larger ones near the rock also responded to her movements. If she stuck out her leg or stamped it against the cobbled surface of the rock they triggered their ingenious sacks and sank effortlessly, retreating from what they couldn't be sure of, from something somewhere beyond the concept of surface that was out of their grasp. The wind brushed her ears; she raised her head and heard singing: *"'Nansi, 'Nansi," said Sea Mammy, "you're not my cousin, you don' belong in the sea."* The accented female voice forced itself on her again. She looked back into the lake and tested her effect on the fish, raising her arm and alternately watching the wing of minnows gliding left, then the three small bass bobbing lower. It was a small display, but she felt it, understood, and stopped, allowing the small creatures their rest in the shade of her body. She would never be able to crack the watery barrier of understanding that separated them.

Something was orchestrating this moment. A strange presence on the lake was blurring the lines that normally divided the earth, the sky, and the water. A wind. Surefoot's chinook met Gerald's hurricane. A thousand names for the wind and the tricks it played. *"'Nansi could call to the winds in their different names and talk in all their different languages. Kee, kee, kee – kee, kee, kee, Clever Anansi, couldn't catch Monkey."* A high, singing rhyme – familiar words she'd never heard before.

She finally saw herself in the way Joanne had described: always below the surface, just on the underside of consciousness most of the day. Not brave enough to love Jennifer and Bill without suspicion, unconditionally. Not strong enough to hold the truth. Not looking beyond her nose to hear her place in the wind, a common wind with many names. She had never actually passed over the first crack; it was the same one over and over that she kept falling into. A crack in time that had continued to shift everything like a great divide.

Her bra was soaked with sweat, and it was starting to chafe the skin over her ribs, so she undid it and released her breasts to the breeze as she rubbed away the sweat. She lay back on the rock. Her eyes became heavy, closed, and her arm fell to her side.

Daphne woke because she was cold; the shadow of the tree had lengthened to cover her. The hours she had slept were disappearing into the horizon. Her muscles were stiff, her skin tight, her head was swimming with sunstroke. Squinting at the sky that was now streaked with orange, she could feel the crinkle of burned skin on her nose. When she touched her reddened breasts her hands left sharp white outlines that faded gradually. Her nipples were dry and sore. She had never burned before and was startled by the festering ache under the touch of her fingers.

To her right she heard a slow lapping of water, as if someone was washing his face, and when she turned, she saw a huge, majestic bird wading along the shore. Dressed in blue feathers, its neck as long as the rest of its body, its beak forming a long menacing point, the heron stood solemnly taking in the scenery, believing it had the view of the lake to itself. Daphne didn't move, barely daring to breathe, but the heron sensed something and leapt out of his evening wading pool and plunged for the sky, its flight heavy yet graceful.

Daphne dressed quickly, carefully pulling her shirt over her burned breasts and shoulders. Her bra remained on the rock. She pulled the diaries from the crevice shelf and moved to the canoe which she dragged clumsily over the boulders into the water. Paddling awkwardly, she tried to head back to the cabin. Her arms tired easily as she crossed back and forth with the paddle, irritating the sore skin on her chest. She rested a moment and stared into the sky. The clouds were a circus of shapes. She thought of lots to say for the childhood game. *There, that's a mouse, a giant mouse with a long skinny tail, riding on the head of a laughing man . . . There . . . it's a dinosaur, a flying one — its pointed head is swooping down on food. A bat . . . look, a deer with a puffy white-cloud tail . . . Over there is a man, his face is startled and his mouth is gaping open. His body lies flat along a white cloud bed, his right leg is shorter than the other . . . no, not shorter, it's gone, it's cut off below the knee.* Gerald. Or a puppet Indian with its leg on fire. Or was the figure a woman? And there they all were at one moment: Daphne, Gerald and the prodigal circus. All moments existing at once in her head, she controlling it like a mighty Greek goddess. *Sing cuckoo, sing cuckoo.*

"*Ooooooooooooooooo.*" Her howl filled the bay and rebounded as a faint warble, *eeeeouw*. It increased her dizziness.

All of the others, she thought, had disobeyed the inevitable, had tried to reverse the current of their circumstances. Her mother had walked into the water to cleanse shame and had never walked out, but perhaps there she'd found the mercy she'd needed. Even in jail, Surefoot would continue her conversation with the pine trees, and belonging would drip from her like blood from a pierced palm. Then there was Gerald . . . he had been alive enough to reinvent himself. She wanted to preserve this act of his, this triumph of the will in the pit of insanity, and it was then that she knew what to do with the diaries. A bow to memory. To let the snow and rain work on them until they became a place in which her own body could eventually be laid to rest. To have the paper petrify and fill the cleft between vegetable and rock, the words silent and grinning in the earth.

She turned the canoe to head farther down the lake and dipped her paddle urgently toward the shoreline. Each stroke produced a piercing in her head. After paddling for almost an hour, she found a piece of waterfront where she could land. There were a few boulders, but it was mostly marsh into which she stepped, dragging the canoe behind her.

She walked up into the gentle slope of the woods. The wind had dropped completely and the trees were silent. Felled trees cluttered the ground and dead branches crunched beneath her feet. Moss covered all the rock and there was a thick smell of dewy earth, the smell of semen. The sun slipped to just above the horizon and the lake turned mauve with streaks of jade. In a large grove, giant cedars oozed a clear and sticky milk that caught her hair. She pushed through broken branches, marched over soft mud. A red squirrel stopped in front of her, quivering and squeaking like a damaged tricycle. Then it ceased, looked at something behind her and out of its mouth came a bizarre chatter – a rapid-fire, high-pitched popping, almost electric; an alarm shorting out.

In its frightened warning, Daphne was struck by how alone she was, and she remembered Jane Eyre alone on the heath, fearing the attack of wild cattle or the stray bullet of a poacher, but trusting and taking comfort in the benign goodness of her twilight surroundings. But in the squirrel's rattle it wasn't Jane's voice she heard; it was that other woman's: the hyena laugh of Rochester's imprisoned first wife. In the drooping branches around her, Daphne could see the big woman's long, black hair, which streamed against the flames of burning Thornfield Hall as she threw herself from its battlements, her tired brain finally relieved in death. Daphne covered her ears and kept walking, resisting the temptation to view her life through another story.

She had to find just the right place, the right soft and holy place. When she reached a clearing near a bed of ferns, it was almost dark, and mosquitoes buzzed around her head, lit close to her ears, and landed on her neck. She had to work fast. Digging into the first layers of moss made her fingers ache, so she searched the ground for a tool and chose a small, sturdy branch to help her dig. When the pit was deep enough, she placed the notebooks in the tomb with the ceremony and seriousness of a dignitary's funeral. "*Bansimande, Bansimande, B-a-n-s-i-m-a-n-d-e, B-a-n-s-i-m-a-n-d-e.*" She cast it like a spell. Her own poem. The word to use when there was nothing else, Sheila had said. It arrived in her mouth sounding as familiar as the call of a hot bird. Her performance was personal – primary – as she patted the earth into a small mound. The building of a monument, one she expected to sprout out of the earth like the curly-haired marble head of Zeus atop its shapely carved and muscular body. The beginning of time. The seed of forgiveness.

By the time she was finished, she could barely see the mound before her in the darkness. Her stomach churned and her belly peeled out a high angry whine of hunger. She was ready to go home. Her joints cracked as she got up from kneeling on the sunburnt skin. Holding her stomach, then her head, she tried not to think about food.

She scrambled up the incline to the next grove on her hands and knees, but something in the sound of the woods at night startled her. A sense of eyes hiding inside holes, waiting. She stopped and felt the ground until she touched soft moss. It smelled inviting, so she tore at some and lifted it to her mouth, tasting first the green moss and then the dark brown of the dirt. The first swallow fooled her for a moment, so she took another mouthful. But when it finally reached her stomach she recognized the hard and indigestible earth for what it was and pelted what was left in her hand to the side. The mosquitoes feasted. The damp soil was cooling, so she began to dig again and to wipe the soil on herself – her face, neck, arms. Using huge gobs of saliva she kneaded it into a cool putty, then lifted up her T-shirt and applied the mud to her stomach, her chest. She had no idea where the canoe was from this grove and feared going deeper into the bush, so she pulled her shirt up over her ears to block out the sound of the annoying mosquitoes and curled up on the moss hoping the night would be short.

# Crescent

The first whisper of sun coincided with the soft *boodee, boodee* call of the loon to his mate. Daphne's neck was sore and her legs and arms uncurled with difficulty. In the patch of sky glimpsed through the branches, the thin curved sliver of the crescent moon was still visible against the growing veil of blue. Her stomach ached. She stood and walked hunched over, stepping carefully, uncertain of which direction to take. Everything around her seemed transformed since the previous day. It was browner, crisper, ready to ignite.

She headed in one direction, then instinct told her that it wasn't right. So she turned another way, circling back around the red spruce. Again, not right. Then, on the other side of the mound of dirt, she spotted what appeared to be a soft print outlined in the moss, leading into the next grove. Her own, she thought.

She followed the tracks, but lost them near a fallen oak. Still she persisted in the direction where she sensed the water to be. An hour passed unnoticed. Eventually, over a high ridge she spotted the glistening of a lake. She ran down to the shore, but when she arrived, she stopped short with a gasp because she knew it was a different lake. Small and weedy, it had one tiny island floating in the middle and piles of beaver-chewed logs were washed up on the shore. No boulders marked the waterfront. She had unwittingly portaged to a neighbouring lake. Dying trees littered the swampy shallows. She turned around and headed back up the slope she had just descended.

Her body throbbed and her skin burned from the scratches of branches and burrs. She searched the ground. Again she saw tracks, but these looked larger than her own. After a moment of hesitation she perceived they were unwavering, steadfast in their course, so she decided to trust them. She tilted her head and pushed back her shoulders to crack the stiffness in her spine. Then, with her eyes on the faint path beyond her, she followed the tracks through the trees.

A breeze came up from behind and she hesitated again, hearing something rustle in her right ear. Fighting for composure, she planted her feet like a sturdy trunk into the moss. She stood and listened. Suddenly, she thought she spotted something moving swiftly among the cedars. It was enormous, a wide human figure – many forms in one – travelling through the bush with the ease and speed of a deer. *You cannot sever me*, she thought, *without rupturing eternity.* She followed the apparition. It was taking her home. Continuing through the trees, she became light in her certainty. Soon there was a boldness about her as she rushed from one tree to the next, following the shape of flowing limbs, stopping only to sniff the wind like a gregarious bird. Beneath the branch of a dry birch she saw a swarm of flying insects, antlike creatures with tiny, almost transparent wings whipping the air. Her hand leapt at one and caught it; she threw the insect on her tongue. After swallowing it, she licked her fingers and grabbed another one.

Following the tracks, she was beginning to grasp what her mother and father never could. She was closing the cracks of time. She pranced on the soul of the world as if it were her own shadow. Rushing through the trees, bending under branches, she wanted to confer with them, to tell them what she knew: that if you surrendered to the hum you could ride it, straddle it like a back or a wing. She wanted to shout it: *Here . . . Listen! I understand . . . Can you hear me? Listen.*

When she reached the road it was late morning. She stopped short in the shelter of the trees, afraid to embrace the hot sun that punished the pavement. Her T-shirt was torn, exposing her mud-caked shoulder. Her legs were scraped and bleeding. A muscle in her calf had tightened into a hard knot. A siren sounded in the distance, and when it had faded away she emerged onto the road. Limping along the gravel shoulder, she set off in the direction of the siren. Her feet burned; the heat was a knife on her neck.

More than an hour later she reached the turnoff to the main highway. She put out her thumb, but car after suspicious car passed her, until finally a pickup truck stopped. The wary driver opened the window.

"You need help?"

"I'd like to go home."

"Ottawa?"

"Montreal."

The man considered it, then swung the door open, signalling that she should get in. She scrambled up on the seat and shut the door. They headed south along the highway as clouds developed in the west.

It was a larger truck, filled with produce, that drove up to Jean Talon market with Daphne sitting in the cab beside the driver. It had taken her four rides in as many hours to reach Montreal, and, finally, at a truckstop, she'd pleaded with this fifth driver to take her with him. Very few words had been spoken on the journey from the woods, only enough to indicate she was in trouble but wouldn't cause any. The drivers had all watched her stare fixedly ahead as they travelled down the highways.

"Thanks," she said to the driver as she jumped down from the cab.

The sky was overcast, and a light wind breathed through her hair and over her tender scalp. The sounds of the market matched the subdued afternoon colours of the potatoes and pears. Relaxing, Daphne made her way down the corridors of the market, her limp barely detectable. The thought of aubergine brought saliva to her mouth. Passing the caged pigeons, she followed the path of tomatoes, stall after stall, lifting her feet in deliberate steps to push back the fatigue, until she reached the largest tomatoes, bulbous and ripe.

The clapper-board sound of a wooden crate falling to the

pavement from across the way made Michel look up from behind his counter. In that second he caught sight of Daphne, who held his gaze for the first time. She walked toward him, the sentence forming easily, spontaneously, as she pursed her flush lips. In a small but firm voice she uttered two brittle words.

"I'm here."

Slender words, but sharp as a deep cut exposing bone.